WICKED'S WAY

WICKED'S WAY

Anna Fienberg

ALLEN&UNWIN
SYDNEY · MELBOURNE · AUCKLAND · LONDON

First published by Allen & Unwin in 2016

Allen & Unwin – Australia
83 Alexander Street, Crows Nest NSW 2065, Australia
Phone: (61 2) 8425 0100
Email: info@allenandunwin.com
Web: www.allenandunwin.com

Allen & Unwin – UK
Ormond House, 26–27 Boswell Street,
London WC1N 3JZ, UK

A Cataloguing-in-Publication entry is available
from the National Library of Australia
www.trove.nla.gov.au.
A catalogue record for this book is available from the British Library

ISBN (AUS) 978 1 74331 990 1
ISBN (UK) 978 1 74336 826 8

Cover design by Sandra Nobes
Cover and text illustrations by Craig Phillips
Text design by Sandra Nobes
Set in 11½ pt Adobe Garamond by Tou-Can Design
This book was printed in Australia in January 2016
by McPherson's Printing Group

13 5 7 9 10 8 6 4 2

Turtle hatchery

Treasure & Honey's house

Will & Wanda's house

Market

River

Highlands

THUNDER ISLAND

Limestone
caves

Wicked's Cave

Reef

Lake

Reef

TURTLE ISLAND

For Kathy Muir, queen of the Cannonball Seas

part one

chapter 1

William Wetherto was born with a talent for the tightrope.

By the time he was eight he could walk a rope as long as a gangplank. And when he was nine, he juggled bananas as he went.

'You're a natural,' his mother told him fondly, as she strung the rope between two mangroves. 'And I should know.' Whenever she said this, she'd tap the side of her nose wisely and wink at him. Indeed, Wanda Wetherto knew everything there was to know about funambulism. She'd even taught him that word – the delicious name for the thing he most loved to do. He thought it right and proper that the tightrope word started with *fun*, because that's what it was for him.

It was lucky that Will had a particular passion to occupy him, as in all his nine years on Thunder Island he'd never met another soul his age, or played a game with a child. Still, he lived happily enough with his mother, just the two of them, in their little wooden house on the hill. *They* played plenty of games together – climbing the banyan tree, swinging from branches like acrobats, juggling pawpaws, and limbo dancing in the moonlight.

But as soon as he woke in the morning, Will ran down the hill to the mangrove trees to practise walking the tightrope.

Now you might wonder at a boy practising his passion so young – although, as his mother often remarked, folk tend to love the things they are good at. And perhaps it was not so remarkable that Will Wetherto at the age of nine could dance on a rope as thin as a whisker, because his own mother had been a star of the tightrope.

Before she met Will's father, Wanda Wetherto worked as a circus acrobat on the Mainland – she could walk the high wire, juggle flaming swords, catch anything thrown at her by the wide world. Ever since he was a baby, Will had watched his mother glide like a ballerina along the tightrope, her eyes burning with concentration. When he could walk, then run, then somersault in mid-air, he begged her to let him learn too. 'I want to have the fun *you* have,' he told her. 'It's only fair.'

Wanda was always persuaded by a sound argument, so she began by fixing a thick rope just a few inches above the ground. Every month the rope grew higher, until he could climb a tightrope so high and thin that when he looked down, the ducks bobbing on the river below were as tiny as the ornaments on their mantelpiece.

Wanda was delighted that her son had the gift. In time, she told him, they'd return to the Mainland together where he could perform on the tightrope and trapeze. 'You'll see, you'll be a star of the circus,' she promised. 'But mind, we can't go until you are grown.'

Will shivered with excitement at the thought of being grown. But for now, when he climbed the ladder and swung himself up into the branches, he was content to see further upriver than he'd ever been allowed to go before. Up here, he felt tall and wise, as if he could manage just about anything. Big things became small and unknown things became known. It was like climbing up to another land. Or being grown.

Will liked to hear his mother talk of the circus and the fun to be had there. At night, she said, bonfires were lit and Travellers read the future in the dancing flames. Musicians played accordions and steel guitars, and acrobats flew around the ceiling of the Big Top like birds. But he wished her stories didn't have to finish with the terrible dangers of the wicked world.

'Mark my words,' she said gravely. 'It's pirates who rule the seas. Those vermin go stealing boys to crew their ships, working 'em till they drop. I tell you, no lad is safe.' She looked far into the distance, as if she could see pirates out there going about their evil ways. 'In this wide world folks like us must have a skill, and if it's a skill that pays in gold, the safer we will be. So keep practising, dear boy – you've got to be an expert in your trade, or you'll be left behind for the pirates to snatch, easy as a shark swallows a sardine.'

Wanda Wetherto believed in telling her son plain truths about the world; all the better to arm him, she said, for when he had to make his own way out there. In the meantime, she gave him excellent advice on the skill of funambulism. Before he set out on the rope, she would point to his stomach, just above his belt buckle. 'Find your balance here, Will,' she said.

'That's the centre of you. And remember this: take your time, check your centre, keep putting one foot in front of the other and your eyes on the prize.'

Wanda Wetherto's words were to be more important to Will than he ever imagined, so it was a fine thing that he listened carefully to his mother. Faithfully, he put one foot in front of the other and kept his eyes on the prize. But in the dark years to come he discovered that the wide world can lead you down paths so mysterious that sometimes it's hard to tell what is the prize and what is the devil.

~ * ~

The dark years began in the autumn of Will's ninth year, when, in the middle of the afternoon, Wanda Wetherto vanished. At first Will thought she must be playing hide and seek. He looked for her in the front garden, through the cinnamon trees and grape vines, and up into the branches of the mango tree. He ran through the tall grasses that grew at the back of their little house. He peered into the chicken coop, the toolshed, behind the newly chopped stack of wood. 'Come out, come out, wherever you are!' he called.

But there was no answering cry.

Will held his breath, listening for the smallest sound. Sometimes when she was hiding his mother couldn't help giggling, but now there was only the sigh of wind catching in the mangroves.

If his mother had heard him, Will decided at last, she would surely have appeared. She'd have leaped to the crack in his voice. When he was battling a nightmare pirate, she'd fly across the hall, her red hair flaring in the candlelight, and bounce on Will's bed. 'Let's bounce on his head!' she'd cry. 'Come on, bounce till he's dead!'

If she wasn't hiding, he thought next, then she must be practising her circus tricks. She'd be down at the river, walking the tightrope.

As he ran downhill, his bare feet slid and slapped on the juicy grass. He fell and righted himself, ignoring the blood on his knee and the sting at his heel. The drum of his heart drove him on, faster, frantic, and now, wasn't that the shape of his mother leaning against the tree?

He burst through the bloodwoods, past the clump of palms and into the clearing. The rope hung between the trees. Empty. Only a great heron stood uncertainly for a moment, then took off in a long curve of wing.

Will looked all around, his head darting back and forth like a hummingbird on a hibiscus flower. His mother was everywhere, in the sudden call of a coot, the whisper of the river; he caught glimpses of her in cloud shadows, the swish of breeze in the leaves.

But she was nowhere. There was nothing of her soft belly or her arms that held him so tight in the night. There was nothing to hold onto.

'Come out come out wherever you are!' he cried. 'You win!'

But his mother had vanished.

~ * ~

Will picked his way upriver, along the mangroves. He searched the river's edge and its wide brown face but he found only upside-down sky reflected there.

In his mind Wanda was tantalisingly close; she was boiling

water for their supper, telling stories of the father he'd never seen. Right there in the stone-flagged kitchen with the crayfish simmering in the pot, she would conjure up the man so that he could almost hear his father's quick laugh and smacking kiss, his pirate promise to come back for his family.

Pickle me toes and pour rum up me nose! had been his favourite phrase. 'And a bit too fond of that particular poison he was too,' Wanda said. But that phrase became Will's favourite, and he and his mother used it whenever a tickling bout or a wrestling match between them got too much. It was their signal for '*Enough!*', stopping a game in its tracks, and it worked every time.

So why the devil didn't it work now?

Because, thought Will, this was a stinking, rotten, snake-poison game that ought to be boiled in oil and buried five fathoms deep. He couldn't believe his mother would invent such a stupid game, he just couldn't believe it. But where on earth was she hiding? For the twentieth time he yelled, 'Pickle me toe…oe…oe … ssss!' but only the sandpiper pecking at the water's edge bothered to call back.

~ * ~

Shadows were lengthening along the muddy bank when Will stopped to rest. He was so weary and his legs were so numb that his terror felt distant now, like thunder heard from far away. He had never been so far downriver.

Ever since Will learned to walk, Wanda had warned him not to go beyond the mangroves below their house. For all her playful games, she was serious about certain things: snake-bite, bug-bite, and wandering out of sight. So Will hadn't ventured around the river's bend to the Cannonball Sea, or the other way, up to the High Lands. His mother said the sea was like a thousand rivers meeting in one, and stingrays with poison barbs and sharks with ten rows of teeth swarmed inside it. Sometimes his mother took their small boat downriver and brought back fish for their dinner. And sometimes she walked the other way, into the hills towards the High Lands where she sold her clay pots at market. But he was never, ever allowed to go with her.

'You are my Secret,' she whispered. 'If the whereabouts of Will Wetherto got out, the Captain of the Cannonball Seas would come to get you – him and his scoundrels! You might be the son of a pirate, but even your father couldn't save you from the Captain. A whisper of you on the Mainland, my boy, a moment's loose talk drifting to other islands, and you'd be in a pickle and no mistake. But never mind, you're safe here on Thunder Island, with not a body for miles around.'

Will didn't know what to make of this. His mother always spoke with affection about his father, who, she said, was a pirate of Some Reluctance. Where in the world that was, Will couldn't figure out – but wasn't his father a man of mystery? Wanda sighed with longing for him, yet in the same breath she swore pirates were dangerous, dire and deadly, no matter *where* they came from. Will didn't like to press her about it as whenever he did, her eyes grew wet and her silences long. All she told him on the subject of love and romance was: 'Know a person for more than two weeks before you marry them. And mind you visit their place of work before you do so.' In his experience Wanda Wetherto was a person as dependable as sunrise, as clear as water. But in the case of his father she seemed, well … different.

~ * ~

Will rounded the bend in the river, then stood still and gaped. Past the stubble of bush, a world of water tipped at the horizon.

'The Cannonball Sea,' he whispered.

Dusk was creeping in, dissolving the line where sea met sky. A chill trickled down his back. But still he stood there, unable to lift his feet. He was awestruck, standing on forbidden land. 'Never go round the river's bend,' his mother warned, 'for there lies the sea. And the sea is the home of pirates.'

Will looked away from the horizon and a flick of red caught his eye. Near his foot lay the thick brown stub of a cigar, burned down to its red paper band. His stomach turned over. He'd seen that thing for the first time yesterday, when a man came to the house looking for work. 'My apologies for disturbing you,' the man had said to his mother, taking the cigar from between his teeth. 'I'm wondering if you've got an afternoon's work for a feed? I'm on my way to the Mainland, but soon it will be night and I'd rather head out in the morning.'

Wanda had seemed uneasy, but she'd asked him to chop the remaining logs, and stack them in the shed. 'It's heavy work,' she said later to Will. 'I may as well take help where I can get it, and you can't refuse a man food in return for an honest job. He's no pirate, I'll swear, but still, keep out of his way till he's back on his boat.' She gave the man a plate of salt fish and beans, and mango juice to wash it down. The man was grateful and polite enough, but somehow Will smelt danger in the drifting smoke of his cigar.

He shivered now, and threw the stub on the ground. What did it mean? He looked out over the ocean, over more water than he'd ever seen. There, beyond the horizon, lay the

Mainland. The place where he would go with his mother when he was grown.

Anything could happen here, couldn't it? In this space where rivers vanished into sky. No outlines, nothing definite. Nothing you could put your hands around. Ghosts could be hiding in the sea spray, pirates looming on the horizon. His mother had known about this shimmering world; she'd done a thousand circus tricks, a million magic acts. For a bag of silver coins she'd pulled a hummingbird out of a man's britches, and escaped from a locked casket – *under* the water! She could vanish a mongoose, a bowl of frangipani flowers, his father's silver sword, even herself. Why, once she'd disappeared in a cloud of blue gunpowder, only to reappear in the toolshed moments later.

What if she'd vanished now, in this strange place? What if she was never coming back?

Will dropped where he stood, his legs turning to water. He didn't care if the bugs came to eat his ears or the snakes licked at his fingers. He was falling asleep and he dreaded waking up.

chapter 2

The sun was rising over the sea when Will opened his eyes. For a moment he was almost blinded by the glory of it, and then he remembered. He moaned as he stretched out his legs. He was thirsty, and something red and itchy swelled above his knee.

He leapt up and ran through the bushes, out onto white crunchy sand. The glare at his feet made him squint. The gold sea dazzled.

A hot panic swept over him; everything was too bright, too big, too much.

Then he saw, down near the shore, a low, curved wall of stones roofed by wire. It was the only human thing in the whole vast place. He made straight for it.

Facing the water, the stone walls only came up to his ankles. But when he knelt to look through the wire, he saw the sand moving inside. A small earthquake seemed to be taking place, sending up ripples to the surface.

Will kept his eyes fixed on the spot. He could hardly breathe with watching. And then, in small eruptions no bigger than his thumb, tiny dark heads squirmed up out of the sand. Two, three, seven, ten appeared, then little arms like fins pulled free. The creatures fell and righted themselves, struggled up cliffs of sand, and collapsed. They had hard shells like crabs...but their necks were long. Were they fish or landed creatures? Would they swim or walk?

So deep was his concentration that when a voice said behind him, 'Oh good, they've hatched,' he yelped.

'Ssh,' said the voice. 'You don't want to frighten them. They must be scared out of their wits already, what with climbing up into the world and about to make the most dangerous journey of their lives. How many do you think? I'm counting twenty-five already. Fancy, the mother can lay a hundred eggs at a time!'

The voice belonged to a girl about his age, or maybe a little older. She had long hair like his mother, only hers was caught at the back in a ribbon. She smiled at him.

'Look, do you see what a hurry they're in?' She pointed at the small sand-splotched bodies tilting as fast as their tiny legs could carry them towards the sea.

Just then a pelican swooped above, throwing a shadow on the sand. The girl squawked, waving her arms like a palm tree in a hurricane.

'*Now* you can yell – flap your arms and curse like a pirate!' she cried.

Will found his voice, and with it came such a volume of fear and worry and hurt that his cries of '*Ahhrrr, ahrrrrhhh!*' startled the pelican and caused the girl to slap her hands over her ears.

'You've got a lusty pair of lungs on you, and that's a fact.'

Will felt a warm glow just under his ribs, right next to where his fear lay. He nodded at the creatures still tumbling out of the sand. 'What are they?'

'Are you pulling my leg?'

Will shook his head. He felt the heat creeping up his cheeks.

'Oh, you must be a stranger here,' the girl said. 'Have you travelled far? *I* want to travel the world one day, and see all the other humans and creatures I've read about. These are sea turtles, who are also great travellers.'

'Did you build their little house?'

The girl nodded. 'The mother laid her eggs too far from the sea. What she was thinking I can't imagine! So I built some protection. See, they need to reach water quickly to avoid being eaten by birds. But you know what? Only about half of them ever survive. That's why they need me around.'

They stood watching the parade of little turtles lumbering towards the water. As a flock of gulls appeared Will and the girl yelled and stomped together, chasing them off.

The girl clapped her hands. 'Isn't that good? We didn't lose *one* —' She stopped and looked around darkly. 'Not yet, anyway. As long as other humans don't snatch them and sell them at market. Some folk have awful habits. Have you ever tasted turtle soup? Me, never. Do you know turtles can live until they're eighty? Can you imagine how many sisters and brothers and grandmas and cousins they must have?'

Will tried to imagine. He couldn't quite, given that he'd only ever known one relative, but he thought that what the girl described sounded mighty precious, and he decided right then

[13]

and there never to eat a turtle either, even if he was starving. Sure as sunrise, it would be somebody's sister or brother.

The girl pulled a pencil and small notebook out of her pocket.

'What are you writing?'

'I'm about to ask you some questions and I'd like to jot down your answers. We don't see many folk from foreign parts, so this is my chance. I'm making a study of different customs and one day I'd like to write a book about it so all the people in the world can get introduced to each other. Which island do you come from? Or do you hail from the Mainland?'

'I, um, live upriver on the hill.'

'Oh.'

In the silence, while the girl frowned in a puzzled way at her notebook, Will tried to think of a new thing to tell her. 'But I can walk a tightrope,' he said. 'My mother is a funambulist.'

'Fancy!' she said, her eyes brightening. '*That's* a new word. I've heard of tightropes in a circus on the Mainland, but I've never seen one. That's exactly the kind of thing I'm talking about – fascinating! Though I must say tightrope-walking looks awfully dangerous. Can you really do it? Did your mother teach you?'

Will's eyes suddenly filled. To distract them both, he pointed to the turtles making their way out of the sand. 'Where is *their* mother?'

'Oh she's swimming off to make more babies, I think. Where is yours?'

'I don't know.' Will looked down at his feet. 'I've been looking for her everywhere, but she's vanished. I'm lost, and I've never been so far downriver.'

The girl put her hand on his shoulder. It felt steady and strong, like something you could rely on. 'It's a good thing I turned up then,' she said, 'because I know every inch of this island, and that's a fact.'

When the last turtle had slipped into the sea, Will followed the girl back along the sand and into the forest. 'Why not come home with me while we think what to do?' she'd said. Her voice hadn't gone up at the end as questions usually do and, like everything else she'd said so far, this sounded like the only sensible plan. Even though she wasn't grown, there was something about the girl that made her seem that way.

'What's your name?' she asked, stopping suddenly, and cocking her head at him.

'Will.'

'Will what?'

He hesitated.

'It's all right if you don't want to give your name. Do you know, on Devil Island, no one even *has* a second name? Or maybe it's so secret, it can never be uttered. What do you think?'

Will wasn't sure. He was thinking about his mother's words, 'You are my Secret,' and how she said he must never tell anyone he was the son of a pirate.

'My name is Treasure,' said Treasure, slapping at a mosquito. 'Do you want to shake hands?'

Her palm was warm and firm. Will wanted to keep holding on to it.

But now the track narrowed and the forest thickened. Treasure strode ahead, flicking back vines and overhanging branches, and peeling away spiderwebs. Will hurried to keep up with her.

Treasure talked all the way, through the swamp bloodwoods and out into the next valley. She talked about hermit crabs and geckos – which weren't *really* bad luck, in her opinion – and how some people boiled up the skins of boa constrictors as a cure for aching feet. Her nanna, who lived on the Mainland and had bad gout, tried it once and said it tasted disgusting. She showed him the Hercules Beetle which had a big horn right in the middle of its chest, and the giant silk cotton tree that seemed to be smoking above the forest.

She told him not to step on the prickly pear as it stung like fire, and to look out for snakes. Sometimes he wanted to say, *I know that*, but he never did. Instead he asked more questions. Her talk was soothing, almost like a lullaby, and even as he walked his heartbeat slowed as if he were being sung to sleep after a nightmare. There was something so comforting about her flow of words after all that terrifying silence.

The climb through the forest became steep, and they had to use all their breath to scramble over rocks and fallen logs. There was just the snapping of sticks beneath their feet, and the whisper of the sea.

Soon there were new noises, a bleating cry.

'Goats,' said Treasure. 'Do you keep 'em?'

'No.'

'You'll see ours soon.'

As they puffed into the clearing at the top of the hill, two fluffy white animals with black faces trotted up. They nibbled at Treasure's face with their pink gums, and then at his own.

He laughed with surprise as he stroked them – their coats were so soft!

'We get milk from them,' Treasure informed him. 'I'll give you some.'

Will followed her up a stone path to a verandah hung with brightly woven cloths.

'Treasure, is that you?' came a voice.

It was cool and dim inside, the stone walls shutting out the daytime heat. A woman was sitting at a long wooden table near the stove. She was bent over her work, her curly dark hair springing out in spirals as if she'd been twisting it around her finger in thought. Will saw that she looked just like Treasure, only older.

'What do you think?' she asked, holding up a string of beads. 'Pretty?'

'Mm,' said Treasure. 'Much better. You were right about adding the blue.'

The woman beamed and said, 'Who's this?'

'Will,' said Treasure. 'I found him on the beach. He's lost and yesterday his mother vanished.'

'Oh dear.'

The woman stood up and came over to him. She was such a brightly coloured person in her red woven dress and rainbow earrings that she reminded him of a hummingbird or a flame flower – something so special you hold your breath when you see it. She looked deep into his face then nodded.

'You'll feel better as soon as you've had some nourishment.'

She brought out a blue pitcher that had been standing in a tub of cool water.

'Goat's milk and honey,' she said, pouring him a glass. 'Cold, sweet and strengthening.'

Will finished the glass in a gulp. But with it a raging hunger ballooned through his body and his knees almost gave way. It was as if the wanting had been waiting, folded down inside him until relief was near.

'Looks like you'll need more than milk to fill your belly. Treasure, light the stove and we'll heat up some sweet potato and that chicken in mango sauce.'

Even though his legs ached and his eyes were heavy, it was hard to keep still. He wandered among the strange coloured balls that swung down on strings from the roof beams like giant painted eggs. They were decorated with scenes of birds and flowers.

'Calabash ornaments,' said Treasure. 'You know, seed pods from the calabash tree. Mamma decorates them and sells them at market.' Treasure waved airily around her. 'She sells necklaces too, and her weavings. What does your mother sell?'

'Clay pots,' he murmured.

Treasure's mother whirled around from the stove. 'That's your mother? Makes those pots? They're wonderful – you can put sour tomatoes on to stew and they finish up sweet. Why, I see her often, and we have a word together. She hasn't ever mentioned me to you?' She tapped her chest. 'Honey. My name is Honey. I gave her that blue-and-gold necklace last year, do you know it?' She gave a low whistle. 'But I never knew she had a child. Why is that now?'

Will shrugged. The lake of things he shouldn't say and

didn't know had grown into a sea that might drown him. So it was better not to open his mouth.

'Well, I'm sure she had her reasons,' said Honey. 'Now, set the table, Treasure, and we'll have lunch.'

Treasure cleared all the beads and string and paints and brushes from one end of the table to the other, and put down orange mats for the three of them. When Will sat down to eat, such a sweet spiciness popped on his tongue that it almost stung. He ate without saying a word, and held out his plate gratefully when he was offered a second helping.

He was grateful, too, that the talk had turned away from vanishing mothers. He learnt that the glossy red beads on the table were seeds from the jumbie tree growing right here on the island, and that you could sell a necklace quick as a wink on the Mainland. But there you had to keep your wits about you as folk would try to cheat you as sure as a mongoose snares a snake. Treasure liked to accompany her mother on those trips, she said, as she always discovered new facts about the habits of Mainlanders and how to handle them.

After lunch, Honey brewed up bush tea for them all. Will ate a generous slice of banana cake too, followed by a bowl of custard. He couldn't remember ever tasting anything so rich and smooth. Then he leaned back in his chair with a sigh. He could feel his eyes closing and there was nothing he could do about it.

'The poor child's exhausted,' said Honey. 'Show young Will out to the hammock on the back verandah, Treasure. He'll catch the afternoon breeze there and have a quiet nap. You'll see,' Honey stroked his hot forehead, 'everything will look better after a bit of shut-eye.'

Will got up wearily, thanking them both for lunch, and followed Treasure out to the back steps. He sank into the striped hammock and almost at once his eyes closed.

~ * ~

Will woke to shadows gathering on the rolling slope below, and voices coming from inside. For a wild moment he thought his mother had come to collect him. He raced through the beaded curtain and into the house.

Treasure and Honey were sitting at the table threading beads. They must have recognised the expression on his face, as Honey said something like *sshhh*, heading straight for him, her arms outstretched. She smelled of paint and something spicy, cinnamon or nutmeg.

'Now we've been talking,' said Honey, 'and made a plan. Tomorrow is market day. I will ask around if anybody has seen or heard about your mother. But we need to know exactly where you live. Is it the little house across the valley on Turnabout Hill?'

Will nodded.

'Good. We've always said those folk at Turnabout Hill keep themselves to themselves.' Honey looked at Will curiously, as if expecting something from him.

'Please, Mrs Honey,' Will burst out. 'If you go to market, you mustn't tell anyone about me. I mean, please do ask about my mother but please don't tell anyone about *me*. My mother said I was her Secret and that's why she never told you about me.'

Honey and Treasure studied him with their dark, serious eyes. He felt the heat rise up to his hairline. He knew they were good folk, but he had to keep his mother's faith.

He waited for their questions.

But there was only the soft *plik* of a bird calling in the dusk outside and the shadows knitting in the corners of the room.

Honey gave a decisive nod, and stood up.

'Fair enough,' she said. 'There's a lot of folk out there we'd all rather didn't know our business, and that's a fact. I'll be cautious in my dealings but I'll find some news of your mother, Will, never you worry.'

Will smiled at her and felt a leap in his chest. Light was stirring in that long dark day. He hoped the next would bring his mother back to him.

chapter 3

From his hammock on the verandah, Will heard Honey moving around in the early dawn. There was the crack of kindling for the woodstove, the rattle of a tea cup. And then the creak of the door closing.

He was glad to hear Treasure stirring on the other side of the wall.

'Do you want eggs for breakfast?' she said as she popped her head through the beaded curtain. 'And you can have toast with guava jam.'

'Yes, please,' said Will. He hopped out of the hammock and followed her.

'The stove needs more wood,' she told him when he asked what he could do to help. 'See, that pile is chopped up, all ready to go.'

As Will picked up the small logs, he tried not to think about the strange man who'd come to chop the wood at home. The smell of cigar smoke was still sharp in his mind. Had the man really been looking for work? He wished he didn't have to think about that now, when the flames were leaping brightly in the stove, and Treasure was humming a cheerful song.

'I made the jam myself,' she said when they were sitting at the table. 'You have to stir it for ages while it boils, with spoonfuls of brown sugar. It's delicious!'

She put a dollop of jam on his toast. The crimson sweetness melted in with the yellow butter and when he put the whole thing in his mouth the juices spurted.

Treasure laughed and swung her legs. 'Mother says it's like eating sunrise. She puts lime juice in too – that makes it tangy. But I like *sweet*. She'll probably buy more guavas today at market. Oh, and she said she'd get some shoes for you, too. You can't go running round barefoot forever!'

Forever. He didn't want that word, it had no shape, it was like that awful drifting place where river meets sky, and nothing is real.

'I have to go back,' Will blurted. 'Now. My mother might have come home and she'd be worried about me.'

Treasure leant over and put her hands on his knees. 'I'll come with you.'

Will tried on the sandals Treasure gave him. They were hers from last summer, and they fit, although the strap at his heels pinched a little, which he didn't mention.

'Excellent,' said Treasure, beaming at him.

He caught the apple she threw at him to eat on the way.

'We'll go down the hill and along the river,' she said. 'It might be shorter to cut across the valley in the middle, but the forest there is too thick.'

Will stopped for a quick pat of the goats as he crossed the garden, and then he was running downhill after Treasure.

It was so much faster going down than up. They followed the rough path they'd trod before, only slowing now and then to squeeze between fern trees growing close together as bristles on a brush, or rock ledges dropping suddenly away. When they reached the mangroves, their faces were damp.

'Further upriver we can take a drink. But here the water is too salty from the sea. It's called *brackish*.' Treasure pointed towards the mouth of the river and its run into the Cannonball Sea. The sun glinted on the horizon, sharp and dangerous. Will quickly glanced away, and headed towards home and the *un*-brackish river he knew.

They picked their way along the bank mostly in silence. Roots rose hard as rocks in their path, and they had to look where they put their feet. As they grew nearer to the track up to Turnabout Hill, Will began to hurry. He felt like calling out, announcing his return, almost as if *he* were the one who'd disappeared, and now he'd decided to come home. He pictured his mother running out into the garden, her apron still tied at her waist after morning chores, scolding and smiling.

'What's that up there in the trees?' Treasure called from behind him.

The tightrope stretched between the mangrove trees. He could see the ladder still there, leaning against the trunk as it had always done. It seemed so long since he'd climbed it, and yet no time at all.

'Oh, is that your funambi-thingummy?' said Treasure.

'Tightrope,' said Will.

'Could you show me how you do it? I've never seen anyone walk on thin air in the true world. We have a storybook about a circus at home, but it doesn't teach you how to walk the tightrope.'

Will hesitated. He just wanted to tear up the hill and see his mother. But a small part of him was afraid of what he might find.

'Well,' he said, 'it takes time to learn the tightrope. You have to practise.'

'I bet it takes days and days and days.'

'More like a year. Especially when you go high. You can't take risks when you're up in the treetops. You have to keep checking your centre as you go. It's your balance that's important. And you have to keep moving, one foot after the other. Never look back, only forward, with your eyes on the prize.'

It felt good to be telling Treasure something she didn't know. He felt more grown up. And he liked using his mother's words; it was as if she were here nestled inside him, whispering.

'I'll show you, if you'd like,' he said. 'Later we can practise on something lower. That's how my mother taught me.'

Treasure rustled in her pocket for her notebook and pencil. She settled herself on a large mangrove root, her face lifted up to him expectantly.

As Will placed his foot on the rope, a calm came over him. His mind went straight to his centre, that steady ticking place in his middle. He let the feeling fill him, and although the sun danced on his skin and a fish leapt in the water, his eyes didn't shift from the prize.

With each step he felt for his centre. He didn't need to touch it; that place just above his navel. It was a ball of liquid gold, balancing the world inside him. No one can take *that* from you, his mother said.

At the other end, he stepped off the rope and climbed into the tree. He heard Treasure call something, but he didn't feel like talking yet. Most folk would probably find this a scary place, where a fall would mean broken bones at best. But here he felt safe. Above him a nest rustled with baby birds. A hummingbird flew in, its wings beating wildly. As it turned in the sunlight, its throat glowed purple.

When Will came down, he told Treasure, 'It was feeding its babies, right at the top there. You have to stay still as a stone to watch. I've seen hummingbirds fly backwards and forwards, up and down.'

Treasure was writing busily. 'Really? Backwards? That's very unusual. I've never seen one up close. What do they use for their nest?'

'Twigs and bark and moss, and once I saw the fluff from my mother's red blanket – the lining has to be soft for the eggs.'

Suddenly Will didn't want any more words. A wave was rising in his chest, bringing urgent thoughts back in. 'I'm going up the hill now,' he said.

He tore through the bloodwoods and the giant ferns with leaves like serving plates. He could hear Treasure crashing behind but he couldn't slow his feet. He vaulted over the garden wall covered in vines and raced up the path.

'Mother! Mother!' he cried, as he ran through the open door. 'I'm home!'

A fly buzzed on the table. Pieces of pawpaw lay on a plate. Ants crawled in the mushed orange flesh.

He picked up the knife lying near the plate. It was caked with dried juice, and a single black seed stuck to the blade. A box of broken eggs lay open, bits of shell glued to the floor in a puddle of yolk. The fire in the wood stove had turned to ash and the iron pot on top was cold. It was so still in that room that it didn't feel true. A spell had bewitched his home, and put everything to sleep.

'What a mess,' said Treasure, clicking her tongue. 'Probably a mongoose. Aren't they like pirates? Always raiding and plundering. Still, I suppose they have to eat like everybody else...'

Will ran through the side door and out to the mango tree. He thrashed at the grasses. He dug his nails into the sweet potato vines and the wild sorrel, pulling up stems by the roots. He kicked the stupid stones in the stupid dirt.

He ran and kicked and swore until his breath was gone. Then he flung himself face-down in the grass. Everything was black beneath his lids. The quiet of the treetops had vanished, the gold had gone. He never wanted to see his home again with those festering ants or that raiding, plundering mongoose. He never wanted to see his home again without his mother in it.

chapter 4

William didn't say much on the way back to Treasure's. He answered when she spoke to him, which was quite a lot, but he didn't like his wobbly voice or the lump in his throat that swelled each time he opened his mouth.

'I'll make us some lunch,' said Treasure in a bright tone, when they walked through her door. 'We can have tomatoes and cheese and then Mamma will be home – maybe she will have some news.'

Will wandered outside and came back in. He set up a fire in the wood stove for the evening, and straightened the table. He fidgeted all through lunch and got up the moment it was finished.

It was easier to keep walking around. When he stood still, there was the grey place at the edge of the world where everything meets but nothing is said. He studied the paintings of ships on the walls and looked at the titles of the books on the shelves. One caught his eye and he pulled it out.

'Do you want to read that?' said Treasure. 'It's about a man who was shipwrecked on an island.'

'What, right here?'

'No, not *this* island. His ship sank and he was all alone, so he had to learn how to survive by himself. Then one day, for the first time, he saw footprints on the beach – a *human's* footprints…'

'Whose were they? A pirate's?'

'Why don't you read it?'

Will made a face. 'I don't know my letters very well yet.'

'Oh,' said Treasure, 'I do. I love to read – my mother says we only get one life but if we read we can live a thousand.'

Will thought about this. 'Has she read a thousand books?'

Treasure shrugged. 'Do you want me to read it to you? I'll trace the words with my finger as I go.'

Treasure sat next to Will on the wicker couch. As she read, pictures of the shipwrecking storm filled his mind. Waves rose up like cliffs but the sailor swam through them. Will wished he had learned to swim too, and remembered that this was another thing on his mother's list to teach him.

He found himself imagining the sailor and his feelings on sighting land, the deathly weariness of his limbs, the foul taste of sea water in his mouth, and he let himself be carried away from this awful day just like the sailor by the waves.

Both Will and Treasure jumped when Honey came in. She dumped a bunch of bananas on the table and a pair of canvas shoes.

Will scanned Honey's face. He had to take a deep breath before he asked his question. But Treasure tumbled straight in.

'Did you hear any news?'

'Yes and no,' said Honey slowly. She picked up the shoes and waved them at Will. 'I met someone who knows you. Who knows exactly what size your feet are, and that you are in need of these.'

'But how is *that*?' said Treasure. She turned to Will. 'I thought you were a Secret!'

Will's throat was dry. But he managed to whisper the one thing he needed to know. 'Did you find my mother?'

Honey shook her head.

'Well, but did you find anyone who's seen her?'

Honey came to sit next to him on the rocking chair. 'I don't know where your mother is right now, Will. It's going to take some time. But there's a woman I see at the market a couple of times a year. She doesn't live on our island, she travels here to buy herbs – medicinal, mostly. She has a Siamese cat that sits on her shoulders. They say she's a Wise Woman. She doesn't say much, and she talks in riddles. But there's something about her. You tend to believe whatever she says.'

'Well, what is her name?' asked Treasure. 'Where does she come from?'

Honey rocked on the chair for a moment. Her eyes weren't focused on Treasure or Will or the shoes in her lap. She looked far away, as if she were still listening to the strange woman's words.

'Mamma?'

'Gretel,' said Honey, coming back to the moment. 'Her name is Gretel, and she sails here in her little boat all the way from Devil Island.'

'Oh!' said Will, glancing up at Treasure. 'That's the place where they have only one name.'

Honey shivered. 'That's right. It's a cursed place. You don't ever want to go there.'

'Yes I do,' said Treasure. 'One day I'm going to visit and find out *why* they only have one name. And then I'm going to put them in my book.'

'They won't tell you, Treasure, my dear. Folks on Devil Island are all hard as nails and thick as coots. They don't bother to learn their letters or do their sums because there's no hope for them.'

Will and Treasure looked at each other.

Honey stared down at the shoes in her lap. 'It's worse for the boys.' She frowned, thinking. 'But then, maybe it's worse for the girls because some of them grow up to become mothers.'

'What's worse?' asked Will.

'Every year,' said Honey, 'sure as the hurricanes blow in, pirates come raiding Devil Island.'

'Pirates?' whispered Will.

Honey clicked her teeth in disgust. 'Vermin of the seas. Scum of the earth. They steal all the twelve-year-old boys and put them to work like slaves on their ships. They keep them for two years, but most don't even live that long. If there were a spell to get rid of every last pirate, I'd be dancing the high jig. Why, I'd not mourn a single one amongst them, and that's a fact.'

Will swallowed. He could never tell them about his father. He knew that now. Pirates, even pirates from Some Reluctance, were unmentionable.

[31]

But Honey was studying his feet. 'Those sandals are wet. I see river weed.' She looked stern. 'Have you been out?'

'We went back to Turnabout Hill,' Treasure said, putting an arm around Will's shoulders, 'to see if his mother had come home.'

'Oh my word,' said Honey. 'You mustn't do that again. It could be very dangerous. Until we know what has happened to your mother, Will, I don't want you or Treasure going there alone.'

Will jumped up, knocking away Treasure's arm. 'But I have to, I have to! My mother could come home any time and what would she do if I wasn't there?'

'Sit down, Will sweetheart, and listen. A Wise Woman knows many things that we don't. I said nothing of you at market. But when Gretel heard me asking at the bread stall about your mother, she turned to me and whispered, "Have you got the boy?"

'Well, I didn't know what to say, I was so astonished. But she just nodded when she saw my face and said, "Good, that's as it should be. He must stay with you, under your protection. He has no shoes, so mind he wears these." And she handed me this pair here, see? "The shoes are charmed and will help keep him safe," she went on. "But I can't give him protection very far from your home. He must not go upriver, and never back to Turnabout Hill. You must tell him." She pressed my hand when she said that, just lightly, but my arm turned icy cold from the wrist to the shoulder. Such an odd sensation.' And Honey shuddered, rubbing her arm.

There was silence for a minute as they all thought about

Gretel's words. Will remembered how hard it had been to stay in his house and yet how unbearable it was to leave.

'But what is the danger?' he burst out.

Honey shook her head, her lips clasped together. 'Like I said, when Gretel talks, you believe her. And you heed her words.'

Will sucked the inside of his cheek. Who was this Wise Woman? Was she a Traveller, could she read the future in the flames? His mother said that not all those Travellers had the gift; some just pretended and made up pretty stories for a handful of silver.

'The fishmonger told me that he'd seen your mother's boat just this morning, tied up next to his like always,' Honey said. 'So she sure hasn't sailed off – at least not of her own choice.' Honey stared darkly at the floor. 'Devil Island's not the only place raided by pirates, you can be sure of that. There are folk about that none of us should like to meet.'

'There was a man,' Will said suddenly. 'Came to our house smoking a cigar. He said he was passing through. Do you think...?'

Honey turned to Will then, lifting his chin with her finger. 'I don't know what to think right now. I only know you can't go back home alone. And I can't risk it myself either, what with both of you to care for. We'll just have to keep our ears open. We'll sit tight and wait until she returns. Your mother will be doing everything she can to get back to you, Will, you can count on that.'

In the quiet of the room a dragonfly buzzed, trapped, at the windowsill.

'And in the meantime you'll stay here and keep us company,' put in Treasure. 'I can teach you your letters and you can teach me the tightrope. We'll be all right!'

Will looked at Honey frowning at him in concern. He felt Treasure's hand squeeze his shoulder. They were kind, honest people and they knew a lot about the world. But the idea of *never* going back was impossible. He would find a way to return, he would, and it would be soon.

In the weeks following the day that Honey met the Wise Woman, Will's world changed. Sometimes, when he stopped for a moment, he wondered who he was now. He used to be content to spend hours alone practising the tightrope or sit, watching, in the trees. He'd absorb things silently, like grass sucking in sunlight. And if he had important things to tell about what he'd seen or thought or dreamt, he saved them up for his mother.

But now there was always someone there, right next to his thoughts. And there was always something new to do. It was as if the world had been a scrunched-up ball of paper and suddenly it had opened up.

'After breakfast,' Treasure said one morning, 'I'll show you my hermit crab. I'm keeping him as a pet so I can learn about him. Hermit crabs are fascinating. Do you keep any?'

'Never even seen one. But I'd like to.'

From under a rock ledge she pulled out a wooden box. 'Hermy,' she said, 'meet Will.'

Will saw a blue-and-white stripy shell, a small bowl of water, some cut-up apple and green leafy vegetables. But no sign of a crab.

'Pick up the shell, that's right. Now give it a gentle tap.'

Will peered inside. He took a sharp breath when a large claw and popping eyes appeared at the opening.

'That's Hermy. Mostly he hides in his shell, but he comes out to eat and drink and say hello. He loves his home but he's growing fast and soon it will be too small.'

Will liked Hermy's surprised eyes and waving feelers. He looked curious and friendly and very smart. Will didn't want him to be homeless. 'What will he do then?' he asked.

'He'll have to move house,' said Treasure. 'That's what hermit crabs do. They have to keep finding a bigger home as they grow. If you like we can go down to the beach later and look for one. Or maybe two, so he has a choice.'

As Treasure changed Hermy's water and refreshed his food, Will wondered how Hermy would feel about his new house, and how much he'd miss his old one. If he'd lived all his life so far in the blue stripy shell, how could he ever get used to something different?

But when they found a bigger shell, and Will watched the athletic way Hermy manoeuvred himself out of the old and into the new, popping his head out again to devour a clump of weed, he saw that Hermy had made himself at home.

Will felt strangely cheered by Hermy's successful move. He wasn't sure why, but somehow he had a special feeling about Hermy, as if they understood each other and had something important in common. Treasure let him take on the job of looking after Hermy's food and water, and that was the first thing he did each morning.

Will liked looking after Hermy. He liked having a routine,

and he would make it last, spending a long time coaxing him out of his shell and watching him eat. Will enjoyed feeding the goats too and running his hands through their fleece. And in the late afternoons he'd take Treasure out to the rope he'd strung up between the coconut palms in her garden, and teach her how to find her balance. She was an eager student and concentrated well, and each day she could stay on the rope a little longer. But the part of the day that Will enjoyed most now was when he sat down with Treasure to read.

Soon he knew all the letters of the alphabet, and could put many of them together into words that made sense. And at the end of the lesson, when Treasure read him a story, he flew away with her to a different place.

They finished the sailor story and went on to read the adventures of tiny folk the size of rolling pins. There was a boy who climbed a bean-stalk into the clouds and a giant who caused an earthquake every time he walked in the forest. Reading with Treasure was like being up in the trees; his own troubles shrank so he could barely see them, so carried away was he by a story.

What he hated, though, was when Treasure closed the book and he was dropped like a brick back into the real world.

Before long he decided he'd have to do extra practice on his own if he wanted to be able to read as easily as Treasure. It would be like having her voice inside him whenever he wanted. And you never knew when a person might be snatched away. Baby turtles could be snatched by birds, lizards gobbled up before they'd lived their first day. And although Will couldn't help being interested in each new thing as it came along, he became wary. Where once he used to just glance at things and accept them, now he looked twice, to make sure. He hung on to things and traced their shape in his mind to store for later in case they vanished.

Through every day there ran the thought of returning home. It was always there, holding him slightly apart from everything else.

chapter 5

Will saw four full moons come and go before the big rains came. Honey said he should move inside to sleep, so they strung up his hammock near the big window overlooking the garden.

Often now he read by the light of the kerosene lamp. He could read for hours without getting tired. He read about all kinds of different people, what they thought, loved, hated, yearned for, what made them angry or sad. Sometimes he felt he'd learnt so much about the world in this short time that if he only read just a little more, he might find a clue as to how to rescue his mother.

The big winds came with the rains as they did every year, and he helped tie down the canvas sheets protecting the goats' pen and the chook house. He patched the leaky spots in the roof and walls and inspected the state of the tool shed, too, even though Honey hadn't mentioned it. Treasure's collection of saws, hammers, and even the good vice on the bench were rusting in the rain. At dawn he began work on the shed's roof and the small high window that invited water in like a drain, and he was finished by lunch.

'You're a gift to us, Will,' said Honey, watching the nimble way he climbed up the walls and swung along the roof.

'And that's a fact,' agreed Treasure.

Will laughed and went in to wash up for lunch. It was cosy in the dry, sweet-smelling house, with the bowls of frangipani and passionfruit flowers on the table. Soon there'd be pumpkin pie and banana fritters for dessert.

Will was glad to be useful. But with each wild-weather day, he worried a little more about his own home, and wondered if his mother was making her way towards it.

In all this time there'd not been a skerrick of news. And since the weather set in, Honey hadn't been able to get to market. The rain was too heavy and the winds too strong, and they heard there'd been a landslide in one of the northern valleys.

In the fourth week of rain a fisherman came by to see if they'd like some salted cod he'd been keeping for the rainy season. Honey was glad of the fish and the company, and they sat around the table scooping up tasty slabs of white fish with fresh baked bread and butter.

'And who's this fine lad then?' the fisherman asked, after he'd told them about the health of his family and his own strapping boys. 'Haven't seen you around here before.'

Will stared at the man blankly, the red rising on his cheeks.

'This here's my third cousin Will,' Treasure said quickly, 'come to see us from the Mainland. He works in a cobbler's shop and has to make eleven pairs of shoes a day or he's sent to bed with no dinner.'

Honey looked at Treasure with raised eyebrows.

'You'll have to excuse him,' Treasure went on. 'He's not used to company, on account of the fact that he spends most of his time in the workshop, cutting and hammering. The master is a terrible slave-driver with red eyes like a demon and great *suppurating* boils on his neck.'

Will had never heard Treasure tell such a story, except when she was reading to him from a book, and he couldn't help grinning.

'Aye,' said the fisherman, 'I used to work for a man like that and soon as I could, I lit out and bought my own boat. Never been happier. When he gets older, he should do the same. Start saving now, young Will, and you'll be sitting pretty.'

The fisherman went on to give more advice about the working world, and Will nodded wisely, trying not to let the bubble of laughter inside escape. But when the man got up to go, he said something that shook the fun out of the day.

'Hear about that bad business at Turnabout Hill?' The fisherman clicked his tongue. 'The woman who lives there, you know, makes the clay pots for market? Disappeared, just like that,' and he snapped his fingers.

'Yes,' said Honey quietly.

'I passed by there the other day, making my rounds – I was shocked to see how the place has gone to ruins. Half the roof hanging off.' He shook his head. 'I mean, the lady kept herself to herself, but she always had a friendly word and she did fine work. My wife loves her clay pots, like most other folk hereabouts.'

After the man left, Honey put an arm around Will's

shoulders. 'That fisherman's talk wasn't easy to listen to, I know. But remember, you're safe here and this is your home now.'

Will winced.

'Only until your mother returns,' Honey added quickly. 'And when she does, we'll all be along to set your house to rights.'

But late that evening after dinner, Will thought about the fisherman's words. His mind turned again and again to his crumbling house; he saw the roof torn off, his mother's precious things open to the ruinous skies. He remembered how in the last two years, since he'd got taller, he'd helped her nail down the tin sheets before the hurricanes hit. He'd helped prepare for the storms just as he'd done for Honey.

A cramp clutched at his belly. The boy in the book he was reading had to leave his sick little sister at home to get help. Only the boy hadn't been able to return to his house because he was captured by villains...

Will felt hot with shame. *He* hadn't been captured by villains, had he? What excuse did he have for not taking care of their house? How would his mother feel when she returned and found he'd left their home to rot?

Enough! he almost shouted. *Pickle me toes and pour rum up me nose – I'm going back to fix it, and nothing is going to stop me.*

He repeated the words under his breath while he went to fetch the tools. The saw was freshly oiled and the hammer and nails in good condition; he wouldn't have time for blunt equipment. He'd have to be back in his hammock before light broke.

He threw a coil of rope into the sack and took the lamp from the kitchen. As he headed for the door, he slipped on his shoes. *They won't protect him very far*, he heard the Wise Woman whisper. *Never go back to Turnabout Hill.*

A trickle of dread started in his chest.

Gritting his teeth, he started down the path. But when he got to the end of the garden, with the wilderness of the forest before him, a fog drifted into his mind.

He shook his head, trying to clear it; he rubbed furiously at his eyes. But no matter what he tried, his thoughts were blurring. The way ahead, only minutes ago shining bright, was meshing into cloud. And still the fog inside him was rising.

His steps slowed to a drag. His feet became clay, as if all the heaviness of the night were pooling in his toes. And a terrible dread gathered inside him.

The fog was thickening, whispering to him. The whisper became a voice, and it grew to a roar that pounded behind his eyes. It welled up from the soles of his feet and broke in waves over his head – *go back go back* – until it washed over everything else.

Will clapped his hands over his ears, but it didn't stop. He tried to become a thing instead of a boy, blocking the noise, cutting it off at the root. He focused on the regular rhythm of his legs, working them like the pendulum of the clock on Honey's wall.

He left the path and trudged on, trying not to hear, trying to notice each real thing he passed: the clump of palms, the silk cotton tree, a mongoose feasting on a snake. Soon I'll be there, he told himself. But when he looked down the hill there was always further to go.

And now, at his feet, a darkness was spreading. It seeped like water, staining the night that had been bright with moonlight. He could no longer see a path ahead and the roaring turned to a dread that stopped him dead.

Will sat down on the ground. He couldn't go on. The noise wouldn't let him.

He took off the shoes and lay them beside him. And he listened to the quiet...

The sweet breath of the night, the call of a bird. Deep inside him, only a sighing was left after the roar, like the wake trailing a boat.

Peace.

He stood up and tried a leap into the air. His knees obeyed him. The little springs in the balls of his feet tightened and released as they should. He gave a wild shout and began to run. The earth underfoot was sharp with small stones and roots but he ran so lightly, it was as if his feet hardly touched the ground.

The moon was silvering the edges of leaves, gleaming in a bird's eye, a dew drop. He leapt down from rock ledges and hurtled over logs, passing through the night like a shadow. He imagined he was a hummingbird, flying over the treetops.

Not once since his mother had vanished had he felt so free and strong – he was in the right place, doing the right thing. And no one could tell him any different.

When he got to the river he slowed his pace through the mangroves. No breeze stirred the water, and his feet splashed still pools of moonlight. Luck was with him – even the weather was holding for the job he had to do.

And yet as he wound around the bend, his unease grew; the night was almost too calm. He remembered his mother calling him in at times like this. There'd be the eerie green light over the river, a strange hush. *Don't get caught in the calm before the storm*, she'd warned. She called it the giant's eye.

The moon was low in the sky. Soon there'd be the bloodwood trees and the tightrope and the climb up Turnabout Hill. If a storm was coming he'd just have to be quick, and make it back before the rains hit.

But as he neared the top of the hill, he couldn't draw a deep breath. Now it was hard to face what lay there, even without the shoes. Keeping his eyes lowered, he crept along the path up to his house.

It was bad. Just as the fisherman had said, whole sheets of tin had slid away from the corners of the roof. When he crept around to the back, he saw that a great tree had fallen across, causing the tin to buckle into a gaping hole.

He made himself walk through the front door. A broken window had let in rain. Mounds of mud and leaves were spattered on the floor. He stood for a moment in the middle of the kitchen. Moonlight shone down through the hole in the roof, puddling in the dirt at his feet.

The house was a ruin.

His eyes moved around dully. He knew he couldn't fix it. It was a nightmare – the snapped-off tree lying crazily on the roof, the tin sheets splintered. He could climb and hammer and tie down ropes, but he didn't have the strength to haul a tree. He was just a boy.

He sat for a while at the table, thinking about nothing.

But his muscles twitched. Couldn't he do something? Maybe he'd start by boarding up the window. He could drag out some buckets to stand under the leaks, roll up the mats that were rotting… If his mother came back – *when* his mother came back – at least she would see he'd tried.

He chewed his lip. His head was so heavy on his neck, he might just lay it down for a little while on the table. Just a little rest. Then he'd make a start.

chapter 6

If Will had known how the path of his life would change in those next dark hours, he'd have turned around and raced back through the forest to Treasure. It's easy to see the wrong turnings when you look back from a distance, but right then, Will was just at the beginning.

He straightened up with a jolt. There'd been a wind moaning at the edge of his dream. He listened to the night outside. Something was growing; a whistling swelling into a howling that rattled at the door and threatened to burst in. Through the hole in the roof he saw clouds scudding through the sky.

A storm was coming.

Leaves and branches were whirling by. Will ran to the window, then to the pantry where the buckets stood. He picked one up, put it back. He couldn't make up his mind what to do first – nothing was *right*. There was no time.

You're safe here with us, said Treasure in his mind. *We'll be all right.*

He hovered near the window. What could he use to patch it? He couldn't think with the wind screaming at him. It was high-pitched as if blowing through a tunnel. Then a low crashing note came, like a tree thudding down. Fat splotches of rain blew through the cracks. He could hear it banging on the tin roof. The moon was rocking in the wind like a boat in the sea. Soon the gale would be so strong it'd pick him up like a leaf and send him flying.

But another sound was riding the air – a squabble of words, a shouted curse. Or was it a trick of the wind? The sounds grew louder, nearer, separating themselves from the whooshing of the wind.

Humans, whispered Treasure.

Pirates, whispered his mother.

He stood frozen at the window.

Then through the broken glass he saw the dark shape of a man. A bolt of lightning lit up his head and shoulders. Will hadn't seen many men, but this one seemed twice the size of the fisherman who'd stayed for lunch. As a cloud clutched at the moon and let it go, Will saw he held a long silver sword in his hand.

Will flung himself under the table. He tucked up his legs and his blood beat loud in his ears.

The door crashed open and a pair of black boots came striding across the floor.

'Where *is* the little varmint?'

The boots kicked a stool just a thumb's length from Will's knee. He gasped, then clapped a hand over his mouth.

Will watched as slowly, like a dream, the tops of the boots

sank level with his eyes. Then came trouser legs patched at the knees, a belt engraved with a skull-and-crossbones, and finally the whole man was squatting on the floor, peering under the table with his beefy face only an inch from Will's.

'There you are,' he cried. He shot out a hairy fist to haul Will up and as he reached across there was a loud crack of bones. 'Oh me flamin' knees!'

Will slithered out the other side of the table and ran for the door. He was on the path with the wind on his face when something blocked him. The clouds parted for a moment and in the terrible white moonlight Will saw another man, leaner but quicker than the first.

The man grabbed Will by the wrist and pulled him into the house. 'You nearly lost 'im, you great bungler!' he said to the first man as they tumbled back inside. 'Lucky you had *me* on the job.'

'Watch it, Squid,' said the big man. 'I'm in charge 'ere an' I'm the oldest too, so you oughta show some respect. The Captain made me First Mate this morning, remember?'

Squid made a face. His breath smelled of rum.

'A...Are you pirates?' whispered Will.

'Where's Dogfish?' the First Mate went on, ignoring Will as if he were a fly they'd just swatted. 'I wanna get out of this weather and back to the ship soon as we can.'

Squid shrugged. 'He was complaining about his stomach again, belchin' like a volcano. Musta ate something that didn't agree with 'im,' and he smirked. His tongue sucked on the black hole where his front tooth was missing.

Will's stomach heaved. He tried to tug away, but Squid still had hold of his wrist, and the man's fingers were as sharp as claws.

'Where's your mamma then?' Squid asked him suddenly.

Will was looking at the iron pot on the table. It was just inches from his free hand. A clout over the head with the pot would surely make this Squid loosen his grip.

'She'll be back any moment,' he said quickly. 'And she'll be bringing my...my third cousin who is a...a wood chopper with eyes like a demon and suppurating boils on his neck, and he'll be bringing his *axe*.'

'Oooh,' hooted Squid, 'now I'm really quakin' in me shoes.' But as he pretended to shiver, his hand lost its firm grip and Will scooted around behind him. He dodged an upturned chair and slid on the mud across the floor. Leaping up, he almost fell into the arms of a third man walking through the door.

'Pickle me toes and pour rum up me nose,' the man cried. 'But he's a lively one!'

Will stood still. 'What did you say?'

'Eh?' said the man.

'Are you my father, sir?' asked Will.

chapter 7

The man's eyes widened with surprise. He looked younger than the others, even though his belly swelled out from his shirt like a pumpkin. But the other men just laughed and shook their heads.

'Come on, get him now before he runs for it again,' said the First Mate. 'I don't wanna spend the night chasin' fleas.'

Squid grabbed Will around the waist and hoisted him into the air. He came down *whumpf* over Squid's knobbly shoulder, his legs stuck in a grip as tight as a cork in a bottle.

'So none of you is my father then? Is that right?' Will managed to ask, his face squashed into the man's back. 'Are you pirates or not?'

The men were striding around the room, opening cupboards, examining the kitchen. They seemed intent on collecting various cooking utensils, together with anything they could eat.

'Well, if none of you is my father,' Will went on, 'how did you know I was here? I mean, it was me you were looking for, wasn't it?'

'Your daddy told us all about you, an' those were 'is last and final words,' the pumpkin-bellied man sighed sadly, as he closed the cutlery drawer.

'You mean, my father is dead?'

'Aye, he told us to look after you when he was gone. And we promised.'

'I don't remember makin' no promise, Dogfish,' said Squid.

'You *are* pirates!' Will burst out.

'And you're sharp as a blade,' sneered Squid.

'A promise to a pirate on his deathbed oughta be kept till the end,' Dogfish reminded Squid, fixing him with a narrowed eye. 'So we ain't gunna hurt a hair on the lad's head, right? He's a pirate's son, and we treat 'im like one of us.' Turning back to Will, he whispered, 'You'll be right as a ship's rat in a galley with us lookin' after you.'

'Aye, eatin' maggot jerky and weevil bread,' Squid sniggered under his breath.

Will was trying to find a way to wriggle out from the pirate's arm and digest this awful news at the same time. He didn't think the hole inside him full of missing people could get any bigger. But it just had.

'What was he like?' he asked. 'My father?'

Dogfish grinned. 'He liked a joke, your daddy. Always playin' tricks, tryin' to liven things up on board. An' he had an eye for the ladies. But he jumped ship to woo your mother. Blimey, did we 'ear all about *her*. A real beauty, a lively lass if ever there was one. And she was right sweet on him, too. He'd have stayed with her till the end, changed 'imself into a landlubber even, if the bloomin' Captain hadn't interfered.

Black as thunder the Captain was, lashed into a fury by the whole affair. In my opinion, he wanted her for—'

'Will yer take a squiz at this!' Squid cut in, holding up a bottle of rum. 'Did yer mamma like a drop then?'

'No!' cried Will. 'That was my father's. She never opened it. She hated the stuff. But it was the only thing she had left of him.'

'Then we'll open it now,' said Squid. 'What a piece of luck!'

Will shut his eyes. He smelled the sickening fumes as Squid popped the cork one-handed and took a swig. He remembered his mother saying she hated the way drink made his father careless...

'Oi, leave that now,' the First Mate said, grabbing it from him. 'It'll come in handy for snuffin' out the Captain's lights when he's in a rage.'

'Parbuckle me timbers,' cursed Squid. 'Why does that devil always have to get the good stuff? It ain't fair!'

'So how did he die?' Will asked. 'He wasn't very old was he?'

'That old dog'll *never* die, worse luck,' muttered Squid.

'The lad's talkin' about his daddy, pickle brains,' Dogfish told Squid. 'He died a noble death, lad, at the end of the enemy's sword. I held him in me arms, and it was then 'e told me about 'is precious son. He'd kept you a secret all these years, told yer mamma to bring you to this lonely place. He was waitin' till you was bigger, till he could escape the Captain... but now it's too late.'

'Aye, an' more's the pity we 'ad to come to this festerin' island in a festerin 'urricane and fetch the little blighter,' said the First Mate.

[52]

Will bit his cheek. Maybe you couldn't miss someone, not really, if you'd never seen them. But he felt hollow. Numb, really, except for the pins and needles under Squid's thumbs. And yet his mother had made his father so real in her stories . . .

He'd think about it all later. For now he just had to get home, back to Treasure.

'But I can't go with you!' he said loudly. 'You can come and check on me if you like, to keep your promise to my father. But please, could you put me down? I need to get going. I have to see Treasure—'

'*Treasure?*' said Dogfish. 'Let the boy loose, Squid, so 'e can talk.'

But just as Squid seemed to be considering it, the First Mate cut in. 'You ninnyhammers, this milksop wouldn't know a diamond from a goat's behind. He's just having you on. How many times do I 'ave to tell you? I'm not yer bloomin' wet-nurse! We gotta go or we'll be curried like chops for makin' the Captain wait.'

Dogfish's shoulders slumped. He burped loudly. 'Oops, excuse me.'

He looked miserable, Will thought, and not so enormously older than himself. The hair on his cheeks was still fluff, not even enough for a beard.

'I always suffered somethin' terrible from wind,' Dogfish went on, rubbing his belly as if it were a crying baby he was trying to soothe. ''Course it's got a lot worse since I went to sea.' He frowned. 'There's a lot of disappointment at sea. Me mam said she was afeard of that. She said: "Heaven knows what'll happen to yer digestion, my boy, on board that rat

[53]

hole. Yer'll finish up just a bag of wind if all you've got to look forward to is pirate swill.' And see, 'er darkest vision has come to pass an all.'

'Aye, and *we'll* come to pass if we don't leg it before this squall hits,' said the First Mate. 'I truly cannot comprehend why you lot ain't obeyin' me every command like the Captain said you oughta.' And he reached out to cuff Squid on the shoulder but caught Will instead, making him wince.

'Oi, no need to hurt the lad,' Dogfish protested. He looked at Will. 'Your daddy was my friend … even though 'e was a lot older than me, we saw eye to eye, like. I swore to 'im I'd look after ye – he was right worried on account of 'e wouldn't be here to protect ye from the Captain if ye was captured. And he didn't mean for the Captain to hear all about 'is personal life, neither. That's exactly what he *didn't* want.' He looked darkly at Squid. 'Mouth like a drain you got an' all.'

Squid shrugged. 'The Cap'n already *knew* about the lad, I told ye. He's got his spies everywhere. I just furnished 'im with a couple of details, like.'

Dogfish shook his head. 'You told him to get into his good books. But you shoulda known. *No* one gets in there, because he don't *have* a good book. That devil can't see the good in no one.' He burped again, moaned, and sat down on a chair.

'Your captain, is he the pirate captain of the Cannonball Seas? Are any of you pirates from Some Reluctance?' asked Will.

'I was reluctant once,' said the First Mate. 'But after a while, well, you stop feelin' anything. You could burn me finger here, and I wouldn't even notice.'

Dogfish sighed. 'Still an' all, we could stay on dry land for one night, couldn't we? We could tell the Captain we was caught in the weather and frantic lookin' everywhere for the nipper. See starboard, that wood all nicely chopped? We could make a cosy fire an' cook somethin' decent for a change – there's a kitchen and everyfink. We could wait out the storm, make ourselves real comfy.'

'There's a stinkin' great tree in the roof and it's leaking like Noah's Ark, you numbskull!' said Squid. But he couldn't help looking around the room, his eyes resting on the woodfire stove.

No one said anything. They could all hear the howling wind outside, and the rain drumming against the roof. Even the First Mate eyed the wood stack and neat pile of kindling, enough to light the night's fire. Will felt Squid's arm around him sag a little with doubt.

'I'll be off then,' said Will. 'If you can just loosen your grip there, Mr Squid, and let me...'

'What are ye sayin, boy?' Squid snarled. 'Our lives wouldn't be worth livin' if we went back without the likes of you. You're bounty. What the Cap'n wants, he gets.'

Will's brain raced. How to make them stay then? He wished he'd brought food... fried chicken, eggs, jam and bread... Maybe he should tell the pirates to come back to Treasure and Honey's house for breakfast... on the way there might be time to slip off...

'We're weighin' anchor NOW, and no shilly-shallyin',' boomed the First Mate. 'The Captain will be lookin' for us with those beady eyes of his. And if we're not back smartly he'll come 'ere with his cutlass and his mean temper and he'll gut you all like the squirmin' little eels you are.'

He shoved Squid hard from behind so that Squid almost fell over, with the load of Will flailing on his shoulder.

'Orright, orright,' muttered Squid. 'But I 'ave to say, *sir*, that your promotion this morning 'as not had a beneficial effect upon yer personality.' And firming his hold around Will's legs, the pirate carried him through the door and down the path, just as if he were a bag of mouldy old potatoes.

chapter 8

'Ahoy there maties, look lively! Work to be done!' came a shout from the deck.

In the berth below, Will lay in a hammock, his stomach crawling with fear. Next to him was a scattering of boys – snoring, whimpering, snuffling, cursing.

'Oi, you,' Will recognised the First Mate pointing at him from the doorway. 'Up 'ere on the poop deck now, Captain wants a squiz at yer. The rest of you swabs, shift yer pegs!'

Will snuck a glance around the gloom, but no one met his eyes. When he had been led down just a few hours earlier, with the wind still rushing at the clouds and shredding the moonlight, he'd searched the sleeping faces. Never in his nine years had he dreamed of seeing so many boys together, and none were much older than he. They must have been snatched from their childhoods too, like chicks from the nest, and he wondered, standing there in the candlelight, if any of them felt as lost and wobbly as he did.

Shakily, Will climbed the steps up to the deck. He had to hang onto the rail, as his knees had turned to custard.

'Excuse me,' he asked a pirate sitting cross-legged, patching a sail with a thick needle. 'W…where is the poop deck?'

'Aft,' said the pirate, without looking up.

'That's down the back of the ship,' said Dogfish, appearing at Will's side. 'You oughta be more helpful, Goose. What we got right 'ere is the son of a pirate. There ain't many in the universe. In fact, this may well be the only one.'

Goose looked up. 'Rare, is he? What, like a precious gem? Could we get money for 'im then?'

Dogfish sighed. 'Come on, lad, I'll lead you to the Cap'n.'

'Cool yer heels a minute,' Goose was interested now. 'Is this the little squib they brought in last night? We sure never 'ad one so young. I threw 'im a length of chain an' he nearly went over the side with it. The lad's weak as a kitten – couldn't hold his own hand!'

'That's as may be, but the Captain wants 'im. They reckon he's got special powers.'

'What, like magic?'

'Mebbe.'

Another pirate cleaning boots overheard them. 'What kinda magic? Makin' work disappear? Brewin' up a feast? Gettin' us off this scurvy ship?'

But Dogfish had taken Will's elbow and was steering him along the deck. More pirates put down their tasks and got up to follow. Will felt his cheeks heat up. Magic – what would they expect of him next? He had a sudden image of his mother, soothing him after a pirate nightmare... *Let's bounce on his head! Bounce till he's dead!* He swallowed hard, gulping down his terror. How could this be true? How would he bear it if this ship, these men, were to be his life now?

As they mounted some steps – 'This is the highest point on deck,' Dogfish informed him, 'with the Captain's cabin below' – the tall figure of a man standing at the rail came into view. He had his back to them, looking out to sea with a telescope to his eye.

'Arrrhhmm,' Dogfish cleared his throat, addressing the stern back, 'Captain sir, this here's the young 'un we picked up yesterday.'

The Captain turned around. He said nothing. Only his eyes flickered over Will's face.

Will shivered. The man's gaze was empty. But when it passed over him it brought a shadow, like a cloud hiding the sun.

The First Mate panted up the steps behind. 'See now, Captain, we caught the little varmint and brought him back to yer, safe and sound. Not an easy job, slippery as fish gut 'e was, but I kept a weather eye an' a tight hand.'

'It was *me* what grabbed 'im when you let 'im go, you bloomin' braggart!' exploded Squid.

'Quiet, you blathering windbags!' the Captain boomed.

Will jumped. His voice was a roar, but no muscle in his face moved. It was eerie, unnatural.

The men stood silent, staring down at their boots. Squid poked the First Mate in the ribs with his elbow. The First Mate ignored him, inching closer to the Captain's side like a dog eager to be petted.

'Sir, if I may be so bold as to make a comment, like,' Dogfish started again. The Captain made no objection, his wooden face unresponsive. 'The lad's younger than the rest but in me own 'umble opinion, 'e'll make a valuable addition to the crew. Like his daddy told me, 'e's got an uncanny head for heights. He's got no meat on his bones but he'll grow fast if we look after … I mean, if we teach 'im well, like.'

'Aye,' agreed Squid. 'Only two days ago we lost that lad what was climbing the mast to the crow's nest. In these big winds we lose 'em like flies. This one'll be for keeps.'

'That's what *I* said,' put in the First Mate. 'Get 'em young, I said, and you'll 'ave 'em for life. They don't know any different; they think that's what they're for.'

'Poor lad,' whispered Dogfish under his breath.

'We was all poor lads once,' the First Mate whispered back. 'But some of us hardened up. You better do the same and be quick about it, or you'll be tossed over the side like a maggoty fish head.'

The Captain's eyes locked onto Will's. 'I have high expectations of you, my lad.' His voice was flat, but an edge of menace poked through like a blade. 'Don't disappoint me.'

'Oh, aye, disappointment's a killer,' sighed Dogfish. 'Gives me wind an' makes me belly feel like there's frogs leapin' about inside—'

'Cut your gibberish, you ridiculous buffoon,' hissed the Captain. 'Did I ask you to agree with me? Do you think I care about the amphibians flourishing in your flabby innards?' Turning to Will he said, 'I hope you don't disappoint me. This crew is always disappointing me – falling off yardarms, breaking their backs, *dying* – they're useless. Now, what's your name, boy?'

'W … Will Wetherto.'

'Whether to what?'

'Pardon?'

'What an absurd, shillyshallying name. You need just one, lad, like everyone else here. Now what'll it be?'

'Well … what was my father's name?'

'Sir,' said the Captain.

'Sir?'

'The Captain wants you to call 'im *sir*,' Dogfish whispered.

'What was my father's name, sir?'

'Wicked,' said the Captain.

'Oh.' Will thought for a moment. 'I'll take that.'

The Captain nodded. 'Wicked it is. Like father like son. See if you can live longer than he did. Now show me how you climb up that rigging to the crow's nest, and be smart about it.'

The men drew in a breath.

'Straight away, sir? I mean, the wind's still blowin' somethin' fierce and the lad hasn't even got 'is sea legs yet,' Dogfish burst out. 'He's all green about the gills. That yardarm swings right over in just a tiddly breeze, sir, and the best of 'em fall into the drink. Pity to lose 'im soon as we found 'im.'

'Have you got wax in your ears, man?' spat the Captain. 'If so, I might have to clean them out with the point of my sabre.'

'Um, there's also something I should tell you, sir,' Will said in a small voice. 'I … um … can't swim.'

'Do I look bothered?' asked the Captain. 'Start climbing, *NOW*!'

Will lurched down from the poop deck after the First Mate. He had to run to keep up. Then he stopped short, almost tripping on the big man's heels. Beside the mainmast was a rope ladder that seemed to go all the way up to the sky.

'This 'ere is the riggin' you gotta climb to the crow's nest.'

Will had to throw his head right back to see the small basket clinging to the yardarm at the top.

'Look at that, the little fellow's startin' up the rat-lines,' came a yell from the crowd of pirates and boys who were gathering to watch.

'Better 'im than me!' called another, and there was a swell of agreement.

Will's stomach flipped like a fish in a frying pan. Glancing at his audience, something sour rose up in his throat and he almost lost his balance.

'Smartly now,' said the First Mate. 'If you're seasick already, by Jove you'll be in trouble up there.'

Dogfish called out, 'Keep yer eye on the rung ahead of ye. Whatever ye do, don't look down.'

The deck under their feet rose and fell. The wind moaned. Cloud hung low and heavy all around.

'That swell is risin',' he heard a voice say.

'Aye, an' you feel it much worse at the top,' said another. 'Last time I was up there in a big wind, I spewed up half me guts.'

Will was trembling with the effort of staying upright as he took hold of the first rung. Spray from the waves blew against his face. He licked the salt from his lips. He didn't know if it was terror or seasickness that was making his head so light. It felt like a balloon bobbing on his neck.

But the rope under his feet was familiar.

As he put one foot after the other he remembered being able to manage anything when walking the rope through the sky.

Lightning glittered on the horizon, blooming briefly against the grey. As far as he could see there was just the rolling sea below and the cloud above. It was like being the only person in the world. The wind rushed at his ears and tugged at his shirt. He could hear nothing but its keening in the rigging and his own heart pounding, but he kept his eyes on the prize ahead, the basket at the top of the yardarm.

A few more rungs now and he'd have to make the leap to the single thin rope attached to the crow's nest. He'd need all his wits about him, and a steady grip.

He waited for his stomach to settle.

It didn't.

He counted the seconds for the wind to die down.

But it didn't.

A sudden lurch of the ship made him sway out to sea. He hung onto the rigging until his fingers went white. Any movement at deck level was wildly exaggerated up here. It was different to walking the rope back home, where you could rely on the ground to stay put. He clung to the rope, swinging out and in with the wind. The bile was rising in his throat. He was going to be sick all down the rigging. What if he fainted and lost his hold?

Find your centre, Will, his mother whispered in his mind.

He put a hand on his middle.

See? No one can take that from you.

[63]

He reached for the thin rope with both hands and swung his body up and into the basket.

A distant cheer came from the deck as he curled up his legs in the small space. His stomach heaved like the waves below.

He sat as still as he could.

So far so good. He waited for the sickness to go, now that he wasn't climbing.

But it didn't. He tried closing his eyes, and keeping them open. He tried fixing his gaze on a distant single point – but there was none. He began to sweat.

You'll be all right, his mother told him. *Stop fighting it. Breathe deep.*

He took a long deep sigh. And another. The minutes ticked over.

The sickness was still there, nagging at him like an annoying mosquito.

But somehow it didn't matter anymore. The stupid thing existed, and so did he. If he stopped thinking about it, it got less noisy. And slowly, he could think about other things.

Like Treasure... and Honey... Hermy, goats, turtles and mangroves...

One day he'd see them all again, he would. And he would hug his mother.

That's the way, she said.

chapter 9

In the next few weeks, Will went up and down the rigging many times. With the first rung the sickness came, but as days went by he learned to quell it until he felt just a slight queasiness in his guts.

The horror of waking to his ship's prison, though, never seemed to abate.

Early one morning when the sky was still pale with dawn, he got the call to go up. He sat for hours in that small basket, his legs crunched up against the sides. It wasn't until the sun was high in the sky that he heard the call to come down. But as he stood, he spied a smudge on the clean line of the horizon.

He took the small telescope from the box beneath him. One, two...three black sails, a huge figurehead of a mermaid, it was coming swiftly, a *ship*.

He leaned out over the crow's nest. His legs ached with cramp. The crew had melted away, but he could make out the steep figure of the Captain peering up at him.

Will cupped his hand around his mouth. *'Ship ahoy!'* He pointed to the dark speck moving slowly but steadily towards them.

In a blink the Captain was on the fo'c'sle with his telescope to his eye. He shouted an order to the First Mate and soon there were pirates dashing about the deck, squawking like a flock of seagulls following fish.

Will began the climb down. He was more than halfway when the First Mate yelled up at him.

'Stop. You're to go back up. Cap'n says it's the Bonny Lasses, a bunch of pirates as greedy an' cunning as they're good lookin'. If they get aboard, they'll sack the ship. You'll be useless down 'ere, a skinny runt like yerself. Here, I'll throw ye a sword. Shimmy back up the ropes an' see if ye can't swing along them rat-lines and fend off any rosy-cheeked women swingin' onto our riggin'.'

'Aye, the Captain's mighty impressed by yer aerial abilities,' Dogfish called up to Will. 'An' yer stayin' power. "For once we're prepared for these vixens," 'e said. "We'll shoot 'em out of the water before they reach us."'

'Cut yer blathering, Dogfish,' said the First Mate. 'Can't ye see there's work to be done? You're all blitherin' layabouts! Wait till the Captain catches you jawin' on.'

'Man the cannons!' came the order from the Captain. 'Every swab on deck!'

Will caught the sword the First Mate hurled up to him. He hoped to heaven he wouldn't have to use it.

As he hooked the sheath over his belt buckle, he wondered why his life just seemed intent on getting worse. He wished for the hundredth time he could wake up from this nightmare.

By the time he was wedged in the crow's nest again, the gunner had fired the first cannon. It exploded in the sea, right in the path of the Bonny Lasses, showering sparks over their bowsprit. Will heard a cheer go up as the crew watched the enemy ship pull away and steer off-course.

He took out his telescope and spotted a nimble figure swinging along the enemy ropes. She had a red bandanna around her head and a flash of blue feathers – a bird – on her shoulder. He couldn't see her face but there was something familiar about the firm and steady way she darted along the rigging. She was joined by another who handed her a bucket. It weighed her down and she nearly lost her grip on the ropes. The sparks across their bow had caught, licking now at the edge of the Lasses' foresail. He saw the first woman hurl the bucket full of water at the flames.

He narrowed his eyes to slits, peering at her. No, he decided now, it had been a trick of the mind. Wishful thinking. That sword at her side and the bandanna on her head were pirate trappings; his mother would have none of that. The Lasses were flying about the deck now, dousing fires wherever they began. And the ship was turning, on course again ...

'Fire the second cannon!' cried Will. 'Enemy ship approaching!'

But the men were so busy applauding themselves and their lucky shot that they didn't hear.

The pirate called Goose was twirling his sword above his head until he fell over a cable and nearly speared himself. Squid found a bottle of rum. Another pirate was trying to grab it from him and a fierce fight broke out. Goose tried to stop it and accidentally threw Buzzard against the tiller, which splintered and broke loose.

The ship shuddered.

Will waved from the basket and yelled down to them. But no one was listening.

And now the Bonny Lasses were gliding grimly towards them with their black sails billowing in the wind. He could see the snarling mermaid bearing down upon them.

'*HELP!*' he cried for the last time. '*DO* something!'

He glimpsed the Captain tearing up from the deck below, glancing up at Will and out to sea. It was too late for the cannons. The enemy ship was almost on top of them.

The Captain strode to the rails and took out a small gunmetal object from a box under his arm. Taking aim, he hurled the thing and Will saw it make a sweeping arc across the sea, landing on the Bonny Lasses' main deck.

A little ball of fire exploded, igniting the mainsail. The Captain threw another exploding object and soon fires were spreading all along the deck until the ship looked more like an island-forest aflame than a ship on the Cannonball Sea.

There was a terrible scrambling now on board. The Bonny Lasses threw water and curses, reefing sails and stamping out fires with rags of carpet, hammocks, their feet, anything that would smother the flames.

The Captain stood gazing at the Bonny Lasses, his body as still as a figurehead on a bow, his arms crossed and his back to the crew. Only Will, making his way down the rigging, could see the clenched fury written upon his face.

The pirates were dancing a hornpipe and slapping each other on the back as they watched the enemy ship turn about and head for the horizon, sails smoking.

But a hush slowly settled as the Captain advanced among the crew. His eyes were as dark as a storm.

'Enlighten me, please,' he said. 'What is it you men are cheering?'

'The Bonny Lasses 'ave retreated, sir,' the First Mate said. 'The lads were just, like, celebratin' the fact.'

'Celebrating? Is that so?'

No one said a word.

'I see. Are they celebrating the fact they were nearly run down and raided?' the Captain enquired, his voice held back like a gathering gale.

Silence.

'Are they celebrating the fact that no one followed up after the first cannon?'

The quiet deepened.

'Are they elated that due to their stupidity it was necessary for their captain to waste two of his precious new grenades to stop 'em?'

And then the storm broke.

'*NEVER IN ALL MY BORN DAYS HAVE I SEEN SUCH LAZY, BONE-HEADED, FECKLESS LAGGARDS! YOU'RE NOTHING BUT A PACK OF DAWDLING DUNDERHEADS!*'

'But sir, our aim was true—' began the First Mate.

'*NITWIT!* If I were you I'd say nothing and keep my head down. I've a mind to strip you of your rank, you great goon.

Now, you are all to set about your work without break until sun-up tomorrow. I want the tiller mended, gunpowder and shot checked, main topmast repaired, empty food barrels broken up and wood stored. You, Buzzard, will build a new wheel if needs be and Goose, patch the jib and the mainsail. See it's done by first light.'

A moan from the crew caused the Captain's eyes to narrow further. 'And we will *not* stop at Bell Island tomorrow to collect supplies as planned. We will keep sailing through the Cannonball Seas, past Devil Island and the Mainland. We may not dock at port for many months, not until I see you've learned your lesson. Do you all realise, we could have been taken, lock stock and barrel!'

'There's nothing 'ere to *take*,' murmured Buzzard under his breath.

'If I don't see that new wheel by sunrise,' the Captain swung around to face Buzzard, 'you will walk the plank at dawn tomorrow. How do you mewling infants think we'll ever find treasure if you can't learn to behave as pirates? Pathetic excuses for men, the lot of you!'

The pirates were as quiet as mice.

'B...but what'll we eat?' a boy asked in a quavery voice.

'Only one boy will eat tonight. This young 'un here, still wet behind the ears,' the Captain pointed at Will. 'He's barely weaned but he saved your worthless lives. If you'd been paying attention, we'd be counting the Lasses' treasure now, feasting on their spoils, swilling their rum. Ah, it doesn't bear thinking about. You men, you're not worth the piece of deck you're slouching on!'

And with that he went below.

The pirates slumped.

'Blimey, I'm hungry already,' muttered one boy.

'We all are,' said another, sliding down on the deck, leaning his back against the side.

'Best not to tire ourselves out, like,' Dogfish said, taking off his shirt and putting it under his head as a cushion. 'The more work we do, the hungrier we'll be.'

Will looked around him in amazement as pirates and boys dropped where they stood, some leaning back to back, using each other as supports.

The First Mate just gazed out to sea, sighing gloomily.

'B...but,' said Will. 'But...shouldn't we be starting those jobs the Captain ordered? I mean, if we get them done, maybe he'll let us stop for supplies. Remember he said—'

'Ooh, listen up, men,' hooted Squid, 'the Captain's pet what saved all our lives is talkin'. He's so *special*, ye better stand to attention while the lad's talkin' or he'll cast a spell on yer.'

'Well, if he's magic, he's not sharin' it with the likes of us,' a pirate with one leg sneered. 'I could do with another one of these pegs, an' all. Maybe he can tell that shark to give it back.'

'I don't know who ever said anything about magic,' Will protested. 'But if you all showed the Captain how much work you were prepared to—'

'What do *you* know, ye little pipsqueak?' said Squid. 'Even if we do everyfink right, we never get to see one drop of treasure, we never get one bite of reward. So what's the bloomin' point?'

'Aye,' said Buzzard. 'How can a body be enthusiastic when he never sees the fruits of his honest labour?'

'But Buzzard, sir, you'll walk the plank if you don't fix that wheel. The Captain needs a carpenter. We all need to have a skill, because a skill keeps folk safe, otherwise they'll be left behind for the pir—'

'Oh, will you listen to this little whelp givin' us the benefit of his worldly advice! Yer think ye know everyfink at nine years old?'

'Ten, actually,' whispered Will. 'Today is my birthday.'

'Well happy bloomin' birthday. We were all ten once too.'

'An' *we* could 'ave had skills as well. Only most of us didn't 'ave time to find out what they were, like,' said Goose.

'Aye, an' I had me fear of the water,' said the pirate with one leg.

'An' I got me disappointment,' said Dogfish. 'Where's the rum?' asked Squid.

'An' you got a drinkin' problem,' said the First Mate.

'I wouldn't have one if ye just told me where you stashed that last bottle.'

'I *told* you I gave it to the Captain to keep him sweet. Fat lot of good that did, but. The man's a bottomless hole. Only gets meaner on the grog. Anyways, swabs, we better get to work or starvin' to death will be the least of our problems.' The First Mate eyeballed Will. '*Bon appetit*,' he spat.

Will stared at him.

'What, ye don't know French? Ye never fought a Frenchie or felt his sword at yer gullet? Well, it means enjoy yer meal, ye little traitor.'

'Steady on,' sighed Dogfish, 'that's a strong word for young Wicked here.'

'Aye, well, he better start livin' up to that name of his.' The First Mate glared at Will. 'This here situation is your fault, yer little try-hard. Showin' us up with yer evil enthusiasm. Ye better put a lid on it, or ye won't last long on this ship.'

'I might start givin' 'im a few fatherly lessons like,' said Squid, rubbing his callused hands together. 'Soon as you wanna give the order, *sir*.'

Will had lost his 'appetit'. He wished he could lose his fear, too, and the memory of the First Mate's ugly words.

As he watched the last of the straggling boys trail off to their jobs at the rigging, he wondered if they, too, had lost their appetites. He wondered if they could possibly be as mean and unfeeling as the pirates. Dogfish didn't seem as bad as the rest. But down in the berth at night no one talked, and never was there a whisper of homesickness or a shared look between them.

Maybe, if Will offered to help with the rigging, there might be one boy among them who could be a friend.

He tried to stop biting his cheek. There was a raw patch now that stung each time his tongue found it. He took a step towards the boys at the mainmast. The offer to help was all ready in his mouth but they gave him such looks of disgust that the words withered before he could get them out.

As he hurried away, he hoped the Captain would forget about his meal. He hoped the man would never notice him again or mention any special skills he had. He almost hoped, standing there, that the sea would rise up and take him so he'd never, ever have another birthday.

And then he wouldn't have to feel anything anymore, just as the First Mate had advised.

chapter 10

The sea stayed where it was and the month of Will's birthday wore on, a heartless sun shining down upon them each day. Then the Captain finally gave the order to drop anchor off Devil Island, and the pirates rowed the long-boat to shore. Waiting on board, the boys heard the islanders' distant shouts as the men raided and plundered the village, returning scratched and bitten but laden with great sides of ham and pickled trout, loaves of bread, sacks of flour and rice, spices and rum and a fresh young crew.

That evening, when the new boys were shown their sleeping quarters and left to nurse their wounds, Will lay in his hammock and listened to the dark. He heard crying, the kind that is quickly stifled. There was a lot of lonely nose blowing too and whispered curses, but the bold words lost their shape in the awful quiet until they trickled into sobs.

He stood up and crept over to a huddle of new boys. He remembered his own dread that first night and his sadness, fresh again, worked its way up into his throat. But before he could say anything, Heartless from the hammock next to him elbowed his way in.

'Stop whimperin', you lot, you're keepin' us awake. You all better toughen up – we don't stand for cowardly little milksops here. You oughta take a leaf out of our Wicked's book, he's Captain's pet.' Heartless grinned, slapping him hard on the back as if it were all a huge joke. 'Wicked doesn't say boo but he climbs the riggin' like a monkey, an' makes us all look like fools.'

Will said quietly to the boys, 'There's ways of overcoming sea sickness and hanging onto the ropes in the wind.'

'Oh aye, Wicked the Know-all,' said Heartless. 'Makes you wanna puke, just listening to him.'

But in the early morning, when the light had barely stolen down into the berth and the boys were still in the clutches of dreams, Will whispered to the boy next to him. 'The trick to climbing high is to locate your centre of gravity,' he began, 'just above your belt buckle…'

'Ah go shove your face down a shark's gullet,' said the boy from Devil Island, 'and let me get some shut-eye.'

But Will kept trying. When they ate dinner at night in the mess, he noticed that many of the new ones just sat in silence – little planets of misery, chewing and swallowing on their own. He sat down next to Scab, a boy with a nervous tic that made him wink continuously as if he knew something everyone else didn't.

'How long have you had that wink?' asked Will. 'See, I've been here a while, and now I bite my cheek. I might know a way to get rid of it if you—'

'Yeah, gettin' off this ship,' said the boy. 'Do you know how to do that?'

'No,' said Will, watching him. The boy rubbed and rubbed at his eye, as if he wanted to rub it out. 'Probably the more you think about it, the more it winks. If you try to think of other things...'

'Like what? Like how to escape? Fat chance.'

'No, because that's too hard right now. I could tell you about some other things to take your mind off it, like...like...'

Will thought of Treasure and the way she had talked to him that first time he'd followed her up the hill. Her words had been like a lullaby after all the terrifying silence, and now he felt an urge to do the same for poor lonely Scab.

'Do you know much about hermit crabs? They're *fascinating* – for instance, they're always looking for a bigger house.'

'Who cares?'

'Well, you can make really pretty ornaments from seed pods. You know the calabash tree?'

'No trees at sea. Why don't you push off and pick yer nose an' eat it?'

It was the same with every boy he spoke to. No one from Devil Island knew how to say please or thank you, or offer a kind word. And no one wanted the comfort of a friend.

These boys weren't so much older than Will. But they seemed like a different species, like plants or cuttlefish or sharks even, for all that they had in common with him. It was the loneliest thing in the world.

After a while Will noticed that up in the crow's nest, where there was just him and his thoughts, he felt less lonely. And he could talk to his mother.

'Such strange folk there are in the world,' he confided. 'How can I be so different? Don't they want what I want? A bit of conversation, a friendly word ...'

Of course they do, said his mother. *It's just that they've forgotten how. Don't you do that, my boy. Remember our games? Remember our limbo dancing in the moonlight? Remember your funambulism in the mangroves? Just keep an eye on your balance and one foot in the front of the other, and you'll be all right.*

Sometimes, when he was up in the crow's nest, he found himself talking to Treasure, too. He told her about the habits and lifestyle of the pirates, how a conversation on board never went anywhere that wasn't planned, or didn't have a purpose. Words were either an order or an insult. *How fascinating!* she said. *When I see you again I'm going to write down everything you tell me.*

His eyes filled then and he couldn't see the horizon. So he tried not to imagine that part too often. But he could hear the lilt in her voice and the little breath she took before she said *fascinating*, and often it was this that got him to sleep at night.

In the weeks after a raid, the crew ate food with no weevils or fungus growing in it. Yet in all their plundering, the pirates had never come across any man or boy who'd known how to cook.

'It's a damn shame,' Dogfish said when Will asked him about it. 'But seein' as the captain shows no interest in food, no one's bothered learnin' how to cook it. We'd only get into trouble.' Dogfish's eyelids drooped as he contemplated the Captain's lack of appetite. 'The man doesn't seem human sometimes,' he muttered.

Will would have liked to talk more about the Captain's nature, but Dogfish was too tired. Though he'd been such friends with Will's father, Will noticed he kept more and more to himself. It was the disappointment, Dogfish said, the disease that took away your conversation. It drained you of enthusiasm so that some days you could barely get up.

The weeks turned into months, bringing more enemy ships sailing into the Cannonball Seas. Up in the crow's nest Will gave the warning, and each time the men were ready. But sometimes a ship got close enough to send out grappling hooks, and once pirates boarded their ship, racing up the rigging to just a hand's length from the basket where Will sat. With his sword strung across his chest, Will learned to fly across the ropes like a bird, swiping at the enemy's feet and faces, causing them to fall through the air and dive, fathoms deep, into the sea. The Captain rewarded him with a fine meal on those evenings, and even though Will secretly shared it with the boys, his skill didn't earn him any favours among the crew.

As one season changed into another and the stretch between raids grew thinner and longer than any tightrope, the men's stomachs were growling. And their tempers grew worse.

'The only one what eats decent is the Captain's pet,' Squid pointed out one day.

'Aye,' agreed the First Mate. 'Yesterday I seen the Captain give 'im some of that beef jerky from the secret stash we was keepin' in the galley.'

'Only because I was up in the crow's nest all day,' Will protested hotly. 'I didn't get to have any breakfast or lunch like you men did!'

The First Mate suddenly leapt up. 'Me belly's eatin' its own self, I'm that hungry. Squid, come with me and we'll inspect those fishin' lines hangin' off the side.'

The two men came back after a while looking downhearted.

'Where's the fish?' asked Goose. 'Not even a one?'

The First Mate shook his head. 'Can't work it out. The lines are all in a tangle. Somethin's weighin' them down under the water.'

'String up new ones then,' said Goose.

'Or we could get one of the boys to dive under an' see what the problem is,' said Squid slyly. He was looking at Will from under his lids.

'I can't swim!' said Will.

'Well none of us would win a race with a snapper,' the First Mate said. 'You don't have to *swim*, like, just get into the water an' see what's the trouble.'

'No, I—'

'Are you disobeyin' an order?' cried the First Mate. His belly gave a loud empty gurgle and he reached over and grabbed Will's shirt. 'You're gunna go over the side like I tell you an' sort it out. Do somethin' useful for once and I'll overlook yer disobedience.'

'Oi, wait on!' cried Dogfish, stirring himself. 'The lad means it, he can't swim a stroke. He'll sink like a stone.'

But the First Mate was already striding towards the tangle of fishing lines, carrying Will under his arm like a package. 'Sink or swim, that's how me own daddy taught me!' he cried. His arms came together around Will's chest and with a grunt, he threw him up and over the side.

The cold of the ocean hit Will face-first. Water shot up his nose and closed over his head. He tried to shut his mouth tight, but he couldn't help coughing and the more he coughed the more seawater he drank. It was so hard to hold his breath. His lungs would surely burst. He kicked and thrashed his legs, flapping his arms. Something long and sinewy slithered past his ankle. He opened his eyes underwater and saw a tangle of fishing line. He was sinking, sinking...

From the dark below his mother smiled up at him. Her fingers trailed pale and achingly close. He drifted down to her, seeing sparkles of sunlight breaking through leaves, mangroves swaying along the riverbank...he could breathe out, let it go.

But oh! Something hard knocked his head. He jerked away, but now the thing stung his ear. He clawed the water with his hands and it flew at him again, coiling around his chest, squeezing his ribs...and hauling him up out of the water, sending him flying over the rail of the ship to land on the main deck, *thump*, like a dying fish.

The Captain stood over him. He stared down at Will, the rope that had lassoed the boy like a horse in a paddock still in his hands. His shadow blocked out the sun.

'Loosen the rope,' he hissed to Dogfish, who hovered near.

'Aye aye, sir.' Dogfish knelt down and put his ear to Will's chest. 'He's not breathing, sir.'

A murmur went through the men like a gust of wind.

'Put him on his side,' ordered the captain.

Dogfish took hold of the thin shoulders. As he turned him over, Will gave a mighty shiver. It racked his body from head to toe. The pirate put a hand under Will's ribs and lifted him a little so he could cough and heave, spewing out a lake of murky liquid from his lungs.

'He'll live, sir!' cried Dogfish, slapping Will on the back.

The Captain said not a word. He watched the boy, eyes empty as the sky, until Will gave his last trembling cough and sank back exhausted on the deck.

Then the Captain turned to the First Mate. 'If you ever give an order like that again,' he spat, 'I'll not only have you stripped of your rank, you'll be keelhauled till you're begging for mercy. Young Wicked is the most valuable look-out we possess, so mind you treat him that way, you spineless lump of lard.' And the Captain turned on his heel and disappeared into his cabin.

chapter 11

William lay in his hammock that night in a darker world than he'd ever known. His throat ached from coughing, but the hollow place inside him ached more.

In the dimness of the berth, he glanced at the boys around him – boys who still inhabited the world Will had known that morning. A cruel and pitiless place it was, but hadn't it held a glint of hope?

There was none of that for him now. The boys wouldn't even look at him.

As he'd lain on the deck, helpless as a beetle on its back, he'd felt the blade of the Captain's gaze pin him right through the middle. He knew as he looked into those eyes that he'd been saved by a devil of a man, and the light inside him would never again burn as bright. It was as if he'd caught the Captain's darkness like a disease, and no one else around him would risk being infected.

He turned on his side, his fist under his cheek. He couldn't help the tears welling up. He made no sound.

But then someone whispered in his ear.

'Here, do ye want a hanky? My mam soaked it in lavender, to remind me of home. No lavender on board a pirate ship, eh? So I was thinking, it must feel bad when someone tries to kill you. On purpose, I mean.'

Will turned over and sat up.

Headlice looked at him earnestly.

Was this some kind of joke? He studied the handkerchief balled up in the boy's hand. Was a stingray's barb wrapped inside it? A stonefish's deadly spike? Even just a mess of maggots?

'Open it up first,' said Will, 'and show me what's inside.'

'Sure,' said Headlice, doing just that.

Will took it from him.

He breathed in the sweet smell of lavender. It smelled just like his own garden.

He smiled at Headlice. And Headlice smiled back.

~ * ~

When Will was ordered to climb up and inspect the state of the top yardarm the next morning, Headlice asked if he could go with him.

'Are you sure?' asked Will. He felt a rush of excitement.

'Yeah,' said Headlice. 'Everyone else falls off the riggin' at some time or other, but you haven't. Maybe you can teach me how. You make it look real easy. An' I'll live longer.'

Will started up the rigging with Headlice just a rung behind. It was a calm, clear day, perfect for climbing.

'You gotta understand, Wicked,' Headlice said. 'Where I come from you have to follow the mob. Anyone sticks out their head, it's chopped off. But I figure that here on board folk have to learn a few new tricks if they wanna last the distance.'

Today Will loved the rough strength of the rope under his fingers. The sky was just a big blue bowl with nothing evil stirring inside it. In the dazzle of company, the Captain's darkness shrank into a speck of dirt under his fingernail. He was going to make sure Headlice learned everything he needed to know to keep him safe.

'Follow each move I make,' he told Headlice, throwing his voice over his shoulder. 'Place your feet in the same position on the ladder, and take hold of the rope with your hands where I do. I'm going start slow and when we're halfway, we'll talk about what to do in a big wind and holding onto your centre.'

And so Headlice learned to put a hand on his middle and feel the solid ticking place inside. When a breeze started up, he saw how Will went with the motion, letting the seasickness ride while breathing steadily into it. Will told him for this first lesson that he could just stay where he was and watch from a safe height while Will swung himself up into the crow's nest and climbed along the yardarm, searching for cracks and gouges in the wood.

'I'll teach you in stages, it's safer that way and you'll remember more,' said Will. 'Next time you'll go further and practise what you've learned. Practice is the most important thing – when you climb high again and again, after a while it feels as natural as walking on the ground.'

Headlice was pleased with his lesson. But when they came down again, a few of the boys eyed them suspiciously.

'Ooh, look at Headlice toadying up to the Captain's pet,'

Scab said to Weasel. 'Waitin' for a few crumbs of wisdom to drop from Wicked's lips?'

'Or a few crumbs of the Captain's special biscuits, more likely,' said Weasel. And they laughed meanly.

Headlice just shook his head at them and whispered to Will that they should go sit up in the fo'c'sle where no one could overhear them.

'I've tried to be friendly,' Will began when they were settled. 'And I always share any extra food I get. But no one except you has ever been nice to me.'

'Where we come from *no one* is nice,' said Headlice. 'Devil Island's a hellhole. You shouldn't take it personally...although you bein' the Captain's favourite makes 'em jealous, I suppose.'

'It's no fun, I can tell you. Gives me the shivers,' said Will.

Headlice nodded. 'He's a strange one, our Captain, isn't he? Take the way he lassoed you in the water – you was nearly sunk but his rope found you somehow. What an aim! It was like a magic trick.'

Will nodded. 'I thought I was dead, and then those eyes of his were boring into me. Like he was snuffing the life out of me, even while he was saving me.'

'Aye,' said Headlice. 'He never seems to eat, either, like other folk. And he never seems to sleep. It's as if... he's a ghost or something.'

Will shivered. It was true. But talking about the unearthly qualities of the Captain was somehow the most cheering thing that had happened to him for a very long time. It was like life coming back into an arm or leg when you'd slept on it. Pins and needles of happiness raced through him, and the words tumbled out of his mouth. It was wonderful to have a friend.

When he woke in the mornings now, the day ahead no longer seemed so lonely. After Will and Headlice had done their chores – running messages for the pirates, cleaning the weaponry, oiling and storing the carpenter's tools – they made plans for climbing lessons or just finding a quiet place to talk. Often Will would be summoned to the crow's nest, but whenever he was free, he sought out Headlice for company.

Will learnt a lot about the folk on Devil Island. Just as Honey had said, nobody bothered with learning their letters – the only thing that mattered was fighting. Lessons in defence and attack began as soon as a boy could walk. Headlice said it was all pointless, though, because hardly anyone escaped capture no matter how many lessons they'd had in wrestling or sword throwing or jumping from great heights. Among his own group, not one boy had managed to fight off the pirates – even Scab, who had the wickedest right hook anyone had ever seen.

'But you're different from the others,' Will pointed out. 'Did your mother ever give you a real name?'

'Mam said she and my daddy would tell me it once we left Devil Island to start a new life.' Headlice looked down at his lap. 'We were all set to leave just before my twelfth birthday. But my daddy got sick. It was real sudden. He couldn't get his breath. It happened to him sometimes but he always got over it. This time…'

Will put his hand on Headlice's shoulder. 'That must be very bad. I never knew my father, so I didn't feel much when I heard he died. Except, well, something…'

Headlice looked up. 'So what's your real name then?'

Will hesitated. His name was like a magic spell his mother had taught him. But the worst had already happened, hadn't it? The thing his mother dreaded most.

'Will,' said Will. 'Will Wetherto.'

Headlice put out his hand to shake. For a brief moment, Will remembered his first meeting with Treasure. Such a mixture of gladness and sadness boiled inside him that he bit down on his cheek and winced, tasting blood.

'I'll still call you Wicked, but,' said Headlice. 'You gotta act more like a pirate. Talk less proper, like. Curse more, and act mean. You don't wanna be different to everyone else – although that's hard for you ain't it, being Captain's pet and all.'

Will looked for a hint of a sneer. But there was none. Headlice was just stating a fact.

Will nodded. 'So how come *you* are different? And your parents? I mean, not many people leave Devil Island or plan to, do they?'

'No,' said Headlice. 'Most folk get used to the way things are – they figure it's the same everywhere, and you just gotta learn how to fight for your life. But my mam had a few years on the Mainland as a girl. She learned to read and when she got back to Devil Island she met my daddy – she persuaded him there was more to life than dodging pirates and drinking rum.' Headlice's eyes suddenly watered. He coughed to hide it.

'My mother lived on the Mainland too,' Will said quickly. 'She worked in a circus. Then she moved to Thunder Island, do you know it?'

Headlice frowned. 'Yeah, I think so. I've seen it on the

maps – it's about as far away as you can get from my home. Lies south-west of Devil Island on the other side of the Cannonball Sea.'

'Can you read maps?'

'Yeah, my mam taught me. I can read and write and draw. She said readin' would come in handy when we were livin' real lives. I don't know what she meant by that, truth to tell.'

'My mother used to talk about her old life on the Mainland. They were good stories. One day I'll escape from this ship, and go to find her.'

'Do you think she's there now? On the Mainland?'

'I don't know. But I'm never going to stop looking.'

Headlice sighed. 'Most boys don't manage to escape. Even if we all want to get off this ship more than anything. Some die tryin'.' He looked thoughtful. 'You know, we're about to sail past Snake Island. The Captain was saying we're heading west to the Dregs Islands. But what if, instead...' Headlice looked like he was thinking aloud, 'we headed north?'

Will stared at him blankly. 'What's north?'

'Turtle Island. It's small, no one lives there. Just coconut trees and lizards. No folk visit, either, 'cause there's nothing to steal or plunder. Not even turtles anymore. They've all been eaten.'

'So why are we talking about it?'

'Well, it's real close to Devil Island. Straight across, only five nautical miles. It'd be just a couple of hours' row.'

'And?'

'What's all this then?' roared the First Mate, striding up and making both boys jump. 'Restin' yer bones, takin' it easy are you? Gossipin' like two old crones! Wicked, Captain wants you up the crow's nest. Headlice, come with me and stow the cannons. Pronto!'

As Headlice was marched off, his ear pulled painfully by the First Mate, he managed to mouth one word to Will: 'Tonight'.

Will scurried down from the crow's nest as the sun set over the hills of Snake Island. In just a few minutes the sea turned from a blazing orange to the heart-sinking grey of twilight.

'What's the hurry, boy?' said the Captain as Will raced by. 'Scared there won't be enough dinner left for you?'

Will said nothing.

'Buzzard's on kitchen duty this evening,' the Captain went on. 'He's got a nice snapper grilling in the galley for me. You can have it if you want it.'

'No sir, thank you, sir.'

'Can't wait to see your little friend, is that it?' the Captain said snidely. 'You better watch it, Wicked. Better not to trust a pirate-boy from Devil Island, you know. Didn't your mother ever teach you that?' And he strode off.

Will went on his way with an uneasy murmur starting inside him.

'Come sit here,' said Headlice as Will came into view. He moved up on his bench. 'Do you want some of these smelly old sardines? I saved some bread to go with them.'

'More mould than bread,' said Scab, his eye winking and twitching furiously. 'Did you save the fish slime too, and the maggoty eyeballs? Here, take some of my foot fungus, it's real nourishin'.'

'Ah go put your head up a dead bear's bum,' said Will.

'Come on, Headlice, let's go up to the deck and get some fresh air.' And he got up, taking his plate with him.

As Will and Headlice stepped up to the fo'c'sle, Will had a feeling of satisfaction. But when they were sitting in a quiet spot with their plates on their laps, he said, 'I suppose that was foolhardy. It's not clever to make enemies on board, especially from Devil Island.'

'We won't have to worry about that for too much longer,' said Headlice, 'if my escape plan goes ahead like I'm thinking.' He picked his teeth. 'See, if we can persuade the Captain to sail to Turtle Island, there might be a way off this ship for good. I'm thinking when the pirates hear that there's treasure buried there, they'll throw down anchor and go digging. And if that happens, well, my plan should work.'

'How?'

'Sometimes my mam used to row me to different beaches on Devil Island so I could go exploring…there's caves, you should see them, lined with salt crystals, sparkly like diamonds. Anyways, I always took this little pocket mirror with me and when I was ready to be picked up I'd angle it into the sun to catch the rays. You ever done that?'

'No,' said Will.

Headlice fished in his pocket. He brought out a small triangle of mirror, jagged at one side where it had been broken off. 'When the sun shines on this glass here, a bright light flashes like a fire signal. Mam would be looking out for it and she'd come to get me. We always said if I was ever captured by pirates, I'd flash that signal when my ship passed near Devil Island.'

Will stared at him. 'But the Captain won't go to Devil Island for ages, the raids are only once a year—'

'That's right,' agreed Headlice. 'Devil Islanders are right hostile, too. Folk always put up a fight. So he wouldn't stop there again in a hurry. But he might stop at Turtle Island. No inhabitants, no battle necessary, just treasure for the taking.'

'Is there really treasure?'

Headlice chuckled. 'Not a bean. But that's not what I'll tell those gold-guzzling pirates. And see, when our ship is approaching I'll secretly signal to my mam, and she'll row under the cover of night to pick us up.'

'Us?' echoed Will. 'You mean, I could come with you?'

'Of course,' said Headlice. 'It's not a big boat, ours, but there's enough room for three. And you're my friend!'

At that last word, Will felt the last of the Captain's darkness fade from him. He saw himself and Headlice sitting side by side in the little boat, telling stories of their escape to Headlice's lovely mother. And then, later, they'd go to the Mainland and start the search for *his* mother. With a stop-off to Thunder Island first, to see Treasure and Honey. He could barely stop himself leaping up and yodelling like a madman.

Instead, he tried to be practical. 'What if your mother doesn't see your signal?'

Headlice scratched his chin. 'Well, that might be a bit of a problem, but not a deadly one. We'd just have to go digging with the pirates. I'll make the location somewhere complicated, inside a cave, under a waterfall … and then you and I can slip off somehow and hide. I know a few places.'

'What if no one comes to rescue us? We'd be alone on the island, no boat, no food…'

'There's coconuts and fish—'

'I can't swim!' shivered Will.

But Headlice was thinking. 'So what's the best way to tell a tale of treasure? We'll have to make it convincing… ten bags of gold coins—'

'And bars of silver, ruby rings, diamond necklaces worn by Spanish queens,' added Will, thinking of the treasure books he'd read.

'Aye, that's more like it,' grinned Headlice.

'And we'll sneak into the Captain's cabin to fetch paper and ink. We'll make a map: you can draw it—'

'Yes, that's good! A map will look proper… and we'll say my own daddy gave it to me so I'd have some comfort and security in my old age. The treasure's rightly *mine*, I'll tell them, but as I'm a generous soul I'm willing to share if they help me dig for it.' Headlice gave Will a friendly cuff on the knee. 'See, soon we're gunna be free as birds!'

And the two boys jumped up and did a little jig around the fo'c'sle until Squid came roaring up to them, demanding to know the reason for their delirium and declaring that if it was because they'd got into his rum, they were grog-faced scallywags who deserved to walk the plank.

chapter 12

Squid's bellowing was a swift reminder to the boys to keep their excitement well hidden. Cheerfulness of any kind was rare among the pirates and created a great deal of suspicion. The climate on board was always the same: dismal and damp as a soggy sponge, with no forecast of sunny days ahead.

But Will and Headlice were bubbling with plans. There was so much to think about. And they had to act quickly if they were to change the ship's course.

The following afternoon, when the Captain was stationed at the poop deck, his telescope to his eye, Headlice whispered, 'Scoot down now to the captain's cabin – you know where he keeps his writing materials. I'll keep watch and if he looks like leaving his post, I'll keep him talking.'

Will nodded and hurried down from the quarter deck. The Captain's door was closed as usual but when Will tried the handle, it wouldn't budge. Of course, why hadn't he thought? The Captain would never leave his door unlocked!

A clatter of footsteps from above. Someone coming down

the steps. Quick as a blink Will slithered down below to the bulkhead. He peeped up through the hole in the boards. Boots…a smell of grog…*Squid*. He was standing at the door of the cabin, pulling out a bunch of iron keys.

Will had to make a lightning-fast decision. This was a rare moment of fortune – he'd have to take his chances and slip in while Squid had the door open.

Silent as a ship's cat, Will tiptoed through the open door. Squid had his back to him, his head stuck in the cavernous drawers underneath the bed. He was grunting with frustration, hands raking through silk shirts and belt buckles, fob watches and decanters of finest painted glass.

Holding his breath, Will crept to the desk and slid open the second drawer.

Creeaak! A soft whisper of wood. Will's heart pounded.

But Squid was snorting now, reaching to the back of a wardrobe. He squatted down on his knees, riffling through fine embroidered coats and piled caskets, swearing under his breath.

Will slipped a sheet from the ribbon-tied roll of paper and stuffed it down the back of his pants. Next he took the little snuff box Headlice had given him from his pocket. Carefully, trying to stop his hand shaking, he poured a thimbleful of ink into the box, shut it tight and stowed it back in his pocket. He was only a footstep from the door when a bony hand came down hard on his shoulder.

'And what the blazes are you doin' here, Master Wicked?' snarled Squid. The fumes from his boozy breath made Will's eyes water.

'I was…um, wondering the same about you, sir.'

They both looked down at the bottles of rum in Squid's other hand.

'Er, hrmm,' said Squid, swallowing. 'My business is none of *your* business, pipsqueak. But since you asked, I'm takin' these up to the Captain.'

'Oh I see,' Will said slowly. 'Well, I'll be looking forward to seeing how overjoyed he is when you give them to him.'

Squid's face reddened with rage. 'Why you little sneak! You low-down grovellin' greedy git! I've a good mind to …'

'On the other hand, maybe I'll just go back to my chores and mind my own business – that is, if you promise to … to …' Will was thinking desperately. He felt giddy already from his own inventions. He had an eerie feeling of being outside his body, looking down at himself and wondering what this strange boy would say next.

Squid was beginning to smirk.

'You've got to promise,' Will rushed on, 'to let us boys alone, *all* of us. Don't pick on me and Headlice or Scab or anyone. Or I'll … I'll tell the Captain it's you stealing his grog.'

Squid grunted with rage and lunged at Will. But as Will was closer to the door and not at all inebriated, he was quicker. He slipped through the passageway, ran up the steps and out into the honest air.

Will and Headlice had to wait until the other boys had gone to sleep before they could start on their map. Will carried the lamp over to the table and spread out the paper.

'Good work,' breathed Headlice as Will brought out the box of ink and told him about Squid's promise. 'You've got a bit of the devil in you!'

[95]

Will tried to smile, but the strange feeling of unease returned for a moment, making him bite his cheek instead.

'Now, I'll draw it up, best as I can remember,' Headlice went on. He took the wood splinter he'd whittled from his jacket, and dipped the sharp end in the ink.

'What a fine pen!' said Will. 'Did your mother teach you that?'

'My daddy,' said Headlice, sighing. 'He was the best whittler and carver on Devil Island. He made toys for me in secret – pity I couldn't share them. But folk would have laughed at us till we wept for mercy.'

Headlice pored over the paper, measuring distances with his thumb and pen, the tip of his tongue stuck out while he drew. Then he printed the names of the islands, the legend at the bottom and the compass at the top. When he was finished he smeared candle grease and sooty fingerprints over it, and held the candle underneath to age the paper. The corners curled a little with heat and the white page turned to a faint smoky brown so that when they held it up to the lantern, they both decided it looked at least as old as Headlice's grandfather.

Will was elected to be the one to tell the Captain of the treasure. 'Even though it's supposed to belong to my family,' Headlice explained, 'you are his favourite, and he'll be more inclined to listen.'

Will woke at dawn the next morning and rehearsed his speech many times before he went to knock on the Captain's door.

'Sir, I'm sorry to disturb you, but I have some news that might interest you,' he began.

The Captain was already sitting at his desk, staring into space with a dark, brooding expression. He raised his brows at Will's words. He looked as if he would pounce at any moment if he heard something to enrage him.

Will's stomach churned. It was one thing to imagine meeting a lion, it was another to be face to face in its den.

'Well, boy, spit it out,' said the Captain. 'I haven't got all day.'

'It's Headlice, sir,' Will began.

'Oh yes, your little friend,' sneered the Captain. 'Telling tales now are we? I'm all ears.'

'Well, in a manner of speaking, sir. He's told me some valuable information and I've persuaded him to share it with you.'

'Go on, I'm intrigued!' said the Captain, yawning.

So Will took a deep breath and told him about the treasure. He put all of himself into his speech, hesitating delicately when he described Headlice's doubt and guilt at betraying his family, rushing on in waves of enthusiasm at the splendid riches there would be for everyone. As he spoke, he almost began to believe his story and at the end, he said something he hadn't planned to say. 'I'm telling you all this, Captain, because you saved my life. And I realise that I never really thanked you. I'm in your debt.'

A strange quiver of light flickered in the Captain's eyes. The empty dark shifted, just for a heartbeat, then closed over again like the sea over a sinking ship. Will's throat went dry.

'Turtle Island you say?' The Captain turned to the globe on his desk.

'Y…yes. It's due north from Snake Island, directly east of Devil Island.'

The Captain swung back to him. 'What's that in your hands?'

'Oh, I…um…almost forgot. It's the treasure map, sir. Headlice entrusted it to me – his father handed it on to him before he died. It shows the exact location of the treasure.'

The Captain took it and laid it on the desk before him. But he didn't look at it. 'You can go now, Wicked. I will consider what you've said and make my decision by noon. But remember this: if I find that any part of what you have said is untrue, both you and your little friend will be fed to the sharks.'

As Will stepped back on the main deck, his guts turned to ice.

What if something went wrong? There was no turning back now. He thought of Headlice and the Captain's warning: never trust a pirate-boy from Devil Island.

But the Captain was wrong. Headlice was his friend.

His bowels squirmed as he remembered the eerie light that came into the Captain's eyes when he admitted his debt to him. It was unnatural, like a marble sculpture coming to life, a tree talking.

He walked up to Headlice near the bowsprit. In a daze, he sat on the deck, waiting for his belly to settle and the cold chill down his back to fade.

'So it's done?' whispered Headlice. 'Do you think he believed you?'

Will nodded. And then he had a great urge to tell everything about it, what he'd said, how he'd almost convinced his own self with his telling, and how at the end he'd thanked the Captain for his life.

'Shiver me timbers, that was pure genius!' crowed Headlice. 'How could he not believe you? You're a natural!'

Will shuddered. *You're a natural* was what his mother used to say when he walked the tightrope. He hugged his knees. He didn't tell Headlice that he'd had no more control over those last words than taking his next breath. Did he say it because he truly felt it? He didn't know. Gratitude…the man *had* saved his life. But as he'd watched the Captain's eyes blaze in response he'd felt a strange power of his own rise – *I caused that*. It was like making an earthquake happen. Moving something unmovable. He'd never felt that kind of power before.

Thinking about it now, he realised it hadn't been a good feeling, not really. Because even as it ran through his veins he felt it change him; it made him feel as small and trapped and helpless inside the Captain's dark world as a fly caught in a web.

Before noon the Captain summoned the crew to announce he was turning the ship about and steering north.

'What?' cried the First Mate. 'Only Devil Island lies that way. We been there already this year, no point in goin' back for more booty. There ain't none.'

'Only a whole lot of heartache,' said Squid.

'An' hostility,' added Buzzard.

'Not to mention aggression,' said Goose.

'That's the same thing, you *goose*,' said Squid. 'You're just showin' off yer vocabulary.'

'Has everyone quite finished?' the Captain asked.

Silence fell over the ship like evening.

'Our destination is not Devil Island, you dunderheads. To the east of it, only six nautical miles off, is Turtle Island.'

'But there's nothing *there*, sir,' called out Squid. 'Everyone knows that. Nought to steal or plunder – well, only if you're partial to coconuts. And there's a tricky reef to steer through an' all.'

'Master Squid,' spat the Captain icily, 'I fear you couldn't steer your way through a school of sardines. You can barely stand up on your two legs, you rum-sodden fool. Now, let me share with you all young Wicked's news.'

Sneers hissed through the crew as they turned to look at Will. He blushed bright red and studied his boots.

'There is a lot more than coconuts on Turtle Island,' the Captain went on. 'According to young Wicked, treasure is buried in one of the caves. No other party is aware of it, so it's there for the taking.'

A crow of excitement went up as the pirates turned to slap each other on the back.

'Now, weigh anchor as I command and use this sou'westerly to full advantage. If it keeps blowing steady and you roll out the sails, we'll be there before dark.'

The First Mate was eyeing the Captain. 'And seein' as I'm yer second in command, sir, I'll be assisting you in dividin' up the treasure this time, fair an' square, among the crew.'

'No doubt,' the Captain agreed, his voice clinking soullessly as stone against glass.

The two men exchanged a long hard gaze. Then the First Mate clapped his hands.

'You heard the Captain, all hands at the ready! Goose, Scab, Heartless, let down the mainsail. Wicked, climb the riggin' an' check the flyin' jib. Heave ho now me hearties, make haste!' And he rubbed his big beefy palms together in delight.

Will hurried along the deck to the foresail. A cold sweat had broken out on his forehead. Everyone was so excited – what would they do when their hopes were dashed? He hoped to heaven that he wouldn't be there to see it. For a moment he felt sorry for them all...

A stab of guilt struck him. It wasn't fair that only he and Headlice could escape. All the boys had suffered the same fate after all. Maybe, when he was free, he would be able to do something for them. Maybe he could organise some resistance, he could work out some way to change things... but as long as he was a prisoner of this ship like everyone else, he could do nothing.

And that was the way he comforted himself through the early hours of the afternoon. He went about his work inventing grand schemes of rescue and revolution; he saw himself grown, with a crew of strong able men behind him, boarding a ship of pirate slaves just like this one. He and his men would take it over, showering the quaking swabs with riches of good food, comfort and the best reward of all, freedom to go and find their mothers!

chapter 13

Will was up on the rigging in the middle of the afternoon when he saw a piercing bright light flash from the bowsprit. There was another and another, in a short intense rhythm. He took out his telescope and saw Headlice at the front of the ship, tipping the small piece of mirror to catch the sun's rays.

Quickly he looked around the boat. No one was near the spot, and no one seemed to notice. His eyes scanned the ship more closely. The Captain was nowhere to be seen – hopefully he was at his desk in his cabin.

When Will met Headlice down on the deck, he pulled him towards the rail. 'So do you think your mother saw your signal? How far are we from Devil Island now?'

'Only about an hour's sail, I reckon,' said Headlice.

'Fingers crossed then,' whispered Will.

'Aye,' said Headlice, his voice shaky. 'All we gotta do now is wait. Hardest thing of all, eh?'

Late in the day big foamy clouds began to gather. The wind

dropped to a whisper and the tall ship lay on a sea as smooth as glass.

'Bloomin' weather,' the First Mate moaned. 'Ye never know what it's gunna do. We was almost there! I was countin' on gettin' through that reef by daylight. Now we're stuck here for who knows how long.'

'Like a painted ship on a painted ocean,' said the pirate with one leg.

'That's real poetic,' said Goose, struck. 'Did you make that up yer own self?'

'Nah, I heard it somewhere.'

The First Mate went up to the poop deck to see the Captain. When he came back he looked relieved. 'Captain said it's no matter if we sail in tonight or tomorrow. No one's gunna fight us for that treasure. We'll just wait for the wind to change, so take yer ease, gentlemen, there'll be a fine sunset to watch this evenin'.'

The pirates cheered, and Squid went off to find his last bottle of rum.

Then the First Mate called over to Will. 'All except you, Wicked. Captain wants ye to go up the crow's nest tonight. We could be in a tricky situation, like, so close to Devil Island. The islanders might send out a boat full of musket shot. Cap'n wants you to spend the night up there.'

Will went hot with alarm. 'Couldn't I just keep an eye from the poop deck? I'll have my telescope, don't you worry.'

'Captain's orders, lad. You're to spend the night in the basket.' For the first time Will saw an expression of sympathy on the man's face.

When he'd gone, Will only had time to whisper to Headlice, 'That's messed everything up! What if I fall asleep? What if I don't hear when your mother comes?'

Headlice patted his shoulder. 'Don't worry, I'll come and get you. It's a good thing I learned to climb the ropes so well, eh? Must've had a good teacher.'

The sun set on the horizon like a fireball shot from a cannon. The sky ran with red and the sea turned to blood beneath it. To the east Will could see the black fuzz of forest on Turtle Island and to the west, yellow globs of firelight flickered along the Devil Island coast. Cooking fires, he thought, and a wave of homesickness made him dizzy.

From high up in the rigging, Will could hear the pirates' laughter on the deck below. He tried not to think how lonely he felt. He tried to think only of tomorrow, when he'd be sitting at a table in a kitchen that didn't float, with kind people who weren't pirates with grudges or drinking problems, or strange empty eyes with weirdness in them.

'And best of all,' he told Treasure, 'soon I'll see *you*.'

Imagine what she'd say when he knocked on her door. Imagine how she would smile! He suddenly felt shy at the thought. What would *he* say? 'I'll tell you how much I missed you, and that you will always be my greatest treasure!' He smiled to himself at his own little joke. When the two of them were safely together on the back verandah with the hill of coconut palms rolling out in front and the smell of roasting chicken wafting from the stove, he would tell her about his adventures – because that's what all the awful things that had happened to him would turn into, he knew, with Treasure at his side.

The moon rose in an inky sky and Will went on imagining his homecoming. Now he knew so much more about the world, he would find a way to get to the Mainland and look for his mother. He might need to rescue her; she may have been kidnapped just like him … He shifted restlessly in the cramped space. Now that his own rescue was so near he couldn't wait. It was as if he could just reach out a little further with his fingertips and catch hold of his mother's hand, touch the back of Treasure's dark head, glimpse the moon glowing hazily through the clouds …

The sky had cleared and was sparkly with stars when Will woke with a jolt. His heart thudded against the wall of his chest. Down below, there was the quiet of sleeping men. A snore, a slurred curse in a dream. Nothing to be alarmed about, he told himself. He must have drifted off for a moment. The water slapped softly at the sides of the ship like voices murmuring, back and forth, back and …

He peered down over the side.

Tied to the hull of the ship, portside, was a small wooden boat. A slender woman was standing in the boat holding up a lantern. In the lemon light he saw her stretch out an arm to a boy about to clamber in. Will stifled a cry; if he called out to them now the whole ship would wake up. He waved his arms wildly.

But the woman and the boy didn't look up.

He scurried down the rigging more quickly than he'd ever moved before. As he got closer to the deck he heard snatches of words from the boat. Headlice's excited chatter, his mother's steadier reply.

'...taught me how to climb that rope ladder like a monkey, he can walk a tightrope, swing on the rigging, it's amazing...Captain's favourite...'

'Come on, dear, hurry into the boat...No, we can't take him with us...No, I said...You know why...dangerous enough taking *you*...I know, but you're still the man's property...no time to argue...think of your little brother at home...Oh, because if we took his favourite, his pet boy, he'd come after us like the devil. No, we'd never be safe!'

Will dropped to the ground and ran like the wind along the deck. His heart was thumping so loud now it was hard to hear anything. He wouldn't take up much space in the boat, he *wouldn't*. It'd be all right as soon as she saw him. She would see he was just a boy, just like her own.

He was almost there when the rope slid from the rail and slipped *thwack* into the water. In the pale starlight he caught Headlice's gaze.

The boy was standing up in the boat, the rope in his hands. He and Will locked eyes; Headlice was the first to look away.

'Haul in that rope and take the oar,' his mother told him. 'Look lively now before some villain wakes.'

Headlice flung the rope into the boat and settled himself on the seat. He didn't look back. He didn't see Will's face or how the life drained out of it as he and his mother rowed away.

chapter 14

William watched the boat vanish into the dark.

He kept looking long after it was gone. There'd been the tiny flame of the lantern, the moon playing on the water. As long as he kept looking, the great black thing inside him wouldn't come out.

When he unhooked his fingers from the rail and turned around, he knew it would get him. He didn't want to face it. He thought instead about Treasure. 'We'll be all right,' she'd said.

But it wasn't all right. Treasure, his mother and now his friend were all floating somewhere out in the world; they were lost in the dark and he was lost too and he just couldn't see how they would ever find each other. He didn't want to think this, but then it was all he *could* think, and the terrible black thing was going to swallow him.

He ran to the bow of the ship. But the empty sea looked no different no matter where he was. What if he called out? For a moment he imagined doing it – the pirates would come rushing, the Captain marching up the steps, 'What's all this racket then?' Maybe they'd even be in time to follow the little boat, bring it back…

Will clapped his hand over his mouth – he couldn't do that, he'd *never* do that.

'Why aren't you up in the crow's nest as I ordered?' asked a low, smooth voice.

He spun around to see the Captain, fully dressed with his sword at his side.

The Captain nodded as if Will had spoken. 'Abandoned you, has he? Your little friend?'

Will said nothing.

'What did I tell you? You've a lot to learn about the world, young Wicked.'

The First Mate burst onto the deck dressed only in his nightshirt. 'Headlice? Gone? Why I'll…that scurvy little sea dog! But we still got the map, sir. We'll still find the treasure.'

The Captain gave a thin smile. 'I am at a loss to know what fills that head of yours. You think the boy would have left something as valuable as a true treasure map in our possession?' He turned to Will. 'Tell me Wicked, just out of idle curiosity, did you believe there was treasure on Turtle Island?'

Will bit his cheek.

Dogfish had stumbled onto the deck, with more pirates behind him.

Will couldn't think. There was only the big black thing inside him. If he opened his mouth it would come out.

He saw Dogfish shaking his head at him.

What did that mean? That he should tell the Captain no, he hadn't believed it? But then his life would be over – the

Captain had said so. Keep your eyes on the prize, his mother had told him. But what *was* the prize in this world of pirates and lies? He didn't know. For the first time he wondered if his mother's advice had covered everything.

The Captain studied him. 'Perhaps we will go to Devil Island now and fetch the wretch. We'll ask *him*.'

'No!' shouted Will. 'There *is* no treasure on Turtle Island, we only made it up so we could escape. And there's no point in going back to Devil Island – Headlice has gone somewhere you'll never find him. He'll be far away by now.'

'And so he has left you to face the punishment. A good friend indeed…' The Captain flicked a smut from the ruffle of his shirt. 'Seems you can't trust anyone in this world. How very sad.'

Dogfish sighed loudly.

'I would have expected more from you, Wicked, I really would,' the Captain went on. 'Regarding your friend, I'll say good riddance. But you – I thought you'd have showed me more gratitude. I am very disappointed.'

'You and me both,' Dogfish muttered under his breath. 'Looking forward to puttin' me feet up for a bit, I was.'

'An' countin' a mountain of gold coins,' snarled the First Mate.

'That's me favourite activity!' put in the pirate with one leg.

'The only way to relieve my disappointment is to punish you,' the Captain said. He tapped his chin lightly, thinking. 'Let me see: there's the lash, the plank, a good keelhauling…'

Dogfish spluttered. 'Steady on, sir, he's only a lad.'

The Captain ignored him. 'But I think, seeing as all these punishments require so much effort, the best thing is to remove

[109]

you from my sight. You'll go up to the crow's nest for three days and three nights to contemplate your sins.' Motioning to the First Mate to follow, he started back to his cabin. 'We'll turn about now. We won't wait till morning. I don't trust those Devil Islanders – we'll head due south and leave this cursed place at once.'

'Aye aye, Cap'n,' said the First Mate.

With a backward glance at Will, the Captain added softly, 'And Wicked, while you're up there, you might meditate upon your curious lack of gratitude. I wonder how you can ever make it up to me?'

Will shivered although it wasn't a cold night. A cloud passed over the moon as the Captain left the deck, and the pirates began unrolling the sails.

Dogfish put a hand on Will's shoulder. 'You're gettin' off lightly, Wicked. I mean, considerin'.'

Will's hands were sweating. 'I'm sorry, Dogfish.'

'Ah, never mind, we would all try to get off this floatin' hell if we had the chance.'

'But Dogfish, I don't want to be alone up there with the thing.'

'What thing?'

Will couldn't find any words for it. So instead, he said, 'I might die from … hunger.'

Dogfish rooted in his pocket and brought out a cold piece of fish. 'Here, take this with yer. I was keepin' it for later but you'll need it more than me. An' next time, be careful who you let save your life.'

'What?'

'Sometimes, like, the obligation you're stuck with is worse.'

Will stared blankly.

'The *debt* you gotta pay 'em,' sighed Dogfish. 'A man like the Captain, it'll never get paid. When you was overboard you'd 'ave been better off learnin' how to swim.'

'But that's impossible – you can't learn in a moment!'

Dogfish raised his eyes to heaven. 'You never know *what* you can do when there's no one else to save you but yerself.'

Up in the crow's nest, Will told himself he'd got off lightly, just as Dogfish had said. He was lucky, really. He'd even got a flask of water to last him. The crow's nest was peaceful, the safest place. He'd try to find Treasure in his mind and remember her fascinating facts. He could talk to his mother again.

But there was the black thing inside him, too. He was alone with it now, and it was frightening. He must have caught it from the Captain. It was fierce, like a dangerous animal kept down in the dungeon. Maybe if he threw it food, it might go back to sleep.

He gobbled up the shark meat Dogfish had given him. He imagined eating Honey's chicken mango, his mother's hot baked bread. He tried to feel the food filling his belly. Often that worked. But nothing seemed to soothe the thing.

And it got out. It was big and dark and shapeless and it swamped him with terror so he couldn't move. It trampled his thoughts. He was stuck inside it, stuck in his dread.

The second time the sun went down, he saw his mother. She was walking the tightrope, high and free, her arms outstretched, balancing her own weight as she went. But she wasn't walking among the mangroves. She was far away in a circus on the

Mainland – a spotlight on her happy face, a crowd cheering at her feet. 'Look at that,' whispered the Captain in his ear. 'Seems you can't trust anyone in this wide world. Even your mother. My word, you've got a lot to learn, young Wicked.'

The sea below darkened, falling quiet. But something loud and angry flared in Will's chest. *I'll keep you safe till you're grown,* his mother had promised. *You're my precious boy.*

'Why wasn't it *you* in that boat?' he shouted. 'Why didn't *you* come looking for me? Where were you when I called and called and called?'

By the time the sun sank for the third time, his eyes stung with weeping and his throat was raw. But he was so tired now he couldn't care. Nothing hurt him. His body seemed to belong to someone else, and his feelings had flown away. When he stood up, he felt as light as air. He was hardly there.

'You've learnt the first lesson, Wicked,' the Captain said when he'd climbed down. 'Friends lie and women betray you. Why, your own mother broke her promise. How long do you think she'd have been satisfied, stuck on that godforsaken island with a mewling puppy for entertainment? Face the facts, you weren't enough for her.' A look of bitterness crossed the Captain's face. 'She wanted more. She'd tasted success, the admiration of men. I've known females like that, dozens of 'em. Listen to me now, lad, and I'll teach you how to get on in this world. You'll be my star pupil. A first-class pirate.'

He gave Will a smile.

And it was Wicked who smiled back.

~ ✳ ~

No one noticed the change. The boys and pirates went about their duties, grizzling about their hunger, misery, bad dreams, the weather. As usual, no one bothered to listen to the other. There were spats over rations of rum, whose turn it was on dog watch, what blaggard took the last piece of dried mutton. Squid nearly lost an eye when he fell over Buzzard's boots and ran into the bowsprit; Buzzard almost lost his hearing when Squid boxed his ears.

But scarcely ever did a man or boy besides Wicked have to climb the crow's nest. Without being ordered, he went up the rigging most mornings and stayed there until he was told to come down. And even though no one was friendly to Wicked since the lie about hidden treasure, they were grateful at least to be spared the seasickness and danger of the bucket.

The pirates fended off a Spanish warship in open seas, then ran aground fleeing the French. But most privately agreed with the Captain that it was Wicked who saved them from the worst battles and certain defeat; his vigilance up in the rigging meant they had time to judge when to change course and retreat, and when to stay and attack.

Now Wicked talked and acted like a pirate; he didn't have to pretend, he just was one. When he got swiped with a sword in a battle, he thought it strange that he didn't feel it. He saw the blood well up from the wound in his chest and drip onto his legs. But there was no pain. Even afterwards, when he'd thrown a bucket of seawater at the gash, he felt no sting, maybe just a slight tingle. It was as if all his nerve endings had been blunted up there in the crow's nest, as if the silence stretching from one end of the horizon to the other had drowned them.

Part Two

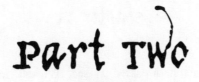

chapter 15

After five years had passed at sea, Wicked gave up trying to figure out on which day his birthday fell. It didn't matter anymore. Time was a droopy, elastic thing. His beard was growing in, thick and dark, making him wonder if his father had been a hairy man.

Tall as Dogfish now, he was, and he'd grown meat on his bones. He remembered, early on, being skinny as a whip. He'd scurried up and down the rigging, swinging out over the yardarm, patching cracks in the mast, keeping busy. These days, he just climbed up in the morning and lolled there all day. His own mother wouldn't recognise him. He felt very old, as far as he felt anything much, and that he had acquired too much experience of the world.

When the pirates raided ports and plundered towns, he went with them. Sometimes, he had a good meal and a drop of ale. But the fear and loathing he saw on the faces of the wenches serving in the tavern made the grog come back up again. After a while he concluded that being on land made him more seasick than being aboard ship. By now, the sea was his home.

Wicked hardly remembered the time when he'd planned to escape. He knew that up in the crow's nest he used to talk to his mother; he'd replayed Treasure's stories about the little creatures with homes on their backs and giant creatures that swam from one side of the world to the other. He did remember that once, when he spotted a whale spouting, he'd almost cried out to her – *look, that's just the way you described it!*

But he didn't do that much anymore. Up in the rigging, he mostly just stared into space, gazing at the empty horizon. He was no longer curious about what might loom upon it. What was the point of thinking about the old life? It was better this way. Childhood was so far away it was like a dream, and this was real. 'You can't lie around all day with your eyes shut,' the Captain said, 'or you'll wake up with a sword through your middle.'

The main prize, he'd worked out, was survival. That meant listening to the Captain and doing what he was told. Loyalty and obedience weren't so hard, after all. And as cold and hard and villainous as he might be, the Captain was still the only one who'd ever bothered to reach out and pluck him from death's jaws – that rotten place his mother had left him.

The other important rules he'd learned were: spot your enemy before he spots you, be first to draw your sword, rob him blind, and trust no one. Everyone was gunning for themselves, so you had to arrive first to get the prize.

When the new boys came aboard, he used to try and tell them these things, but he didn't bother with all that now. They'd find out the hard way, just like he did.

One year, summer came with a hurricane. The hold was flooded and a pirate was washed overboard by a wave as tall as a mountain. Soon after, three pirates never returned from a raid on the Dregs Islands. They were found dead by one of the Captain's spies at the bottom of a cliff. That same summer, two boys, Scab and Heartless, managed to escape by bribing a passing fisherman. And when the ship stopped near the Mainland, even the pirate with one leg braved the short distance from ship to shore on a moonless night, swimming his frog-paddle and vanishing into the bush.

The Captain was in a stormy mood for days afterwards, and disappeared with a bottle of rum down to his cabin.

The autumn brought unusually cool weather and several pirates came down with flu. Two developed pneumonia and had to be buried at sea.

'We'll sail to Devil Island earlier than usual,' the Captain decided in exasperation. 'Crew needs topping up.'

The pirates ground their teeth and exchanged bitter looks.

'He's got absolutely no human feelin',' Dogfish remarked for the hundredth time. 'Toppin' up indeed. Like us men are just rations of rum that need renewin'.'

'Aye,' agreed Squid. 'Talkin' of which, has the old devil taken the last drop?'

The crew were wary of the folk on Devil Island. They were a feisty lot, and their boys were famous for fighting back. They dropped on pirates from rooftops and treetops, pelting them with their poisonous pets. The pirates often returned scratched and bitten to the jolly-boats, the boys slung over their shoulders now as quiet and limp as wet sails.

'But just think, maties,' Squid said, rubbing his hands together with glee as he contemplated the next day's capture, 'won't it be good to 'ave a fresh supply of varmints to order about?'

'Aye,' agreed the First Mate. 'I feel like having a proper vacation – putting me feet up an' lettin' someone else trim the sails for a change.'

And so, the next evening, a new batch of boys came aboard like a delivery of fresh baked buns. Wicked cast a careless eye over them: Mischief, Hoodlum, Rip, Rascal ... all loudmouths, all easy enough to manage. Even that big bossy one, Bombastic, who kept his poisonous pet frog secretly in his jacket. Wicked had spotted it lapping at spilt rum. The frog was always escaping, lurking around Squid's secret stash. If the Captain ever got wind of it there'd be hell to pay. The Captain loathed amphibians. Wicked couldn't see why. He remembered Treasure saying amphibians could live in water *and* on land. She found that fascinating. The Captain said it was infuriating: 'Wishy-washy creatures, why can't they make up their minds?' For the Captain, you had to be one thing or the other, gilled or legged, friend or enemy, *for* him or against him.

But what did Wicked care about a poisonous pet frog or the lumpy boy who was hiding it? What did he care about any of them – they were all the same every year, and nothing different about this lot.

Except for one. The lad who'd *pleaded* to be taken aboard.

After the first week, Wicked had to agree that in all the Cannonball Seas, there'd never been anyone like him.

The boy called Horrendo.

chapter 16

'Anyone for garlic prawns? They're delicious even if I do say so myself. Dogfish? That's right, take a decent helping. Don't worry, plenty left for you, Mr Goose,' Horrendo said, spooning a generous portion of Seafood Delight onto the pirate's plate.

When they'd finished, the crew lay back against the sides, sighing in contentment. It was just noon, and by now everyone looked forward to lunch and dinner as the best times of their lives.

Horrendo, the star of the last catch at Devil Island, was proving to be a wizard in the galley. Not only could he throw together any bunch of ingredients and turn them into a mouth-watering feast, he'd gone to the trouble of finding, mending and plaiting the old nets in order to catch fresh fish every day.

'Size isn't everything, you know,' Wicked heard him confiding to Dogfish one day. 'See these tiny whitebait? Why, just roll them in flour then fry in oil – hey presto, you have a tasty, crunchy snack to fill those little corners when dinner seems so far away!'

At first the pirates mocked him. The First Mate had wanted to swat him like a fly, irritated by Horrendo's constant buzz: 'What would you like?' and '*Do* try the shark fin soup' and 'What about a little herbal tea to settle your stomach, sir?' His eternal politeness in the face of rudeness was beyond reason, Squid declared; was he the village idiot? But once Squid tried the soup and followed it up with crusty French toast drenched in sweet syrup, he changed his tune.

Wicked couldn't fathom it. Back when *he* was a kid, even younger than Horrendo, he'd climbed those rat lines like a monkey, saving the men from the job they dreaded most of all. From his first day he'd suffered up there alone in the crow's nest, sick as a dog, rocked by the high winds and drenching storms, sword-fighting enemies twenty feet above deck. But did anyone ever thank *him*? Did anyone ever say a kind or grateful word to *him*? Not bloomin' likely – all he ever got was black looks and the vicious slur of 'Captain's pet'.

Wicked refused to eat that slop Horrendo cooked – it was making the men stupid, telling silly stories about their childhoods. It smelled good, it was true, but like the Captain said, it made them soft. Didn't they run straight to Horrendo with their cuts and bruises, sitting still like well-behaved infants while he cleansed and dabbed? And why were they acting that way *now*, after all these years that he, Wicked, had had to swallow their insults and jibes, their calls to 'toughen up!' and 'stop yer bally-hooing, yer spineless lump!' at the slightest sniffle of homesickness. What, suddenly the men had *feelings*? It was as strange as a fish suddenly getting up and walking, the moon falling from the sky. And Wicked was having none of it.

Neither was the Captain. The pirates warned Horrendo that the Captain wasn't interested in food or having his wounds tended. 'The man ain't like anyone else,' Dogfish explained. 'Yer concern for his stomach annoys him. An' ye don't want the Captain annoyed.'

Horrendo nodded and agreed, as he was always polite, but the boy just couldn't help himself. It seemed to Wicked that Horrendo must have a tic of some sort, like Scab who'd had to keep rubbing his eye even though it hurt. Or even like himself back in the day, when he used to get nervous and bite his cheek till it bled. Horrendo's unfailing *please* and *thank you* was a kind of reflex, maybe. Wicked saw him purse his lips sometimes after he'd said something pleasant or urged a plate of lobster mornay upon a pirate who, only seconds before, had deliberately put his foot out to trip him, 'just for a laugh'. The boy wasn't able to exclude the Captain from his dinner invitations either, even though the First Mate warned him many times that if he kept that up it would be bad for his health.

'He's got a curse on him,' Rascal explained to the men one evening. 'Had it ever since he was born. It's the Wise Woman's doing – he'll never be able to swear or fight. Even if you jumped on him with a drawn sword, he'd say, "Oh, so sorry, was I in your way?" Nah, under that curse he's helpless as a kitten.'

'And we'll never know what he'd of been like without it,' put in Mischief.

Curse or no curse, Wicked knew that even if he'd gobbled up every bit of Horrendo's lobster or swordfish or whatever bloomin' thing it was, he wouldn't have liked the boy anyway.

He just wouldn't. So what did all the others see in him? And why hadn't they ever liked *him*, Wicked, when he'd been skilled and eager and done the worst jobs willingly? No, perhaps it wasn't strange at all that it was just he and the Captain against the rest. The Captain was the only one who'd ever thought Wicked was worth something.

'Wicked is the most valuable look-out we've ever had,' he'd said after a battle, right in front of everyone. Wicked used to hate being singled out, but he knew now it was the reason he'd survived. The others mightn't like it, but what did he care? They were all unreliable, as wishy-washy as amphibians, as stupid as that frog the boy Bombastic tried to keep hidden in his jacket.

And now, Wicked's guts were playing up. In the mornings it was worst – awful griping cramps that clutched at his belly and wouldn't let go. He had to hang over the side for ages. Nothing much came out after a while, but he felt like it would, so he had to stay there. The others teased him and blew raspberries whenever they passed him. 'Old Wicked's worse than Dogfish now,' they said. 'Soon we'll 'ave to toss you overboard with the fish heads!'

Horrendo circled him like a demented bird, squawking about the benefits of his calming chamomile and simple rice dishes for a 'complicated tummy'. Wicked even ate some of his offerings, specially prepared with no fats or spices. But nothing seemed to make any difference. Somehow it made Wicked feel lonelier than ever, this inability of his to enjoy what the others enjoyed. He must be different to everyone on earth or at sea – except for the Captain, maybe. But then the Captain never looked lonely.

His stomach grew so bad that it wouldn't let him climb the rigging. The pain when it came was crippling, and once he almost fell from the yardarm – which would have meant certain death. He had to go down to the Captain's cabin and tell him. It was the worst thing he'd had to do since he'd come on board.

'I'm real sorry, sir,' he said, standing behind the Captain's desk, his fingers tapping anxiously on his thigh. 'Maybe if I just lay up in the berth for a few days, it'll pass. But if I keep doin' the climb I might fall and then I'll be no use to anyone.'

Wicked stared down at his feet. Strange, a sharp lump in his throat made his eyes water, like a fishbone caught right where he swallowed. He didn't expect sympathy from the Captain. He just hoped for a day's mercy. But the Captain's next words surprised him.

'I agree,' the Captain said. When Wicked looked up, he saw the Captain nodding. 'We'll send that boy Rascal up there. He's a shirker and a weakling, always mooning about, coughing and spluttering. This will give him something to do, get him trained up and fit to be a sailor.' He looked straight at Wicked then and it seemed that the light in the room shifted for a moment, dulling to grey, as if a candle had flickered. Goosebumps sprang up on Wicked's arms, and the black thing stirred inside him.

'They're a useless lot, this crew,' the Captain said evenly, his eyes never moving from Wicked's own. 'But you, on the other hand, I need.'

And with that, the Captain went back to studying his maps, motioning to Wicked to close the door behind him.

~ * ~

Lying in the gloom in his hammock, Wicked's thoughts returned often to the Captain's last words. His mind kept saying them, the way his tongue kept finding the hole in his tooth, tracing it over and over.

The Captain needed him. He'd actually said it. Being *necessary* was even more important than being *valuable*, wasn't it? No one else cared if he lived or died, but the Captain of the whole Cannonball Seas needed him. That was something.

Wicked watched Rascal shiver and shake up the rat lines. The boy was as trembly as a jelly. It was obvious the seasickness was ruling him. And he had the flu – well, he *always* had the flu, that one. The lad possessed a faulty pair of lungs, no doubt about it. Those coughing fits could be fatal when you were up high on the rigging.

Truth to tell, when you first started, the job was hard enough even if you were well. For a moment Wicked remembered his own fear in those early days, the bleakness of that crow's nest and the empty sky once he'd got up there. He almost called out to Rascal one morning, thinking he'd teach him about balance and discipline. But when he saw the boy wearing those stupid mittens that his friend Horrendo had knitted him, something closed over inside him until he couldn't remember even a twinge of whatever he'd wanted to say.

Those two boys were as thick as thieves. Or best friends, maybe. They were always whispering together at dinner, and Horrendo had gone to the trouble of sitting up every night for a week making those mittens, even after he'd cooked dinner and washed up and wiped down the galley. No one had ever knitted mittens for Wicked. No one had ever cared a fig whether his hands were cold or raw or numb. He'd only ever had one friend on board. And Headlice had deserted him, like everyone else.

So Wicked lay low and rested, and then he went back to light duties on board. Every now and then he went up the rigging, but the Captain seemed to prefer to 'use up' the boys.

'You should ask Horrendo to fix you something special for your stomach,' Dogfish said to him one day when he saw Wicked wince from sudden cramp. 'He works miracles, that lad.'

Wicked just shook his head. What was the point of talking?

'He's taken a set against the boy,' the First Mate said to Dogfish. 'Can't figure it, meself. At least now we've got somethin' to look forward to when we wake up. What's on today's menu, do you know?'

'Fish pie, with garlic and rosemary,' Squid put in. 'Can't wait, can you? How long till lunch?'

After a conversation like that one, Wicked just wanted to be alone. But when he went up to the crow's nest, he couldn't seem to find any comfort in his thoughts. Treasure hardly ever appeared anymore and when she did, she looked at him oddly. 'Why *don't* you like Horrendo?' she asked one day. 'Why not try that soothing fish soup? You're getting strange, you know. I almost don't recognise you!'

His mother made a sudden appearance, too. She was very small and far away. From over the horizon she called, 'You're losing your balance, dear boy. Remember to check your centre!'

He put his hand on his stomach. But everything heaved and gurgled in there now, and was never still. It was like the sea, driven by currents that he couldn't see or fathom.

chapter 17

When the Blue Devils came sailing in, it was Rascal who spotted them. But the boy was too late, of course. 'Pirate ship, pirate ship!' he yelled when he was halfway down the rigging. 'They've got their cannons out!'

What had the lad been doing up there, daydreaming? If it had been Wicked in the crow's nest, he'd have seen the Devils when they were just a dirty speck on the horizon. Timing was everything; it gave you the advantage, letting you shoot first and avoid battle.

And the Blue Devils were dead nasty, too. They'd attacked before and done a lot of damage. Wicked didn't relish another fight, not with his guts the way they were.

Watching the ship glide in, his stomach heaved with alarm and bile rose into his throat. Or was it the grub left in the galley that made him want to spew? Earlier, he'd been so hungry his guts were growling. He'd given in and wolfed down Horrendo's famous garlic prawns but they'd tasted foul to him, and he couldn't figure why everyone raved about them.

He stopped wondering when the first cannon flashed like lightning over the deck. The mast exploded and the Devils swarmed aboard yelling blue murder. Cutlasses clashing and boots kicking, they were all over the ship like an outbreak of pox. It wasn't until the Captain appeared and caught the Blue Devil captain in a headlock that they got the upper hand. He made the Devils drop their swords, but not before Buzzard lost an earlobe and Goose's pinkie finger was sliced clean away.

Wicked had offered to go up the ratlines to defend the rigging – achy guts and all, he was the only one who could do it.

But halfway down, a pain stabbed him, taking his breath away. He burped sour prawns, breaking out in a sweat. That bloomin' Horrendo was killing him, and just when he needed his strength!

That night, as he lay exhausted on the deck, Horrendo ran past with an empty soup tureen, and tripped over Wicked's foot.

'Oh sorry, I didn't see you there. Are you all right? You don't look it. Oh, I meant nothing personal about your ... er ... complexion, though a healthy diet might help with ...'

'No, I'm not all right, you little ship rat. You ought to be sorry, leaving bad prawns in the galley for me to eat. It's a miracle I'm still here.'

Horrendo was puzzled, then horrified. 'You didn't eat those? They'd been out in the sun for ages!' He shook his head. 'I was so tired I forgot to throw away the leftovers, but I didn't think anyone would be silly enough to ... oh!'

Wicked gave him a hard look. But just then such a wave of nausea washed over him that he couldn't be bothered saying anything more. He could still hear that milksop Horrendo tending the pirates – spooning out soup, bathing their wounds. He was coddling them, and in response, the pirates' talk grew all loose and soppy.

'Oh what a terrible injury, does it ache awfully?' he'd asked Goose, who was wailing about losing his pinkie finger. Rascal was coughing fit to burst, and that boy Rip was cracking his knuckles till Wicked wanted to crack them for him. Squid even started talking about his mother: 'Remember when she hugged you if you was hurt?'

Blimey! Truth to tell, at that moment, he was sure something inside him was about to explode, and it wasn't just that pimple on the side of his nose.

But it was the Captain who exploded. So fed up was he with Horrendo's courtesy and cooking and donkey-brained talk that he ordered him to walk the plank. And that's when the boys planned their escape. Who'd have thought they'd ever have the gumption? The night before the plank-walking, in the quiet dead hours, the young scoundrels silently lowered the longboat. And in the morning they just rowed away, taking Horrendo with them.

'We're better off without them,' Wicked told the men. 'I mean, take that little try-hard, Horrendo. He pretended to care about you all but no, soon as he could, he snatched his opportunity and vanished. Your little angel just abandoned us without a thought.'

'Well, that's a bit harsh,' said Dogfish. 'The Captain was going to make him walk the plank!'

Wicked shook his head. 'Never trust a soul. Haven't you all learned that by now?'

'Still an' all,' sighed Squid, 'the lad did leave us with his recipe for lobster mornay.'

'Aye, it was right thoughtful of 'im, an' we still got those good fishing lines he set,' Buzzard said, as he blinked away a tear. 'I'm gunna miss the little fella.'

'You great greedy guzzlers,' thundered the Captain, stomping up the deck. 'Stop thinking about your bellies and think about getting rich.'

The men suddenly went quiet. The Captain told them that while they'd been losing the battle with the Blue Devils, he'd leapt to the enemy's ship and stolen into the captain's cabin – and snatched a treasure map right off the desk! Shipwreck Island was where they were bound.

The men quickly cheered up.

'But we gotta bite the bullet an' take the most direct route,' the First Mate told them when the Captain had gone. 'Through the Scorpio Strait.'

'We'll die in those killin' currents!' cried Squid. 'Waves as big as houses! Anyone with a brain would avoid 'em and go the long way round.'

'Aye, ye gotta still be *breathin'* to appreciate a bag of gold,' said Buzzard.

The First Mate shook his head. 'The old devil's made up his mind. You know what he's like. Scorpio Strait it is.'

The men tried to argue. 'We're too young to die,' Goose protested. 'Why, we ain't even really *lived* yet.'

'Aye,' agreed Buzzard. 'We only just got acquainted with the Continental breakfast.'

'An' next week we're gunna have a stab at Seafood in a

Basket,' Goose put in, 'with a bit of decent dinner conversation to go with it.'

The Captain wouldn't stand for their wails and protests. That evening he pointed his sword at the men huddled at the bow. 'The next pirate who opens his beak will be spliced so far down the middle he'll be talking to his *twin*.'

A glowering silence fell. But the next morning, the muttering started up again.

Wicked decided to keep to himself below deck and nurse his belly. He could have told the men to save their breath, but it seemed too much food and stupid talk had mushed their minds.

And so the Captain set his jaw – and their course – for Scorpio Strait. That meant Davy Jones' Locker for them all. The pirates knew their fate, like they knew the nose on their own hairy faces.

'Well, I for one ain't ready to be fish food,' said Squid. 'Who's gunna stand with me?'

There was a short intake of breath, a minute's hesitation. Then each man stepped forward to pledge his sword. And so when the sea rose before them in a wall of water, the men ganged up on their Captain.

Mutiny, that's what it was, plain and simple. The cold-hearted bunch snuck up from behind and threw him in the jolly-boat with nothing but a lousy bottle of rum. It all happened so fast. Quicker and meaner than a shark bite. Wicked remembered stumbling up on deck in time to see the back of the Captain's head as he bobbed away over the waves. He'd never seen the man's head without a hat on it. His hair was dull and thin, like old string.

It was a strange, anxious moment. It made Wicked think of Headlice as he'd drifted away and how every second had put more distance between them, and the pit in his stomach where all the lost things were buried opened out, making him run, sick as a dog, to his berth.

The Captain had always seemed indestructible – wrong or right, that devil at the helm was something you could depend on. And now he was gone.

But the men were doing the high jig, lifting their knees and slapping each other on the back. They couldn't stop laughing and congratulating each other.

So Wicked squeezed his anxiety down to a fly-speck and swallowed it. He concentrated on thinking about the treasure they'd said was buried on Shipwreck Island. Blimey, if it weren't for the Captain, that wool-witted crew would never have *known* about the treasure, or how to find it. Wicked wondered if they had thought about that when they bundled their Captain into his dinghy.

'Now the old demon's gone we won't have to watch treasure slip through our fingers no more,' the First Mate had cried. 'By Jove, I'll grab it with both hands!'

'*We'll* grab it,' Squid said, narrowing his eyes with threat. 'With *all* our hands. Plural.'

'Aye, aye!' shouted the men, wriggling their fingers in the air to show just how many they had.

'That's what I meant,' said the First Mate hastily. 'No need to get yer whiskers in a whirl.'

And so the pirates set their own course, taking their own sweet time. Along the way they experimented with Horrendo's recipes, frying, baking and sautéing, conducting long and tedious conversations about their culinary catastrophes. But when they did finally step ashore on Shipwreck Island, who did they spy hiding behind the bushes but the grubbiest, greediest set of young scallywags they'd ever had the misfortune to sail with!

'It's *so* nice to see you again,' said Horrendo, putting out his hand to shake.

The pirates went silly with surprise. But Wicked didn't even raise an eyebrow when he heard that it was Horrendo who had masterminded the boys' whole escape.

'Didn't I tell you the lad's tricky as a two-tailed coin?' Wicked muttered to Squid. 'He must have known about the map all along, and made sure the small fry got to Shipwreck Island first.'

Squid just shrugged, but Wicked was seething. How those boys got there in that rickety longboat, he couldn't figure. They said something about the dolphins 'guiding them to safety', but it was all a lot of hot air.

Within minutes Horrendo had the men slapping him on the back, as happy as clams. And when the lad suggested that 'we boys' help find the treasure, the First Mate brought out the map at once. 'How interesting, a *volcanic* mountain, do you see the symbol?' piped the little know-it-all, studying the map. As speedy as hounds after a rabbit, men and boys followed Horrendo up the mountain – and right into the hut where the treasure lay buried.

Wicked stared into the deep dark hole they'd dug, mesmerised by the bags of gold inside. Coins glinted through rips in the cloth. All the past was forgotten … irritating boys, unfaithful friends, who cared when this gold glittered here for the taking? He couldn't wait to run his hands through those beauties.

But now, *what?* Here was Horrendo, the greedy pipsqueak, telling the pirates to share it all out with the lads as *well*. How much would be left for each man? Only a mountain of treasure would make up for all those lost years at sea. *Sharing* – what a mangy, flea-bitten idea!

Wicked was having none of it. He leapt right into the hole and grabbed as many bags as he could carry. He would have got away with it too if that great lump of a lad Bombastic hadn't jumped on his back and squeezed the breath out of him like a python. They all ganged up on him then, same as always, and who knows what they might have done if, sudden as a clap of thunder, there hadn't been a terrible cry and a thud, then another and another, outside the hut.

Wicked rushed out to see four, no, five men trussed in rope, lying on their backs in the grass. Another pirate went down, and it was then that Wicked saw, striding towards them, the dark silhouette of the Captain against the flaming sky.

Right rum it was to see him standing there on Shipwreck Island, strong as twenty men, lassoing the pirates as they ran, felling them like trees, and all with the rope that had saved Wicked's own life.

'Why ain't he *dead*?' Bombastic moaned. 'Why ain't he eaten up by all the little fishies in the sea?'

'I already told you why,' Dogfish replied dully. 'Ye just can't kill the man.'

'Hand over the treasure, you *dogs*,' roared the Captain.

The men fumbled in their pockets and down their shirts, their hands full of coins and fear. But Bombastic was clutching at his waistcoat, trying to cover a squirming lump.

'What's *that*?' As the Captain reached for the boy, Wicked smelled the rum on him, strong and sweet.

Bombastic's pet frog must have got a whiff of it too, as, delirious with the aroma, it hopped from the safe little waistcoat pocket right onto the Captain's beard. The Captain's mouth dropped open in horror, and, seeing its chance to lap at the sweet stuff, the poisonous pet took a death plunge right inside.

'Aaarggh!' choked the Captain. Even as he coughed and spluttered, the frog must have been working its way down the man's throat, slithering in a rum-soaked frenzy.

Wicked watched as the frog's poison took its effect. It was a terrible thing to see. The Captain swallowed, turning wine-red to purple, charging off through the forest like lightning. Shuddering and shaking, crashing into trees, he galloped over boulders like a stampeding beast. He'd turned into a wild thing and Wicked, racing after him, felt deranged just witnessing the transformation.

When the Captain streaked uphill to the top of the volcano, Wicked saw sparks shoot into the sky. The ground rumbled beneath his feet and he shouted in warning, 'Come back! Danger *ahead!*'

But the Captain wouldn't stop. At the edge of the abyss he teetered and swayed, his head swinging crazily on his neck. And then his body went loose and he pitched forward, hurtling down, down into the boiling mud below.

No one could come back from that. Not even the Captain.

'He might be supernatural,' Dogfish said later. 'But nothing could survive a *volcano*.'

Wicked couldn't say a word.

He stayed silent, too, when later that night on the sand, the pirates divvied up the bags of treasure, allotting a 'fair share' to the boys. Then, as men and boys climbed aboard the ship, stumbling under their bags of gold, he crept into the berth like a shadow. He was cold with shock and he didn't know if he'd ever get warm.

But look at the men now, *they* were happy. Ecstatic! They were making plans. *Plans!* And right at the centre of it all, as usual, was Horrendo.

'Let's take the treasure back home,' Horrendo was urging them as they set sail under the moonlight. 'If you help us rebuild our lives, the villagers of Devil Island will forgive you. All that fighting and kidnapping – it was the Captain's doing, and now he's gone! Aren't you sick of swords and starving? Don't you want to sleep in soft beds?'

'Imagine,' Buzzard had said dreamily. 'No more fear of losin' our ears.'

'Or our pinkies,' Goose added. 'I only got one left.'

'Well how many ears do yer reckon *I* got?' said Buzzard.

'Imagine,' Squid had put in, 'no more puttin' up with yer absurd conversations. I'm for it, as long as I get to build a mansion in the hills with me share of the treasure.'

Even the pirate Scabrous had agreed with him. 'I want sunken baths in me powder rooms. With gold taps an' all.'

And so they sailed back to Devil Island, bristling with hope and dreams. When they drew near, Horrendo suggested that the boys take the longboat into shore first, so that the villagers knew their sons had returned to them safe and sound. 'And we'll need to take a good share of the treasure with us,' added Hoodlum, eyeing Wicked distrustfully. 'Just to make sure, like, you pirates are gunna do the right thing.'

'Orright, but only if I'm aboard with you,' said the First Mate. 'Just to make sure you *boys*, like, are gunna do the right thing.'

Villagers were gathered on the shore to watch the boat come in. They ran forward, their fists at the ready, but when they saw the shining faces of their own dear sons, the battle cries turned to howls of amazement.

'Am I dreaming?' cried Rip's mother, dashing towards her boy. 'Oh, don't wake me up!'

Mothers and fathers, aunties and grandmas couldn't believe their eyes. And when the boat came back again with the men, their eyes grew even wider. Here were real live pirates greeting them civilly with 'Good day to you!', and 'Excuse me', and 'Fine day for it!'

Horrendo sat between his parents, their arms joined around him. Lone boys and men were among their families again. Pirates were crying. Even old Squid found his mother.

~ * ~

But Wicked didn't find *his*. No, *his* mother never came to find *her* boy. Not bloomin' likely. He had to watch instead all the stupid hugging and kissing, mothers with their lost and found boys, the cries and sighs of grown men. It was enough to turn your stomach – even if it wasn't turned already.

[137]

Still, there was a moment on that first night, when he'd sunk into a bed and every muscle in his body relaxed so deeply it seemed he'd found heaven in a duck-feathered mattress, that he thought village life could be all right. And even the next morning, when the sun beamed through a clean window and there was the smell of freshly brewed tea, he wondered if he might stay.

That morning he went to the meeting in the square. The villagers exchanged thin-lipped smiles with the pirates, the peace between them new and fragile. Wicked wandered through the crowd, stopping at the stall selling cakes and coffee. Up ahead, at the front, was a table laden with pirate treasure. A huge pile of jewels glittered in the sun, so bright it was blinding if you looked too long.

Wicked blinked. He thought he saw Headlice, standing with a tall, curly-haired woman.

A smile burst from his mouth. A flood of memories flashed behind his eyes and somehow the warm sweet feeling was stronger than anything else. He hurried towards them but as he drew near, he saw they were talking with Horrendo.

'Pleased to meet you,' Horrendo said. 'And this is your mother?' The three all shook hands. 'Headlice, weren't you once a friend of Wicked's?'

Headlice nodded. 'Is he here? I want to see him again, make things right.'

'Yes,' said Horrendo. 'But, well, I think I should warn you first. Wicked mightn't be quite as ... er ... willing to become a good citizen as the others. What I mean is, it might take him a bit longer to ... rehabilitate. I don't want to sound unkind, but he's had a bit of trouble with the idea of sharing the treasure.'

'Oh, Headlice told me all about him,' Headlice's mother said. She turned to her son. 'Best to keep away from him, dear. He's the one snatched so early. Poor mite, why was his mother not minding him? *I'd* never leave my child alone like that. Terrible, some people, they just shouldn't have children.' She shuddered. 'It's sad, but there it is. No wonder he's so badly behaved.' And she took her son's arm, thanking Horrendo and moving away.

Wicked flushed with rage. Something black and wild rose up inside him as he pushed his way to the front.

'Steady on,' muttered a villager as Wicked shoved past.

But Wicked couldn't stop. The darkness inside him was loud as a hurricane. It blew away any sweet drop of memory, it blew him forward until all he could feel was the heat of his anger and all he could see was that treasure gleaming and dancing in the sun. Badly behaved, was he? Well, he'd give 'em badly behaved.

Horrendo was standing on a stool now, asking for understanding from both sides. 'And before we share out the gold, everybody, I'd like to tell you my idea. If we each took only half of our share of the treasure, and put the rest…'

Wicked gave a howl of fury. He lunged out of the crowd, snatching a bag of gold from the table. 'This is *pirate* gold,' he cried, 'and no landlubber's goin' to tell me otherwise!'

A storm of protest broke out from the villagers, and the crowd split apart just as surely as if Wicked had thrown a cannonball into the middle of them. He didn't care, why should he? None of them cared about *him*. It would always be like this, people making up their minds about him before they even gave him a chance.

The villagers were complaining their sons had been kidnapped – well, his whole *life* had been kidnapped. He'd lost everything, and the only thing to show for it was this haul of treasure. Wasn't that the prize? These families hadn't ever been to sea or fought a man twice their size or known what it was like to have your guts ripped in half while you're up in the rigging. No, they'd just spent their lives looking after their kitchen equipment and pretty gardens, and now, pickle their gums, a wheelbarrow of gold was arriving in their laps!

Curses were hurled back and forth and it might have become bloody, too, what with the pirates putting up their fists, if Dogfish hadn't caught Wicked's wrists and held him down. Then Horrendo suddenly began to shout.

'You selfish, lying, cheating pig!' he bellowed at Wicked. 'Can't you see, if we all put some of our treasure into a common pool we'd have enough to build a wonderful life for *everyone* here? But no, you slimy apology for a human being, you dung beetle, you lousy smear of cockroach pus, you smelly...'

The torrent of words stunned Wicked. The little angel was swearing – at *him*.

The villagers fell silent, staring at Horrendo, their faces blank with amazement.

'What'll happen next?' said one villager. 'Will fish fall from the sky?'

And when the crowd turned to look at Wicked, the pirate who'd turned their little saint into a cussing fiend, he felt himself to be smaller and shabbier than ever before.

'So *this* is how Horrendo will be now the Wise Woman has lifted her spell?' Rascal whispered to his sister, Blusta.

'It can't be true!' she whispered back. 'He's never said a bad word to anybody. No matter what was done to him.'

'Aye, and you should have seen what happened to him at sea!'

Wicked felt woozy, as if he might faint.

Truth to tell, he didn't know what to feel. He just knew he had to get away from this hellhole and never, ever return.

chapter 18

As Wicked rowed away from Devil Island, the sun was low and the voices of the villagers grew as faint as the moon's shadow in the east. He didn't know where he was headed.

It was strange, that's what it was, as mysterious as a catfish with legs. Now *he* was the one escaping, with as much treasure as a pirate could carry, and yet he felt worse than at any time he could remember. Almost without noticing, they'd let him take his own share, steal the dinghy, and only bothered to murmur 'good riddance' as he'd sailed off.

'And good riddance to you too, you rotten *rubbish*,' he'd yelled back, but the wind off the sea had lifted his voice up with the spray, and thrown it away.

Heading into wide open sea, Wicked tried to concentrate on the simple stroke of his oars, the splash as they hit the water. His eyes scanned the horizon – no land, no nothing interrupted the flat gilded world ahead. It didn't matter; right then, he didn't care where he ended up. He'd never known what was coming, or what to do about it when it came, so what was the point of planning anything now?

You took it in the teeth, same as always.

All around, the darkening ocean spread out as empty as Wicked's future. He could see no sign of life to the north, south, east or west. But he rowed on. For a while his arms ached, but then he stopped feeling it. The motion of the oars dipping down and up, down and up, almost sent him to sleep. He was tired, so bloomin' tired.

But wait, up there, what was that on the horizon? A shape looming up like... like the humped back of an animal. He blinked, wondering if he was dreaming. He looked again.

Land. Definitely land.

Wicked felt a rush of relief. For hours now he'd been wondering if he was turning into the Captain, alone in an old dinghy, drifting on the seas...

As he rowed nearer, he realised that this must be Turtle Island. He remembered sailing towards it once before, his heart full of hope.

The first star rose, twinkling brightly like one of the diamonds in the sack at his feet. Wicked felt his spirits rise with it. His toes felt for the rough canvas with the lumps of treasure inside. He'd taken his share before he left, all right. Spanish gold, bars of silver, strings of pearls, diamonds, rubies the colour of burning coals. He'd worked for it like everyone else, hadn't he? It'd buy him anything he wanted. They couldn't take *that* from him, no! He just hadn't wanted to spend his lot in that blasted place with those blasted villagers and their happy, everything's-rosy-now faces.

Rosy for *who*?

Wicked wriggled uncomfortably in the boat.

How they all hated him now!

Even Horrendo. That lad was the worst. He'd only been nice to Wicked because he was under a curse – of niceness! But now the lad was roaring like the most pernicious pirate on the Cannonball Seas. No, just like everyone else, Horrendo wasn't to be trusted.

Wicked shuddered, hearing the lad's words again. He wished he could burn them from his mind.

Well, he thought, now there are no ratlines to climb, enemies to spot or yardarms to repair, nobody wants me. And that's all right with me.

Turtle Island, eh? Look, he was almost there. The place where no one came to steal your gold. Coconut trees. He thought of Treasure. He could hardly remember what she looked like, or the sound of her voice. He knew her hair had been dark. She'd said something about turtles...

Never mind. She was lost now too, like everything else. Well, he didn't care. The peace and quiet would be like medicine, wouldn't it? No mothers clutching their long-lost sons, crying with happiness, reminding him he was an orphan.

The sea was shark-skin smooth, the breakers near the sand just a wobble. Good. So killingly tired. He took the precious sack of treasure and tied it around his waist. Then he climbed out into shallow water and hauled the boat up to the sand. His arms ached so badly, he could hardly lift it. The boat was heavy, the dark coming fast... he felt for the rope at the bow and tied it with a hasty knot to the palm tree leaning out over the beach.

As he dropped down on a patch of grass, he listened to the sighing of the sea. The tide was low, the moon rising. He stroked the canvas sack beside him like a pet. Now there'll be time, he thought. In all this quiet it might come to him what to do next.

Right now, though, the world was too big and he was too weary.

Tomorrow.

chapter 19

His mother was pointing up at a palm tree.

'Breakfast,' she said, as a coconut came loose, falling slowly through the sky.

'Look out!'

Wicked's eyes snapped open, his heart racing.

He rubbed his forehead where the coconut had almost landed. Waves tumbled onto the sand, louder than last night. High tide now, he supposed. The sun was blazing.

He listened for a moment. Beneath the sound of the water, such stillness. No cursing or complaining. No cruel words. No kindness, either, but when had there been? Too far back to remember.

He lay on his back, trying to remember where he was. It'd be easy to get jumpy in all that quiet. Already it began to prickle under his skin.

Wicked stood up, stretching his arms above his head. His back creaked. He thought of Rip's nervy knuckle-cracking, how he'd hated silence, needed to break it. He gazed out to sea, and it was then that he saw it. Or rather, *didn't* see it.

The boat.

It had gone.

He shut his eyes and opened them. Everything was still the same. The foamy line of breakers, the white sand, the palm tree where he'd tied the boat that was...

Gone. As if someone had just come along and cut a hole out of the world. Where was the missing piece?

He ran down to the shore. He felt along the trunk of the tree, saw where the rope had chafed the bark. There was no sign of it now.

He couldn't believe it. What would he do without a boat? Miles from any land – why, he could be stranded here his whole life...

Alone. Only coconuts to eat. Trees to talk to.

It would be fine for a week, but for his whole miserable *life*? Another sting of panic shot through him. His treasure?

He ran back to the grassy mound where he'd slept. Thank heavens, the little beauties, safe and sound! He hugged the blessed sack to his chest. He spread out the pieces of gold to count, ran his hands through the jewels.

But the tingly breathlessness he expected when he looked at the treasure didn't come. Instead a cold sinking feeling, like an anchor dropping into the sea, settled at the bottom of his stomach. What was he going to *do* with the treasure, stranded here on an island? Could he eat it? Could he drink it? Could he talk to it?

Oh, hang the pirate dogs! All because of that stinking rope of theirs – old and thin as a rat's tail. The pull must have been strong with the tide coming in but a decent rope would have held. Blast them!

He leapt up and ran back up the sand, to a higher patch of scrub. He looked out to sea, as far as he could to his left and right. He peered at the horizon. This just didn't feel true – the foreverness of it. If he blinked, the picture might change and the boat would be back.

No.

'*Stupid old rubbishy rope!*' he burst out loud, jumping up and down with rage.

'A bad workman always blames his tools,' a voice cut in.

Wicked froze.

He squinted up at the trees, and behind him through the bushes. But he couldn't see anything that looked like it could talk.

So now he'd gone mad. Hearing voices.

'Blimey,' he cried. 'I can't even trust me own mind. I've landed in hell!'

'One man's heaven is another man's hell,' said the voice.

Wicked dug his toes in the sand. He held his breath. To his right, from the bushes, came a rustle of leaves. Out stepped a large blue and yellow bird.

'The devil take you!' yelped Wicked. 'I'm seeing things as well as hearing 'em. A talking bird, what next?'

'A bird in the hand is worth two in the bush,' the bird told him. 'Bless you, my son.'

No, it wasn't just a bird, it was a parrot. He'd seen one like it on board the Bonny Lasses' ship, through his telescope. But he'd never met a parrot who could hold a conversation.

'Where did you come from?'

The parrot peered at him sideways. 'You can kill a man, but you can't kill an idea.'

'What?'

The parrot looked awkward. He scratched under his wing with his beak.

Wicked noticed both wings were clipped. Even though the bird was probably an illusion, he felt a sudden pang. The bird was trapped, just like him. 'Who did that to you?'

The parrot's feet shifted on the ground as if he were embarrassed. He cleared his throat. 'A man with one clock knows what time it is, but a man with two clocks is never sure.'

Wicked stared at those black, yellow-ringed eyes.

Strange. This was almost the strangest thing that had ever happened to him, and by now he had a long list.

The bird was studying the grass. Every few seconds he made a little click in his throat as if about to say something, but then thought better of it.

Wicked decided to act as if the bird were making perfectly good conversation. It seemed kinder.

'Oh, yes, I see,' he nodded wisely. 'Too many clocks.'

'When all you have are lemons, make lemonade!' screamed the parrot in response. The feathers on his head stood up with excitement and he ran around in happy circles. 'Get me a jug of ale, ye lively lass!'

'Never a wiser word said,' agreed Wicked.

The bird hopped right up to Wicked. 'A friend in need is a friend indeed.'

Well, thought Wicked, now *that* was sensible. The parrot seemed to be waiting for something. But it wasn't easy talking to a...bird. Still, shouldn't he keep up his end of the conversation? He searched for something to say. 'Um, check your centre, keep putting one foot in front of the other—'

'And your eyes on the prize,' finished the bird.

Wicked gasped. 'Where did you hear that?'

The parrot found something between its feathers and ate it. Then he gave a little hop, almost apologetically, and cleared his throat again.

Wicked waited. But the bird found something interesting in the sand.

This would drive him mad. Maybe the parrot wasn't real after all. He reached out a finger. The blue feathers were silky. The parrot let him stroke his chest. Wicked felt the warm little heartbeat under his hand and a strange melting feeling spread over him. His stomach gurgled.

'Ease off the grog, you dogs,' the parrot said. 'An army marches on its stomach.'

Food. The bird was right. He had to learn what to eat on this island, and what to drink. First things first. Even madmen had to eat. He was so thirsty he could suck the sap out of a palm tree.

'Any fresh water round here?' he said.

The parrot looked at him sideways. 'Doubt is the beginning not the end of wisdom.'

Wicked sighed. He gave the bird a last little pat and stood up. 'Better use my deadlights then and climb that hill,' he told him. He didn't know why he was bothering to explain, but it felt like the right thing to do. As he trudged up the sandy slope the parrot waddled after him.

Wicked had only taken a few steps when he realised the bird was having trouble keeping up. He stopped and turned around, waiting for him to catch up.

The bird hopped onto his foot and without thinking, Wicked picked him up, one hand under the leathery pronged toes, and put him carefully on his shoulder. The parrot nibbled his ear.

Wicked laughed. 'Blimey, that tickles!'

'Take the bitter with the sweet, Pirate Pete,' the parrot told him.

At the top of the slope the patchy sprinkle of grass became a carpet of green. Both pirate and parrot gazed out over the view with satisfaction. The hill fell away into a small valley where a lake shimmered, surrounded by reeds. Giant ferns and coconut palms towered over the little oasis.

'That's my waterhole right there,' said Wicked. 'Maybe you're my lucky charm.'

The parrot pecked excitedly at his ear, then ran up and down his arm. 'There's nothing good or bad but thinking makes it so,' he squawked, but Wicked had stopped trying to understand.

He almost ran to the lake, the parrot clinging on firmly. He knelt down and cupped his hands, gulping the clear spring water. When he'd finished, he burped with satisfaction.

'Better out than in,' said the parrot, hopping off for a moment to drink with him.

Wicked sat back cross-legged and said, 'Next thing is grub

and shelter.' His eyes travelled up the trunk of the coconut palm to his left. Fat green bunches of nuts hung amongst the leaves at the top. He'd often eaten coconuts when he was a boy, and drunk the milk inside. It would be a challenging climb – that straight trunk, no branches, no rungs. He'd have to think how best to do it ...

A knife would be handy, to get at the tasty white meat inside. And how would he lop off its head? Pity he had nothing useful with him – not even a decent bit of rope to hold him as he climbed the tree. What had he been thinking when he left Devil Island?

'And where will I sleep when it rains?' he wondered out loud.

'All the world's a stage,' said the bird.

It was going to be difficult to make shelter without any tools. He tried to remember back to the book Treasure had first read him, about the sailor shipwrecked on that island. But each time an image came, a pain crept in behind it and his mind went blank. It was the same when he tried to picture her face. Well, that was a waste of time now. He had to find some kind of shelter before night fell. The sky had been cloudless all day, but storms came before you could say curse the catfish.

In the quiet, another thought prickled: what about hurricane season? He flicked it away. With any luck he'd be rescued before that happened.

Mind who saves you, Dogfish's words echoed in his head.

'Damn and blast,' said Wicked, his spirits sinking. 'Who'd bother to come looking now?'

'Anything that can go wrong will go wrong,' added the bird, like doomsday.

'Aye, thanks for reminding me,' muttered Wicked. He put his head in his hands. Then he gave himself a shake. 'I'm gunna call you Doomsday. Is that all right with you?'

'A rose is the same by any other name,' said Doomsday.

Wicked couldn't help grinning. 'I suppose that's a yes. Come on, let's go and see how bloomin' impossible it is to find some shelter.'

It was late in the afternoon when they gave up the search. They were standing under a cliff bordering the northern side of the island. It rose sheer from the rock pools but when they followed the crag inland, towards the forest, it hollowed out into a series of caves below. The first one was deep and dark and endless; Wicked felt a shiver go through him. He'd rather not sleep in a place with a mystery at his back. They wandered in and out of hollows, startling a colony of bats, walking into curtains of cobwebs.

And then Wicked found his cave. It sat beneath a tuft of scraggly bloodwoods. As soon as he stepped in, it felt like the right one. The roof was just a few inches taller than he was – he could stand up comfortably – and in just four paces he reached the back wall. He ran his hand along the rough stone. No wet seepage, no bat dung. He could see the beginning and the end, and the space caught the last rays of afternoon light.

'Home sweet home,' he said. Then he clucked his tongue at the parrot. 'Blow me down, I'm gettin' to sound like you.'

'Better to have loved and lost than never to have loved at all,' said Doomsday.

The ground was hard and rocky – he'd have to go looking for something softer to put beneath him. He was turning to go when he saw a glint in the corner. It was lit up by a shaft of low afternoon light.

'Pickle me toes,' he whispered. 'Will you look at that?'

He reached down and picked up a knife with a bone handle. He slipped off the sheath and tested the point. Sharp as blazes. The blade ran the length of his hand, ideal for cutting the top off a coconut, splitting saplings for kindling, scaling a fish … On his knees he sorted through the small pile of precious objects. There was a flint for fire, a long whittled spear, a satchel, an old hammock and half a coconut shell, ideal for a drinking cup.

'I'm rich!' he cried, jumping up so suddenly that Doomsday squawked in protest and bit his ear.

chapter 20

Over the next few days, Wicked was busy. It surprised him that in a place where there was not one order to obey, hours could go by before he found a chance to sit down. When he did, his mind turned to the sailor who'd lived in this cave. He got to wondering how long the man might have spent there. Had he left long ago, or only the day before?

Wicked didn't like to think about the alternative – that the poor sailor was still on the island, having dropped dead of old age or something worse, his bones lying naked and lonely under a rock fall somewhere. In a strange way, Wicked had grown fond of him. Having use of the man's treasured possessions made him wonder what it would be like to have a father, and Wicked felt grateful for this lucky inheritance.

By now he had explored most of the island. The lake spilled out into a shallow creek that emptied into the sea. In the valleys the coconut palms clustered, and he'd spent much of the first day working out the best way to climb them.

As he had never gone up or down anything without rungs or branches, he had to try out different holds.

'Better safe than sorry,' the parrot agreed, watching him at the foot of a tree ripe with coconuts.

Wicked gave a little spring, and leapt up. First his hands grabbed the trunk, then his bare feet found grip and his knees hugged tight. Steadily, hands advancing first, he began to make his way up. It was a slow, hard climb. He was heavy, and his limbs weren't as flexible as they once were. He didn't look down. It was only when he reached the first green coconut that he realised it wasn't going to come loose. He shook and twisted it, but it wouldn't budge. The knife – he'd forgotten it!

Wicked didn't waste his breath cursing. He was too exhausted.

As soon as he hit the ground, he fetched the knife and went straight back up. This time it was a little easier. Because he knew he could do it, his confidence was greater and he was able to gain a little more height each time. And when he got to the coconuts, he hacked them off with the blade.

He didn't watch where the nuts dropped. His eyes were fixed on the prize at the top. He nearly lost his hold when he heard a shrill squawking from below. Then it suddenly stopped.

Wicked peered down through the leaves.

Doomsday was lying flat on his back, his little wrinkled feet sticking straight up. But Wicked scrambled down, and when he leaned over him, the bird staggered up, wobbling in circles as if he'd drunk too much rum.

'While there's life there's hope!' cried Wicked, surprised at the sharpness of his relief. He studied the parrot, checking for injuries. Doomsday was undented – although his feathers on the left side looked a bit crushed. It must have been only a glancing blow. But the bird did seem more confused than usual.

'Lie down with dogs an' you get up with ... zebras,' muttered Doomsday groggily.

The next time he went up, Wicked decided, he'd be more careful. Although he'd only met Doomsday two days ago, the parrot was now the most precious thing he had.

That afternoon Wicked went in search of rocks to build a cooking fire. Along the creek he found some good-sized stones and he put these, together with his collection of sticks and dried leaves, into the satchel. Back at camp he arranged the stones in a ring, placing the kindling inside with a couple of bigger branches on top.

'I wish I had something tasty to cook,' he told Doomsday.

'If wishes were fishes then no man would starve,' the parrot replied.

'Aye, and a fire will send a signal to any passing ship,' said Wicked.

By now the parrot's conversation felt normal. It was funny how quickly you got used to things, he reflected. Before Horrendo came on board, pirate conversations only lasted long enough for a yes or no. Talk never wandered away from the point. With the parrot, there *was* no point, and it was no use looking for one. But somehow, he didn't mind.

Wicked put his flint to the dry twigs and leaves, and blew on it. A spark caught, and then another, and soon a bright flame leapt up.

The two sat together on the sand, gazing at the fire. As the sun sank into the sea, Wicked thought how much cosier he felt with their own little source of light, right here at their feet. Every now and then he wandered into the bushes to collect more kindling, always able to find his way back to Doomsday, and their camp.

And by firelight he was able to prepare the coconuts, ready for breakfast. He scalped the green rind from the top and split open the shell with his knife. Catching the milk with his cup, he offered some to Doomsday, before swilling it down. Wicked savoured the sweet white meat – delicious! He wondered if it tasted even better than he remembered because he'd worked so hard to get it.

It was a good thing that Wicked liked coconuts, as that was all he found to eat in that first week. Doomsday brought him some lizards and once, a small dead green snake, but he just couldn't face the idea.

The bird shook his head. 'Don't put all your eggs in one basket.'

'I know,' said Wicked. 'But what can I do? I wish we *did* have eggs. This here is Turtle Island, but where are they all? I haven't spotted one!'

He dimly remembered something Treasure had said about turtles – she hadn't been keen on eating them, he thought. But maybe he'd dreamed that, dreamed her ...

By the end of the week, coconuts lost their thrill for Wicked. Every day his eyes searched the horizon, and with every fire he lit, he hoped for some sign from a ship. Coconuts were all right if you thought that one day you could eat something else. But what if help never came? What if this was it?

One morning when he was slicing the top off his twentieth nut, he felt his stomach heave. A cramp made him wince and he remembered the bad old days on board ship when his guts had given him strife.

'Blimey,' he complained to the parrot, 'I hope I'm not going down that road again.'

He moaned and lay back down. But an hour later Doomsday came back with something in his beak.

'An oyster! Well, what do you know?' Wicked remembered the time they'd stopped at Bell Island and Horrendo had made such a show of collecting oysters from the rock. He'd served them up with a slice of lemon and handed them around. Wicked had taken one, just to show he wasn't yellow-livered, but as it had slipped down his throat he'd thought it was like eating your own snot.

'Aye, but beggars can't be choosers,' he sighed, and took out his knife.

'You get what you pay for,' nodded Doomsday. 'The best things in life are free.'

The oyster tasted just like he remembered – slimy. But it made a change.

'Show me where you got it,' he said to Doomsday, and they walked down to the shore.

There were ten, twenty oysters within easy reach, and Wicked went to work with his knife. He saw more around the rocks where the water was deeper, and glimpsed the slim white shadows of fish. With sudden longing he remembered the smelly hunks of mullet Dogfish used to keep in his pocket, the fresh swordfish Horrendo once caught...

'By thunder,' he groaned, 'what I wouldn't give now for a fish on my plate! Look, there's a whole sea of 'em out there.'

'Give a man a fish and he eats for one night, teach him how and he eats for life.'

'Aye, but you gotta have the equipment, right? What, am I just gunna wade in there and catch one with my hands?'

The bird looked at him and shook his head. 'There's more than one way to skin a cat.'

Hmm, thought Wicked. But what if you don't want to eat *cat*?

That day Wicked followed his usual routine, collecting kindling and coconuts, replenishing his water supply. But as he worked he was thinking about fish. Surely he could find a way to catch that sea of food out there. What kind of sailor *was* he?

Every time he thought of wading in, his guts turned to ice. He remembered the feeling of water closing over his head.

And then, facts were facts. He didn't have a fishing line.

But all day, niggly fishy thoughts twisted and turned in his mind.

That evening, when the fire was lit and dinner eaten, Wicked stared into the flames. How wonderful it would be to roast a snapper over the coals. He licked his lips, imagining the tasty grease dripping down his chin.

He had to try. Tomorrow morning, soon as the sun rose, he'd wade into the shallows.

~ * ~

It must have come to him in the night, the idea of using the spear.

'I'm gunna catch me a fish with this,' he told Doomsday.

'See?' He showed the parrot the little white bone that was stuck to the spear, near the sharp chiselled point. 'I don't know why I didn't think of it before.'

'Beware!' said Doomsday as he hopped after him down to the shore. 'Never leap from the frying pan into the fire.'

'Can't you be encouraging for once in your life?' Wicked called back.

Doomsday said something but Wicked couldn't hear it now. The water was up to his knees. He looked back at the bird pacing anxiously up and down the shore. Then he turned to face the water.

The unease in the pit of his stomach swelled with each small step he took. His toes sank into the sand. His fingers clenched around the spear. There – a flicker of ghostly white near his thigh. Quick! He lunged with his spear and the point came down in the sand near his foot. Any closer and he'd have stabbed himself.

Blast. He waited, focusing on the clear shine of water. Stars of sunlight dazzled the surface. Another fish! He stabbed at it again, and missed.

He went out a little further. Now he was up to his thighs. His lungs tightened at the thought of deep water, the sinking into darkness.

He looked up ahead, past the ripples of breakers. A cloud of bigger fish was circling just below the foam – a whole school of them, ripe for the picking. If he just had the mettle to go after them.

How could he get out there? He'd have to drown first. Even here, now, in a sea like glass and with the water only up to his thighs, he was anxious. He was never going to catch a fish like this. Stuck to the shore like a barnacle to a rock.

He was the one who should be called Doomsday, he thought. Doomed to be a landlubber, a coconut-eater, a snot-swallower for the rest of his days.

~ * ~

Wicked tried four more stabs at tidbitty fish who came to tease him. Nothing. He dragged himself back through the water, and flung himself down on the sand. His stomach growled with hunger.

'Hopeless,' he sighed.

'You can't teach an old dog new tricks,' agreed Doomsday.

'Aye.'

'If you always do what you always did, you always get what you always got,' the bird added.

'Blimey, that's about the most depressing thing I ever heard,' said Wicked.

Doomsday waddled to his side and hopped onto his chest. He pecked at Wicked in a soothing way, flapping a wing against his ribs as if trying to pat him.

'You know we're alike, us two,' Wicked told the bird. 'You can't fly and I can't swim. We're doomed to stay here for the rest of our lives. The only cheery thing is that mine won't last too long – a man can't live on coconuts and snot forever.'

'Better to light a candle than curse the darkness,' said Doomsday. 'Who took my boots?'

'Bird-brain,' Wicked muttered, 'why can't you say something sensible for once?'

chapter 21

Wicked took his spear into the water again the following day. He stayed till late afternoon. Once, he almost speared a fish. But it swam off as if it had only been flicked by a rope.

He tried boiling up seaweed and eating that – it tasted like old underwear. He cooked little pipis in their shells and ate oysters. And coconuts. But he was always sickeningly hungry.

The next time he waded into the sea he told himself that if he didn't get a fish, he'd give up. He'd turn his back on the sea, and all the cruelty it held. As he ventured further, he cursed until his throat hurt.

He glanced back at Doomsday. He was doing his usual pacing along the shore. Wicked felt a twinge of … he didn't know what. But it was good to have someone back on land watching him.

When he turned to face the sea again he saw a bottle bobbing on the waves. It was just beyond his reach. The familiarity of its shape stirred a strange longing for company.

If you always do what you always did, you'll always get what you always got. That bird said a lot of crack-brained things, thought Wicked, but maybe there was something in this. Maybe it was time to try something new.

He took a stride through the breakers until he was up to his waist. A bottle would be handy to fill with fresh water for the nights. Funny, he thought, why doesn't it sink like me? He watched it bob along the water, drifting where the current took it.

The bottle was empty, just full of air.

Air is lighter than water, he thought excitedly. Water was just about the heaviest thing he knew. He remembered carrying those brimming buckets across the deck. Back then he'd wondered how the slippery, shapeless stuff could weigh more than something solid, like wood. Wet rope weighed more than dry; sodden sails were murder to lift…

That hadn't seemed important back then.

Now it was everything.

He took a deep breath.

He imagined his lungs expanding, filling with air. How light I am, he thought. If I lie on my back like the bottle, perhaps I'll float too.

~ * ~

But he didn't. The back of his head sank up to his ears, and the water ran up his nose. Even though he clenched his body tight, ready to fight, the nasty stuff kept winning. He tried again and again, locking his jaws together in determination, lying rigid as a plank. Even his toes curled under with effort. But he just kept sinking and spluttering and spewing.

When he stood upright and shook out his ears, he heard Doomsday screaming. The bird thinks I can't do it, Wicked muttered. Thinks I'm gunna drown. Can't teach an old dog new tricks, eh? Well, I'll show him.

His eyes searched out the bottle. It was floating calmly on the waves. He remembered watching Horrendo drift like that on his back, puffed from diving down to fix the nets. The boy looked like he enjoyed it. Calm. Every now and then he'd kicked his feet – that's right! And when he wanted to come back to the boat, he'd flung his arms back behind his ears, and pulled the water through his fingers.

Wicked tried again. This time he let his muscles go slack. He stayed up a few seconds longer. *Relax*, he told himself. When he felt himself sinking, he kicked his feet like Horrendo, slow, then fast, turning the water to froth. The power in his feet was surprising. All his life he'd tried to keep them still, carefully poised on the rope – hadn't that been his strength? But now his feet were wild things!

He was kicking, breathing, floating … *oh!*

He gave a crow of joy and the stinking stuff rushed into his mouth.

He came to a standstill and coughed out his guts. Then he lifted himself back up. This time he spread out his arms like a starfish and flapped his wrists at the same time as his feet.

Wicked floated in the sea well past noon.

It felt amazing.

It was mysterious.

It was the most fun he'd ever had.

He would keep practising until he was perfect. Until he was at least as good as Horrendo.

Until he could swim.

chapter 22

Doomsday didn't like the new routine.

Each morning, after his coconut juice, Wicked ran down to the beach. Doomsday hovered on the shore.

'A leopard can't change its spots,' Doomsday told him one night as they sat by the fire.

'No,' said Wicked, 'but a man can learn to swim.'

Doomsday looked at him sideways. 'A little learning is a dangerous thing.'

'That's why I have to practise,' said Wicked. 'I have to get really good, so I can chase fish with my spear wherever they go. One day I might even make it back to Devil Island. Then I'll get a boat and sail to the Mainland, or anywhere else in the world!'

When he said that, Doomsday's head sank onto his chest. For a change, he didn't comment. He didn't even look at Wicked. He just poked his beak into his feathers, and shut his eyes.

But Wicked was thinking about the next day. By now he could float without having to concentrate. And he could cover a bit of distance on his back. Tomorrow he would try turning over. He'd keep his face out of the water, moving his arms and legs like a frog, the way he'd seen Horrendo do.

He felt a lurch in his belly. The idea was scary and exciting at the same time – a bit like those early days when he was learning the tightrope. He had a sudden memory of his mother looking up at him, smiling. 'That's the way. Check your centre. Don't look down!'

A pain just under his ribs made him stop thinking about that, so he thought about tomorrow instead, when he was going to try real swimming.

Like floating, it wasn't easy at first. He swallowed a lot of seawater, and didn't get very far. But he kept trying.

Each morning after breakfast, he'd race down to the water. He always said goodbye to Doomsday, but the bird wouldn't look at him. He didn't chat as much as he used to, Wicked noticed, especially in the mornings. But Wicked was so taken up with his swimming, he couldn't think about anything else for very long.

When he came in at sunset, Doomsday didn't want to talk about Wicked's swimming.

'Give you enough rope and you'll hang yourself,' was all the parrot said.

Every day Wicked was learning something new and important: if he kept his fingers closed and his hands cupped, he went faster. If he kept kicking while he moved his arms, he went at maximum speed. He had to concentrate at first, or he got mixed up. But after a lot of practice, he began to move naturally in rhythm with his breath.

And he started to love it. At night he would wake, a strange excitement tingling in his chest, and remember that he could swim. He could hardly wait until the morning. He wanted to try a new kind of stroke, or see if he could last longer in the water before his breath gave out and he had to stop. It was splendid, this feeling. Why, he had his own little boat tucked inside him, taking him wherever he wanted to go. He could change direction in a second, he could hold his breath underwater and glide like a fish. And now, when he spotted his prey, he could go after it.

The first night that he roasted his own dinner was the happiest in his life so far. It was a fine snapper, twice as long as his hand. It had given him quite a challenge, disappearing past the rocks, leading him to a whole school of them. He let the flames die down, then carefully laid the fish over the coals. The smell of roasting meat made the juices dribble in his mouth. Tears came to his eyes. He held his face over the fire, taking in great draughts of frying fish.

And when he took his first bite, he cried out with pleasure. '*Have* some,' he urged Doomsday. 'It's bloomin' wonderful!' On the bark plate next to him, he served up a fat piece for his friend.

Doomsday came over and picked it up with his beak. But when Wicked added, 'You know, I'm gettin' so good I'll be able to swim off this island soon – I won't even need a boat!' Doomsday spat it out.

'One man's loss is another man's gain,' the bird muttered gloomily, but Wicked was too busy savouring the snapper in his mouth to notice.

Wicked knew he had to go into training in order to swim

the long miles back to Devil Island. And he knew it would take some time. But now he didn't mind. One day he could leave; knowing *that* made all the difference. He could hunt and cook his own dinner, he could keep himself warm and dry, and he could feel himself getting stronger and leaner with each week that passed. It was like growing down, not up, his limbs remembering their childhood grace, his mind waking up.

He enjoyed the beginning of the day and the end. He liked having something delicious and rewarding to look forward to: the dinner he'd caught with his own hand. He never went hungry. It was a marvellous feeling to know that the sea was full of riches and he had enough skill to take from it what he needed.

So he decided to give himself tests to pass before his big swim. Out on the wide Cannonball Sea there would be no rock to rest on. He would stop and float when he needed to, but that wasn't the same thing.

When he'd first rowed here from Devil Island, he remembered drifting, going wide, daydreaming, not sure at all where he was headed. He'd been past caring.

He calculated now that if he'd rowed directly to Turtle Island, it would have taken about two hours. To swim that distance, it could take twice as long. You'd need strength and breath and skill to do that. And he'd have to carry a weapon. There were killers in the sea, he knew too well, and he'd be a fool to swim such a distance unarmed. He'd tie the knife to the belt at his hip.

To swim such a length, he'd need to be able to make it first from one end of the island to the other. When he could do that without resting, he'd judge whether he was ready to swim all the way back to Devil Island.

It was good to have an aim. It made the days even more fun and purposeful. Swimming became so natural that his mind slipped off its leash, free to wander in and out of thoughts like the fish that flowed around him.

The morning Wicked was ready to swim to the other end of the island, he marked off his one hundred and thirteenth day. Because it was a special day, he made an extra-large cut with his knife on the wall of the cave. He liked to see the neat lines standing all in a row, marking out the path of his progress.

The sea was a deep sapphire blue when he set out at dawn. He headed west around the reef at a steady pace, only slowing a little now and then to rest his arms. When he swam into open sea, the water spread fathomless around him, but he kept his mind focused on his breath, each one a small stepping stone towards his goal. Once, for a few minutes, a school of sardines swirled in a silver cloud beneath him, keeping his pace. He'd settled into a rhythm so right it was like finding the path out of a maze.

When he reached his destination at the southern end, he let himself be carried by the waves, floating in like a piece of driftwood. He had never felt so weary. But he'd made it without stopping.

He rested in the green shade of ferns until the sun was high in the sky. Then he waded back into the sea. If he had kept going then, when the day was still dazzling, the journey back home might have gone as smoothly as the start.

But Wicked discovered dolphins. They were leaping in and out of the waves near the shore. He'd seen dolphins before, when the ship was heading for the Shipwreck Isles. He remembered pointing them out to the First Mate, who hadn't bothered to take more than a squiz through the eyeglass. 'Only good thing about dolphins is they ain't sharks,' he'd said.

Wicked didn't agree. Now, when a dolphin took off on a wave, he took it too. He tried to keep up, his arms flung out ahead of him, his legs kicking, but it was only when he dared grab a fin that he felt what it was like to fly like a bird.

When a school of fish swam in – striped bass, he thought, just like Horrendo had once served – the dolphins herded them into a huddle and he was able to spear one with his knife. He forgot everything then... Devil Island, his training, his plans. He was just another part of the sea.

The water was darkening with dusk as he made his way back. It rocked and slapped before him, jagged as cut glass. He felt uneasy as he swam. 'The end of days brings sharks, and sharks bring the end of days,' he remembered Doomsday tolling.

He swam faster. How could he have delayed so long? At a reef, midway, he wondered if he should try to swim in to land. He felt for the knife at his belt, the fish he'd strapped in with it. Maybe he could make a fire, cook his dinner, spend the night there. But then he remembered the coral riddling the reef, and knew it would cut his legs to pieces.

He swam on.

He was rounding the point when he saw the fin.

Please, please let it be a dolphin.

But he knew it was not. The sickening thud in his heart told him. He watched the way it stalked him, a steady black triangle against the flaming sky. It was moving in slowly, surely, like a ship set on its course. Fear rose out of him like vapour from a swamp. Could a shark smell fear? He didn't know. But it could smell the fish on him ... the bloodied head where he'd banged it on a rock.

He tore the bass from its strap, and flung it wide. Without glancing back he sped through the sea, his breath tripping and tumbling inside him. *Go for the fish, leave me alone.* His heart was bursting when he opened his eyes underwater and saw a dark shape circling below. He slid the knife from his belt and drew up his feet. His eyes searched the depths for the shark. But when it came, he didn't see it.

He sensed a movement behind him, a quick swirl of water. Without thinking he kicked out, and his foot met something cold and massive. The shock of flesh hit him like lightning. He whirled around and saw a glistening eye, a strip of gill and he thrust at it with his knife. He kicked and stabbed at the churning water, staining red. He couldn't feel his body; he was lost in a trance of survival.

And then, he was stabbing only cloudy water. His pulse boomed like a drum in his ears. He peered through the murky nothingness. The shark had gone.

He ran his hands over his feet, checked his legs and arms. Pirates claimed you couldn't feel a shark bite – there was no pain, just a tug. He imagined bleeding to death out here, silently, half his body swallowed.

But it seemed he still had everything he came with into this world.

He floated on his back and took great thankful breaths.

He thanked his mother and Treasure and Doomsday. He thanked the father he'd never seen and the man who'd given him the knife. Tears ran out from the sides of his eyes and melted into the water. His chest heaved with sobs. He felt good. Clean.

Grateful.

Slowly, shuddering all the way, he swam home beneath a rising moon.

He was barely conscious when he dragged himself into the shallows of the bay. Perhaps that was why he ignored Doomsday, who came screaming in to meet him, the stick legs splashing, feathers wild. Wicked didn't stop to wonder, either, why the bird clung so painfully to his shins, the sharp little claws pricking him as they waded awkwardly into shore together.

Wicked was too weary to walk all the way up to his hammock in the cave. He dropped down instead on the sand where he stood.

But Doomsday wouldn't be quiet. He was cursing like a pirate, furious and terrified at the same time. He hopped up and down on Wicked's chest. The feathers on his head stood to attention and he flapped a wing towards the cave, pointing wildly. He bit Wicked's ear, tugged at his eyebrows, pulled his hair.

'*OW!*' cried Wicked. 'You're a proper little pest. Will you shut up and let me rest?'

'No rest for the wicked!' screamed Doomsday.

'Oh, go to the devil.'

The last thing Wicked heard before he fell asleep on the sand was Doomsday's chilling call, 'Beware, the devil is here! The devil is *here*!'

chapter 23

Wicked woke in the night when he turned over onto something sharp. Through the slit of his lids he glimpsed a pool of silver moonlight on the sand and there, floating in the middle, was his boat.

He closed his eyes again. He was dreaming. He *must* have been dreaming. Because even more impossible than the boat was the Captain's face above it, white and cold in the moonlight.

In the morning, Wicked's whole body ached. Sleeping on the beach had not been his best idea. His shoulders and arms groaned from the long swim, and his back was pock-marked with the dents of little shells.

'Doomsday? Where are you?'

Only the waves sifted in and out. In a flash of memory he saw the frantic bird, and heard again his warning.

A shiver passed through him.

Gingerly, he sat up. His eyes travelled down the beach.

He hadn't been dreaming.

A boat was hauled up on the sand, just like the one he'd

sailed in from Devil Island. He wiped the sleep from his eyes. The boat was still there.

He crept down to the shore to inspect it. It was green, not blue, but his fingers traced the same deep grooves along the right side. He straightened up and looked around. Just sand, and palm trees.

'Doomsday?'

There, on the sand, a feather. The edge was smeared with red. Wicked remembered the limp, the way the bird had staggered as it scuttled up and down his chest.

He started back up to the cave. Probably the parrot would be there, sleepy after all the fuss last night. He'd be perched as usual on the little ledge next to the hammock and they'd share a coconut juice as they always did first thing in the morning. Maybe he'd cut his foot on an oyster, or got nipped by a crab. Wicked would find a fresh strip of palm leaf to bandage it.

But as he hurried over the hill, a bad feeling gurgled in his guts. Last night, Doomsday had wanted his attention. A splinter of regret niggled. He wished he hadn't told him to go to the devil. He wished he'd taken a look at that leg. He tried not to think about the rest of his dream.

He arrived panting at the mouth of the cave. Then he stopped short. Someone was crouched at the back wall, riffling through his pile of possessions.

Wicked squinted into the gloom. He made out a man with a hat … maybe this was the sailor who'd left the precious things! He wanted to shake his hand. But when the figure straightened up, shock made Wicked gasp.

'Well, well, sleeping in till noon like a lazy landlubber, eh?'

It was the Captain's voice, sure enough. How was that possible? Wicked took a step closer.

The same hooded eyes, dull and weatherworn as wood. The Captain stood just as he always had, tall as a mast, straight-backed, swayed by nothing.

But something was different. As Wicked watched the man lift his hat in greeting, he saw the hair on his head was gone, and the bushy black eyebrows had been burnt to stubble.

Wicked cleared his throat. 'Is it ... you?'

The Captain smiled, his jaws cracking into dangerous lines. His eyes didn't change. As he smoothed down his jacket Wicked noticed his nails were singed black.

'Are you a ghost?' With a shaking hand, Wicked reached out to touch him.

But before he could, the Captain flicked him away with the spear. 'Show some respect,' he spat. 'I'm still your Captain.'

Wicked cringed as if he'd been hit. That tone took him back to the ship, to all the years of cruelty and harsh commands. Without thinking he blurted, 'Yes sir!'

The Captain's face relaxed. 'You still have so much to learn, Wicked. A badly tied knot cost you your freedom. Bad manners may cost you still more.'

Wicked looked down at his feet.

The Captain tapped the spear lightly on Wicked's chest. 'Now, let us start again. As you see, your Captain is hale and hearty, even though you squabs committed the worst of crimes against me.'

'I never had any part in that mutiny,' cried Wicked. 'I swear!'

'But you were silent. You were lily-livered. You, in particular, should have been loyal.' The Captain gave him a thin smile, even though the point of his spear lay directly over Wicked's heart. 'Still, you are young. I am prepared to overlook your cowardice. So, tell me then, are you pleased to see your Captain?'

'Yes, sir,' said Wicked automatically. 'But how did you…?'

'You doubted me? Shame on you. As you see, I possess powers far greater than those of mere men. Now, you are lucky, Wicked. You were my apprentice from the time you were a nipper. There are things I know, things I can do, that ordinary folk only dream of. Wouldn't you like to continue your education?'

Wicked met his eyes, and looked away. The man had saved Wicked's life, shown mercy when he was sick. So why now did the Captain's gaze feel so crushing, his attention like the weight of the ocean pressing down on him?

'Well?' the Captain barked.

Wicked felt himself shrinking inside. Not since he'd come to Turtle Island had there been a moment like this. In his mind, the smaller he became, the taller the Captain grew. He was no longer a child but even so, the illusion of the man's height and power lingered like a stain that couldn't be removed.

'Things aren't always what they seem,' a voice piped up from the folds of the hammock.

'Doomsday!' cried Wicked. Like a wand breaking a spell, the bird woke Wicked from his dread. He started for the hammock but the Captain stepped into his path.

'Talking to the birds now, are you?' he said. 'You've gone

soft in the head, lad, like those other jellies you left behind. We can't have that.' The Captain turned and kicked the hammock hard so that it swung crazily in the gloom.

'Oi, watch *out*!' cried Wicked.

'WHAT?' bellowed the Captain. Wicked had never heard him shout so loud. 'You're giving me orders now? I'll have to teach you some manners, like this bird here.' In one swift movement he upturned the hammock and *thud*, Doomsday fell out on the stony ground.

Doomsday tried to stand, trembling. Wicked saw the cut on his leg, jagged and open. He reached down but the Captain barred his way with the spear.

'When folk step out of place,' he said silkily, 'they get hurt. All you have to do is listen, Wicked, and learn.' He ran a finger over the point of the spear, testing its sharpness.

'Now, we were having a nice chat, just the two of us, before windbag here interrupted. I imagine you're as happy as a pig in mud to see your old boat again, lad. Spruced up, a new coat of paint, eh?' The Captain's tone had changed completely. 'By Jove, you must have been convinced you'd die in this godforsaken place, no one to talk to but feathers-for-brains! Now, I have an excellent business deal for you.'

Wicked squirmed. He'd have sworn the Captain was trying to be...friendly. As if the man were standing at the door of his house, inviting him in. But the welcome was brittle, and Wicked knew he'd crumble into a thousand pieces if he stepped in.

'Aye,' nodded the Captain, agreeing with himself. 'You're a lucky young rascal indeed. Your Captain has come to the rescue, *again*. You can tell me how grateful you are when we set sail.'

Wicked felt a hot storm rise inside him. 'I wouldn't have to be grateful if you hadn't stolen the boat in the first place!'

The Captain's eyes fixed on him, unflinching. '*Your* boat? You mean the boat you stole from Devil Island? It was floating in the ocean, nitwit.' His voice was hushed with menace. 'You've made free use of my possessions, I see. Fishing with my spear, sleeping in my hammock. But don't mention it, lad, glad to be of help. Now it's time for you to get off this island. And your Captain here will provide your escape.'

Wicked wrenched his gaze away. Escape? If this was escape, why did it feel like prison? Like being kidnapped all over again?

'Say your prayers, this ship is going down!' came a muffled cry from the corner of the cave.

'Shut your beak or I'll shut it for you!' the Captain hissed, giving the bird a jab with his spear.

Wicked froze. The blade rested on Doomsday's head and suddenly Wicked understood, with a terrible certainty, that it was the Captain who had clipped the bird's wings.

Wicked scooped him up and put him on his shoulder. He could feel the bird trembling.

'Sink or swim,' Doomsday whispered in his ear.

Wicked drew himself up to his full height. He squared his shoulders and the muscles rippled in his arms. The bird was right. He was grown now. Everything was different. He wouldn't drown, he wouldn't go under. He could *swim*.

Wicked took a deep breath, as if he were about to dive deep. 'I've made my own plans. I'm gunna swim back to Devil Island.'

[179]

The Captain laughed. 'Swim? Are you mad? Do you have a death wish?'

Wicked bit his cheek. 'I taught myself. I've trained hard.'

'Oh, dear,' sighed the Captain. 'Your ignorance never fails to amaze me. I gather you haven't made the acquaintance of the sharks that patrol these waters?'

'I have, but I've found ways to deal with 'em.' Wicked couldn't help a small swell of pride.

The Captain shook his head. 'You might have been lucky once. You can't bank on a second time. Don't be such a fool – what kind of poxy lunatic chooses to swim in shark-infested waters when there's the offer of a boat? I've never heard such a crack-brained scheme in all my life.'

Wicked flushed red. Put like that, his plan did sound crazed. And it was a risk, truth to tell. Perhaps too big a risk. But if he accepted the Captain's offer, the price he'd have to pay was more than he could bear. He'd rather die free than live as a slave. That much he'd worked out for himself.

'You can kill a man,' Wicked said, lifting his gaze to the Captain, 'but you can't kill an idea.'

The Captain rolled his eyes. 'Oh don't start boiling your brain, you'll hurt yourself.' He paused, then looked at Wicked with mild curiosity. 'Tell me something. If this bird has become such a friend, why are you planning to desert him? The parrot can't swim, even if you can. You're willing to leave him where you found him, on the island? Is that your *idea* of how to treat your friends?'

Wicked blushed to the roots of his hair.

Doomsday was silent.

The truth was, it struck Wicked now, that he hadn't even thought about the bird. Not yet. So taken up was he with his swimming that he hadn't...

'I'm sorry,' he whispered to Doomsday. 'I just didn't think.'

'No, you only thought about yourself,' the Captain said cheerfully. 'Bravo! You had the right idea this time. You know, Wicked, you and I are more alike than you realise. The sooner you learn that, and start taking lessons from me, the better. Devil Island is where we're both headed. I've got a bit of business to take care of there. We can begin lesson number one on the way.'

Wicked said nothing. He felt Doomsday quivering, the bloodied foot sticky on his shoulder. Some friend he'd been to the bird. No better than useless.

The Captain glanced at Doomsday, shaking his head. 'But if you're swimming back, of course, the bird will provide a tasty meal for a stranded sailor. Such a pity the poor maimed creature has no one to... protect him.' The Captain licked his lips. 'Ever tasted roast parrot? Delicious.'

The Captain waited, idly twirling his spear.

Even if I'm a useless blighter, Wicked decided in the silence, *I'm better than no one.*

'I'll come,' he said finally. 'But only if the bird comes with me.'

The Captain was in a hurry now.

Wicked didn't have long to say goodbye to Turtle Island. After he'd filled up the bottle with water, collected some coconuts, and picked up his sack of treasure, he put Doomsday on his shoulder and stepped into the boat. It was the right thing to do, but Wicked felt a hopeless weight settle in his heart.

When Wicked was seated at the oars, the Captain pointed to the knife in Wicked's belt. 'I'll take care of that,' he said smoothly. 'We don't want you having an accident, do we.'

Wicked passed it over, wondering if he would always do the Captain's bidding. The thought made his shoulders collapse.

'Every cloud has a silver lining,' Doomsday squawked.

Wicked gritted his teeth. I'll do this one last thing, he thought. But I won't take any more lessons, or listen to any deals. I've done my years at sea. We'll get to Devil Island, then Doomsday and I will disappear. Maybe we'll go to the Mainland, or even back to . . .

'Weigh anchor!' shouted the Captain.

'I'll look after you now,' he whispered to Doomsday.

How he was going to do it, Wicked didn't know. Or even if he could. But he was going to try.

chapter 24

The Captain leaned back in the boat, watching Wicked row. It was mid-afternoon and the sea glinted like treasure.

'Head west around the peninsula,' the Captain said. 'When we get to the red cliffs, you'll turn south-west. Put your back into it and we'll be there by dusk. That'll be just right. We'll need the cover of dark.'

Sunlight scattered gold coins on the water and the sky shone opal blue. It didn't seem right, Wicked thought. The dread in his belly sat like lead while the world sparkled around him.

The Captain was unusually talkative. He laid his arm casually across the rim of the dinghy, sliding his back against the side to get more comfortable. He kicked off a boot. 'You know, I wasn't surprised to hear that you left Devil Island so soon. Seems you didn't enjoy the company.' He snorted. 'Pack of pigeon-hearts, those men. Call themselves pirates? Bowing and scraping to that child, fawning in front of those ridiculous villagers. Pirates, my foot! Wet-nosed puppies not fit to haul anchor. Makes you want to puke.' He shook his head in disgust. 'But tell me, as you rowed off, what did you think you were going to do? Where were you headed?'

Wicked said nothing.

The Captain dusted something off his coat. The ruby on his finger glittered. 'You never think very far ahead, do you, lad?' He waited. 'Well, am I right?'

'Yes sir.'

'That's why you need me. Your Captain will do your thinking for you. I heard all about it, you know, your escape from those mewling do-gooders. "Share this, share that", bleating lambs, bleeding hearts, the lot o' them. Now if you'd gone a bit further and holed up at Snake Island or even the Mainland, I might have saved you a lot of time and trouble.'

Wicked shuddered. Doomsday pressed into his shoulder.

'That's where *I* headed, after Shipwreck Island. I had nothing on me, not even one bar of silver, but I made do. A pocket picked here, a sweet deal there. Of course I had to take another name for my business dealings, a nobody name – called myself Wicked, hope you don't mind. I don't mind telling you, my own reputation had been dragged through the mud by those pirate dogs.' The Captain sighed, and fiddled with his ring. 'But never say die! I've got a ship together and a new crew waiting for me on Snake Island. A burly bunch of sea dogs they are, just waiting till I give the signal.'

Wicked felt his guts loosen. 'What are they waiting for?'

'You.'

'Why me?'

'There's something I need,' the Captain said smoothly, 'that only you can get for me.'

The sea slapped against the sides of the boat. The oars slid through the water.

'Well?' The Captain's tone was still pleasant. 'And here I was thinking you would be eager to help the man who saved your life.'

Wicked's throat went dry.

'Beware the devil's creep, softly softly in your sleep,' croaked Doomsday.

The Captain gave a grunt of rage and lunged at the bird. But Doomsday had slithered down inside Wicked's shirt. Slowly, the Captain slipped the knife back into its sheath. A shallow nick, the length of a fingernail, welled red under Wicked's ear.

'That is an annoying creature,' the Captain said mildly. 'Drives me to distraction. If you can't control its beak I will silence it for good myself.'

Wicked felt Doomsday huddled against his middle, trembling.

'As I was saying before that drivelling gasbag piped up,' the Captain went on, 'you have an opportunity to help me, Wicked, as well as participate in an excellent deal for yourself.'

'Thank you sir, but no, I have other plans,' Wicked stuttered.

The Captain gazed at him. 'Ah, Wicked. What am I going to do with you? It seems that like a cat, you have had many lives. Yet I am the one who keeps giving them back to you. One day that may have to stop. For now, I don't ask anything in return, except your gratitude.'

'Yes, sir.'

'Gratitude comes in many forms. Let me tell you briefly about the developments in the real world these last months.

While you've been stuck nowhere talking to birds, those Devil Islanders have been busy. You wouldn't recognise the place. The tavern is doing a roaring trade and they've built an inn to sleep scores of happy customers. Money is being made! Tourists are coming from all over the Cannonball Seas ... and the secret, they tell me, is the food.'

The Captain stroked his chin. Wicked could feel Doomsday still shuddering against his ribs. The bird was a constant itch of feathers. Wicked was dying to scratch but he didn't dare stop rowing.

'Nowhere in the world, so folk say, can you get a feast like that on Devil Island. People are spending a fortune holidaying there. Horrendo of course is in charge of the menu, but they say he has help ... a small slice of magic that he adds to his pie.'

'I always *thought* there was something unnatural about the lad,' Wicked burst out, his sudden anger surprising him. 'An unfair advantage, like. You know he was under a spell? But not anymore.'

'They say a Wise Woman lives on the island, whose garden boasts a special herb. Add a sprig to any meal, and it will have the diner delirious with delight. I want you to steal that herb for me, Wicked. For us.'

Wicked slowed the oars. Under his shirt Doomsday pecked fluff from his navel.

'Why would you want that? You don't even *like* food.'

The Captain smiled grimly. 'How astute of you, my lad. You're right. But others want it badly. In this world you have to discover the thing people value most. First code of business: pay as little as possible for it. Second code of business: sell it for as much as possible. Pirate's code – steal it, and you'll maximise your prize.'

'Check your centre, keep your eyes...' whispered Doomsday.

Wicked shooshed him with his hand on the bird's beak. Where *had* Doomsday heard that? An icy chill seeped into Wicked's blood. 'Can you tell me where you first met Doomsday?'

The Captain spat with irritation. 'What's that got to do with anything? I don't remember. The bird's a dimwitted fool, repeats anything he hears.'

'Has he sailed with many pirate ships? I thought I saw... that time with the Bonny Lasses...'

'One parrot is no different to any other. We were talking of things of *value*.' The Captain's face had darkened. Wicked watched him clench his jaw in the effort to remain calm. 'Now, I'm offering you a deal that will make you forget you cared one jot for a mangy bird with limited conversation skills.' The Captain's voice turned to silk. 'Prick up your ears, my lad, we can sell this herb for more gold than you ever dreamed of.'

'But I already have my share of the treasure,' Wicked said, picking up the oars again. 'I earned it fair and square.'

'See, right there is your limited thinking. *Earned* it, indeed. What kind of a pirate are you? I don't know where you got that notion from. Are you referring to the piddly pile of coins you keep in your jacket? That's not enough for a luxurious life. A life that is special. A cut above the rest. And you, my lad, can have one! Bigger and better than any of those other pirate dogs on board my ship. Because you are different. Look at you, the only one to leave that absurd child's game on Devil Island.

You went to look for a better life for yourself. And you'll find one with me.'

As the Captain talked, he rubbed his hands together and smiled, gazing off at the horizon as if spellbound by the shimmering possibilities awaiting him there. Frequently, he glanced back to check Wicked was listening. He seemed to enjoy having an audience, stretching out his legs, waving a hand in the air as he described a palace he'd seen with a marble staircase and a hundred servants. Even his eyes looked more alive, reflecting the gold dazzle off the water.

Wicked was struck by the change. If he yawned or looked away, the Captain shrank a little and grew grumpy. This was definitely a new side to him, thought Wicked. He'd only ever seen the man giving orders or demanding favours. As far as he knew, the Captain had never put any effort into trying to, well ... *persuade* a pirate to do his bidding. He was different away from his ship – that must be it. Wicked remembered how strangely stirring it had been, years ago, when the Captain of the Cannonball Seas had told him he was valuable. Now he just couldn't wait to get away.

'I've done things in my life you can't imagine. And not just at sea. I've owned gambling houses and circuses, gold enough to fill a ship.' The Captain frowned, the shadows in his cheeks deepening. 'Lady Luck just deserted me for a while, that's all. Don't depend on her. Rely instead on your Captain.'

'Circuses? Did you ever meet my ...'

'You see, you don't have a choice, Wicked,' the Captain rode smoothly over Wicked's voice. 'You have a debt to me. But your payment of service will be your reward, too. This is *your* time now. All the work and suffering was for this moment – it will be your crowning achievement. That herb will make you rich. It is your prize.'

Wicked didn't believe in prizes anymore. And he was stuck on something the Captain had said… But right now, Doomsday was shivering against his ribs. Wicked wished he could tell him everything would be all right. A sudden memory of Bombastic talking to his frog flashed across his mind. For a brief moment Wicked understood something, and he felt a pang deep in his guts.

Then the Captain said, 'Can you see the shoreline? We'll be there soon.' And the place in Wicked's mind where the boy and his pet had appeared closed over, like high tide rolling into shore.

The sun was still blazing above the horizon when the boat neared the harbour of Devil Island. 'We've made good time,' the Captain said. 'Maybe too good. We'll drift here a while, cool our heels until sunset. Have a drink, relax, while I tell you how this plan will proceed.'

To the north-east of the harbour, the Captain said, lay a huddle of limestone caves. The biggest cave was miles deep, running back into a tunnel that stretched inland and opened up at the edge of a thick forest. Directly ahead, in a small clearing, Wicked would find the house of Gretel, the Wise Woman, and her prized garden.

'The herb you will be looking for has a very particular leaf. Long and narrow but with a curious system of veins. Here, I've got a drawing of the plant to… remind you.' The Captain passed Wicked a tightly folded square of paper, holding his gaze. 'Keep it safe.'

Wicked took the drawing and shoved it deep into his pocket.

'I want you to dig up every one of those plants by the roots and bring them back to me. Mind you speak to no one on the island. In four days from now I'll be waiting in a longboat with a couple of my new crew.'

Wicked swallowed. 'Four days? Surely it won't take long to dig up a few plants!'

The Captain shook his head. 'You're not using your head, Wicked. You're dealing with a Wise Woman here. She will have powers you're not acquainted with. Survey the scene first. Pick your time. Trust your instincts. I don't want any mistakes.'

Will's stomach dropped. A Wise Woman. A memory was coming towards him from far away. Like a landscape emerging on the horizon, it was sheathed in mist and distance. His feet felt heavy.

'Why don't *you* do it?' he burst out.

The Captain's lips thinned into a snarl. 'I'm not well-liked in these parts.'

'Neither am I!'

'You'll use the tunnel and be careful not to show your face. Now, you'll need this flint here to light the torch for your passage through the tunnel, and this hat to pull down over your eyes.'

'But what about digging the plants up? I'll need that knife, too.'

The Captain's eyes narrowed. 'No, you'll use your hands,' he said smoothly. 'A tool won't be necessary.'

Wicked held his gaze for as long as he could, but his lids lowered finally, as if they had a will of their own. 'Well, am I gunna sleep on hard ground then?' he muttered. 'At least let me have the hammock.'

The Captain clicked his teeth. 'You're getting soft. What do you want with that? It's *mine*, remember. I might need it where I'm going.' The idea of giving up anything of his own seemed to hurt the man, even something of such little value. There was a groan of resignation, and reluctantly, the Captain passed it across. Then he glanced to the west, and nodded.

'Time to go now,' he said, his voice resuming its even tone. 'Pick up the oars. We won't row into harbour. Too visible. I'll drop you off near the caves. Remember, you are to be back at dawn in four days. If you lose your way, never fear, I will come and find you – and your feathered friend.'

In the mauve twilight, Wicked waded ashore. Doomsday poked his head out to investigate.

'Hop up now,' Wicked told him. Clinging to a finger, the bird scrabbled up to his preferred place on Wicked's shoulder. He was still trembling.

'You're safe,' Wicked murmured. 'He's gone.' But Doomsday continued to shake.

Wicked felt nervous, too. Strange, he thought, as he stared ahead at the sinking sun, he left this place months ago, at twilight. So much had happened in between. There'd been Turtle Island; he'd learnt to swim. But it was hard to think clearly now, just as it had been then. When the light faltered and outlines were smudged, how could you see the right path ahead? The past rose up like the cliff in front of him, and a decision taken just hours ago blurred into a question. Over his shoulder a faint moon shared the sky with the melting sun.

He came ashore on a rocky promontory, lacy with rock pools. Spikes of stone pierced his feet and he had to go slowly, picking his way over sharp little shells and ridges. Along the shore to the south-west, he made out the lemon light of fires blazing through windows. The village square beyond was lit by flaming torches and on the breeze came the opening bars of an accordion, the tinkle of laughter. His own path instead lay in darkening shadow.

When he made it to the beach, he stopped to light the torch. He held it high and there, straight ahead, beyond the sand, were the grass-covered boulders that housed the caves.

He came to an opening larger than the rest, and stepped in. The mouth of the cave yawned as wide as the doorway to an abandoned palace. As he passed through, he imagined the bones of dead kings and queens weaving around him. He stood still, the breath frozen in his throat.

The limestone walls were a dazzling white, studded with crystals. Light bounced off columns of stone that flowed down from the ceiling like candles upended, dripping wax to the ground. Mist pearled his skin. It was a ghostly place. His breath was white and thick in front of him.

As he crept further into the cave, he saw no end, only a tapering into a tunnel that veered into pitch darkness. He shuddered so hard that Doomsday nearly fell from his perch.

'When you venture into the black, you don't come back,' said Doomsday.

'Aye,' said Wicked. 'Thanks for that. And we can always die tomorrow but for now, help me find somewhere to hang this hammock. I'm not going nowhere till daylight.'

part three

chapter 25

The tunnel was the only route to the headland above. To enter, Wicked had to stoop. Narrow and dark, the path wound around corners, the ground rising and falling beneath his feet. The morning light made no difference, he realised, when you walked under the earth. He held up his torch to see the way ahead, praying the flame would last the distance. Sometimes he had to squat down and lurch along like a crab. He tried not to think how cramped it was or about the creatures scuttling in the crevices; and always there came the steady drip, drip, from the water gleaming down the walls.

Only once he saw a breakaway road to the right. He stood for a moment, looking this way and that.

'What do you think?' he whispered to Doomsday. 'Which path should we take?'

The bird inched up his shoulder. 'There are two sides to every question.'

Wicked sucked his cheek. The bird was as helpful as a hat in a hurricane. But he turned and took the road to the right.

He'd only gone a few paces when the ground fell into a steep descent. He held the bamboo torch high, a cold sweat breaking out on his forehead. Now, as he stopped to listen, there came a roar of cascading water. When he peered down he saw the dark close over an inky pool, swallowing the way.

He turned back to the original path. 'See, now I know the way to go.' The sound of his own voice, loud with relief, gave him courage. 'You gotta keep your eyes peeled,' he told the bird, tapping his nose with his finger, 'as well as trust your instincts.'

'Instincts,' repeated the bird.

'Guts,' said Wicked.

'Guts,' said Doomsday. 'I'll have yer guts for garters!'

Wicked grinned, and they sang *guts for garters!* to keep their spirits up until the path began to climb and a pinhole of daylight beckoned ahead.

The sun spread deliciously over his back as Wicked hauled himself up into the world. He kneeled on the grass and lifted his face to the breeze. Squinting, he made out fern trees and figs, and beyond, a forest of bloodwoods. Somewhere in the middle would be a clearing, and the house of the Wise Woman.

Here, in this wild windswept spot on the edge of the forest and the beginning of the sea, there was nobody. He pulled his hat down over his eyes. Something in his stomach was churning.

'He who hesitates is lost,' croaked Doomsday.

'Guts for garters,' said Wicked, and stood up. He stretched his arms and straightened his back. His bones cracked. 'Now we'll go and see about that herb.'

Doomsday said nothing.

'I know, I *know*, but who can tell what the man'll do if he doesn't get what he wants,' Wicked burst out. 'His reach is long and deadly – I was thinking it over all last night. He'll turn real nasty. To you, and to me.' Wicked bit his lip, glancing at Doomsday. 'I'll just do this one more thing, and then we'll be free. And anyway, it's only a plant, no one's gunna *die* if we take it. Wouldn't be the worst thing to happen at sea, either, if Horrendo's lobster mornay lost a tad of its flavour.'

'Food for thought.'

'Aye.' Wicked quenched the flame and laid the torch on the ground beside a rock for his return. And then he took his first steps into the forest.

It was dark and cool with the trees thickening around him and the ferns crisscrossing above in a green roof, whispering in the wind. Secrets rustled in the leaves. The ferns gave way to taller trees, and there was the scent of nutmeg. His breath tightened – how long it had been since that spice had tickled his nose! He drew in great draughts of it as he crept forward, sticks snapping underfoot. His eyes watered and he wiped them with the back of his hand. Doomsday clucked and clicked near his ear, trembling.

And then, directly ahead, he saw it. In a clearing on a small rise of hill was a wooden house. A chimney was smoking even though the day was warm, and to the side was the vegetable garden, bordered by hibiscus bushes.

He picked his way towards it, keeping to the thicket of trees. He peered out from behind a bloodwood. So close now, he could reach out and touch one of the hibiscus flowers.

Then, from the house, there came the rise and fall of voices. A door opened and he ducked down so suddenly that Doomsday almost lost his hold. '*Ssh!*' Wicked warned, shutting his beak with his fingers as the bird began to squawk.

Two people, no, three were coming down the stone steps. A cat, draped like a rug around the tall woman's shoulders, yawned in the sun.

'But Gretel,' the boy with the floppy hair turned to ask her, 'why do *you* think the other plants died?'

Wicked started at the voice. He stared. Irritation rose like steam under his skin.

The woman shook her head. 'The herb has been in my family since the time of my great grandmother. No one ever knew how she came by them but the original wise seeds were sown in her garden, right here where we're standing.'

'So maybe the soil anywhere else, even just an arm's length away, mightn't be right for it?' the girl behind them cut in.

'That's a good hypothesis, Blusta. You're learning so much in such a short time.'

'Isn't she, though?' agreed the boy warmly. 'You should see her broccoli and spinach at home – her garden's keeping the whole tavern supplied! And as for her strawberries, I've never tasted anything so sweet and juicy.'

The woman smiled. 'Your enthusiasm helps to keep everyone blooming, my dear Horrendo.'

Nitwit! Wicked had to bite his cheek to stop from cursing.

'Thank you,' said Horrendo. 'But you said there's only a couple of your seeds left, and they're not sprouting. What if...'

[197]

'The dried herb in the library will see us through the year. Only a speck is needed in any pot, as you know,' said Gretel.

'You worry too much,' said Blusta, and kissed Horrendo on the cheek.

'Old habits,' smiled Gretel.

Horrendo blushed a fiery red.

Wicked ground his teeth. *Typical!* Now the dunderhead even had a girlfriend. And look at that pair of females, worrying about him *worrying!*

'Talking of hypotheses,' Horrendo went on. 'I've asked Rascal to look into how to care for the last remaining plant. And how we might get new seeds. You know, he's come on tremendously since we built the science laboratory. He spends hours there after class, experimenting, mixing his chemicals. He's so keen to learn.'

Gretel nodded. 'It's a great gift.' She turned to Blusta. 'I think it runs in the family.' She stroked the cat's paw thoughtfully. 'Work with your brother, Blusta, and share *your* botanical gift. You two are going to make some important discoveries, I know.'

Horrendo groaned. 'But that's just it. If Rascal could focus on the one thing he would get somewhere, but he's so ... scattered. He's into *everything!* You know he's mad about those salt crystals from the caves? He reckons if you mix them with, well, I can't remember exactly – this and that – he can turn things invisible. That is, it only lasts a few minutes, but he's working on it. *Time* is the problem, he says. Yesterday, he disappeared Bombastic's puppy, right in the middle of its dinner. Everyone got a terrible shock. The hound stayed vanished for half an hour. He wasn't just invisible, he'd sort of melted away completely! Rascal was ecstatic about the "longer duration of the invisible state" but

Bombastic said it might scar the poor dog for life. "No it won't," said Rascal. "Just look at the evidence before you." And he pointed to the puppy, who'd gone back to wolfing down its dinner as if nothing had happened. Well, Bombastic was ready to jump on him. He tried to grab the potion but Rascal was too quick – he fairly flew back to the laboratory to find out what ingredient was responsible for this "great improvement in durability", as he calls it.'

Horrendo gave a loud sigh after this long speech and collapsed on the garden bench. Blusta sat down next to him.

'It's just, well, I feel so responsible for everything,' Horrendo said quietly. 'You know, this whole village changing, the tourist boom, all the villagers' hard work, the well-fed holiday makers – it's because of my … well … and it all rests on that herb, doesn't it?'

Gretel put a hand on his shoulder. 'We will see,' was all she said before she wandered back up the steps. At her door, she turned and added, 'Visit the library whenever you wish, Horrendo, and take your supply of the herb. But remember, only a pinch. It's important that the store stays safe in case we have no luck with the seed,' and she passed through the doorway, and was gone.

'I hope you heard: just one pinch,' said Blusta, pulling Horrendo up beside her. 'You know how you overdo things sometimes. What you need is more confidence in your own cooking.'

'But she didn't say *whereabouts* in the library the herb is. Tucked into a book? There are hundreds of them. What, am I supposed to have a magic nose, as well?' He let out a small grunt of anger. 'Why does she have to be so...mysterious. Infuriating. Frustrating. *Maddening!*' He looked surprised, then guilty. 'You know, it still feels strange to say bad words out loud.'

Blusta grinned. 'They aren't so bad, and the herb is in the Reference section, under the first letter of the Librarian's mother's name.'

'Oh! Why didn't she tell *me* that? So what is it?'

Blusta quickly glanced about her, suddenly looking doubtful. 'I shouldn't have even told you that. Not here, out in the open. It's like a password, we mustn't say it out loud.' She pulled Horrendo up beside her. 'I'll tell you later, but now we've got to go and help Squid get ready for his opening night.'

'What, the Beach Bar is finished?'

Blusta nodded. 'Buzzard put the last touches to the carpentry last night. He was up for hours varnishing tables. They're perfect – so shiny you can see your face in them! And Mischief has painted a mural on the back wall.'

'Will there be some kind of show?'

'Yes!' Blusta grinned. 'Rip is going to play the accordion and Hoodlum is doing his magic tricks. It'll be fun! And afterwards, there'll be limbo dancing...' Blusta glanced at him from under her lashes.

But Horrendo was worrying. 'Maybe I should bake some of my sticky date cakes and chocolate-filled sponges. No, I should be at the tavern early to prepare, there'll be a full house for dinner...'

'Oh, heaven give me patience!' Blusta burst out. 'The kitchen can do without you for one night.'

As they wandered off hand in hand, their heads together, Wicked sucked his cheek. Even as the two disappeared down the path back to the village, he could hear them chattering on, clackety clack, like crickets on a summer night.

He sat back on his heels. He didn't know what to think about first. With a shock he realised that the Captain didn't know the herb was dying. That seemed odd – and yet oddly useful.

For a moment he imagined returning empty-handed. He shivered, even though the morning was warm. 'We're gunna have to sneak into town and find that library,' he told Doomsday, leaping up.

A sudden cramp made him bend double.

Breaking into a library seemed worse than digging up dirt. Just the thought made the bile rise in his throat. And he didn't know that password. Who was this Librarian? And her *mother*? Blimey, how would he discover that? But then he straightened. If he had to go into town, at least he'd get an eyeful of that famous tavern. He had to admit, he was curious. He wanted to take a squiz at that laboratory, too. And just fancy, old Squid – with his own bar! It was amazing…

Doomsday climbed up to peck under Wicked's hair. He found something tasty to eat. Wicked's scalp prickled. And his skin felt sticky with salt and grime. He hadn't looked in a mirror for months.

'Hmm, maybe I should have a wash before I go.' But his stomach rumbled like a storm brewing. 'I'm so hungry I could eat the hoofs off a horse. Maybe I can snatch something tasty from the market.'

He smoothed his shirt and combed his beard with his fingers. Then he and Doomsday followed the sandy path to the village.

The track wound through low brush that thickened into forest on either side. Out past the bloodwoods on his left there was the ocean but up ahead the track took a sharp turn to the right to avoid a deep ravine.

A loose rope-bridge was slung across the cavernous drop where a river rushed to the sea. The bridge cut straight across to the village, towards the first scattering of grey peaked roofs. Some of the wooden planks had fallen away, leaving the ropes slack. It was so frayed in parts, Wicked didn't know if it would hold his weight.

'It'd be a short cut,' he told Doomsday, 'but I've got no stomach for heights anymore. Besides, that fall would be deadly. I've got you to think about now.'

'Remember to stop and smell the roses,' Doomsday remarked.

A rope between mangrove trees swung into his mind. A lazy river. *You're a natural,* whispered his mother. *You can walk anything.*

Wicked shook his head and kept to the main path.

It was hot trudging through the bush and as the path rose steeply, bees swarmed in the honeysuckle, their wings throbbing in the moist still air. It was going to be tricky, Wicked thought. He'd have to keep his hat over his eyes ... and maybe he could walk with a limp. He'd keep to himself. With any luck the villagers would all be out and about, and quite a crowd of them there'd be, if he remembered rightly. No one would notice one bearded, hungry, hatted fellow with a parrot on his shoulder, would they? No one ever noticed him when he *wanted* them to, so why would things change now?

chapter 26

The village square was bright with stalls selling nuts and beans, rice, fish, pumpkins, plantains and barrows of watermelon. There were wicker baskets of mangoes splendidly done up with ribbon, and barrels of live blue-crabs. Wicked darted among them, his eyes under his wide brim bigger than the two oranges he picked up and pocketed. Folk milled about him like a school of sardines. He'd never seen so many different people herded together in all his born days. *Odd* people. They wore strange clothing in styles he had never seen before, and even the men sported necklaces of beads and bracelets on their wrists. They strolled about unhurried as if they had no work to go to or any burden on their minds. He watched them enjoying the day, tasting coconut milk and mango juice from a stall offering free drinks. They slapped each other on the back and chatted about the weather and their children, discussing the various bargains they had found.

'That tourist boat came in early this morning, eh?' said a familiar voice.

Wicked spun around to see Goose standing behind a stall from which the most intoxicating aromas were rising. Was Goose talking to him?

'Aye, we weren't expectin' them, neither,' Goose went on. 'The tavern will be right full tonight, not to mention the B&B.' He was turning over a whole pig on the spit, basting the sides with oil. Next to the barbecue were roasted chickens kept warm over a potbellied stove. At the sight and smell of it all, a dizzy sensation started behind Wicked's eyes. When he blinked, stars prickled in a night sky and he saw the stove his mother had cooked on, remembered the smell of her roasting hen.

'What can I get ye, sir?' Goose asked him now.

'Oh, err, well,' mumbled Wicked, pulling down his hat.

'Just havin' a once-over like, before ye decide, eh?'

'That's it,' replied Wicked, dropping his voice a few notes. Next time he might try a Spanish accent, he thought, or French maybe.

Goose didn't seem worried that he didn't want to buy. 'You take yer time, sir,' he said in a friendly way, grinning widely. ''Ere, 'ave this to help ye consider me merchandise, like,' and he offered Wicked a chicken leg in a folded napkin. 'And take this for yer fine-lookin' parrot.' He popped a morsel of meat into Doomsday's beak.

'*Merci*,' muttered Wicked, and sidled away.

He found a space to sit down on the grass behind the market, and lunged into his drumstick. Oh, the joy of it! Grease gleamed on his mouth and cheeks, and he wiped it with his beard. In his other fist he had a small crusty loaf that the baker – who looked like an older version of Bombastic –

Lexington Park Library
St.Mary's County Library
My Place to Learn, Discover, Relax

Customer name: Smith, Harmony
Circulation system messages:
Patron status is ok.

Title: Wicked's way
ID: 35920001987401
Due: 07/31/2017 23:59:59
Circulation system messages:
Item checkout ok. You just saved $9.99 by
using your library.

Total items: 1
7/10/2017 7:34 PM

Circulation system messages:
The End Patron Message is OK

Renew items at:
www.stmalib.org
301-863-8188, press 2

had given him 'to tickle his fancy'. In the pockets of his jacket he had the oranges, a nice ripe avocado, a small kerosene lamp a stall holder was giving away, and a banana cake. He felt rich and full, fat as a fly, as Doomsday said, swooning in the sun.

He lay back for a moment and closed his eyes. Happy voices drifted over him like music. It sounded good to his ears, that trilling flute of a woman's laughter. He thought about the dark cave he would return to and the silence; the drip of musty water on stone and the dungeon where he'd sleep. Why didn't *he* work here, like Goose, finding his ease in friendly banter, snacking on pheasant?

Because he had a job to finish. A wave of nausea passed over him and he burped up chicken. He had to get that herb before his life could be his own.

He stood up and dusted down his trousers. The sooner he got on with it the better.

But on his way out he couldn't help stopping to examine the little footstools and night tables at the homewares stall. The dark wood was polished to perfection and just begged to be touched. As he gave a secret pat to a silken surface he felt a hand on his shoulder. He jumped, and his hat slipped. Quickly he jerked it around to cover his eyes.

'Can I interest ye in this 'ere *tavola*, sir?'

'Tavola?'

The man grinned. 'It's foreign, like, for *table*. The Librarian at school told me that, an' all. Goes down well with the tourists.'

'Librarian? Where is …'

'I noticed you appreciatin' our fine woodwork,' the man

said proudly. 'That table you're lookin' at is pure polished mahogany. Made it meself.'

'Aye, it's a fine piece of furniture. But what I wanted to know was—'

'I 'aven't seen the likes of ye 'ere before, I don't reckon.' The man eyed Wicked thoughtfully. 'Are ye a tourist yerself then sir?'

'In a manner of … er, speaking,' said Wicked. 'I'm a … er, merchant, looking at … er, wooden goods.'

'You've come to the right place then, yessir!' In his eagerness the man pushed back his long hair and Wicked saw half his ear was missing.

Buzzard! Wicked wouldn't have recognised him. The man had round rosy cheeks and a lively sparkle in his eyes. The hard set of his jaw had loosened into a smile so that the whole shape of his face seemed different. Wicked couldn't help smiling back at him and he nearly came out with his name, but stopped himself just in time.

'Bein' in the trade as you are sir,' Buzzard said, 'you'll appreciate fine work. Will ye take a squiz at this fine walnut finish?'

'So you made this, all these … er, things did you?' asked Wicked in wonder. All Buzzard'd ever done on board was slap together a barrel, or repair a yardarm. But this was the work of an artist.

'Aye, got me own workshop at the school back there.' Buzzard jerked his thumb at a circle of rainbow-coloured buildings behind the square. 'Got more work than ye can poke a stick at, but I like to help out, ye know. Teach the little varmints on a Thursdy and Fridy. Here they come now, me two best pupils.' He smiled proudly.

Two boys, one short and one tall, came up and tugged at Buzzard's arm. 'You want us to take over the stall now for yer, Mr Buzzard?'

'Aye, lads, soon.' He rubbed his hands together. 'When I go an' get me afternoon tea, like. There's scones today.' He looked at the boys fondly. 'This 'ere's Rowdy and Hoodlum. I'm teachin' 'em everyfink I know. Me apprentices.'

The two boys beamed at him like healthy apples. Wicked wouldn't have recognised them, either. It wasn't just that they were rounder and stronger, it was more that they looked sort of glowing, as if they'd been polished with great tenderness, just like the tables.

Buzzard leant forward confidingly. 'See, now I'm busy doin' what I *like*, if ye can comprehend. An' each project is a challenge. Back when I was a pirate, losin' a challenge meant death. But now, see, it just means ye do it again, only *better*. It's like I died and went to heaven. I mean, ye get the chance to use what ye learnt the last time, you understand me?' He turned to the boys. 'Isn't that wot I'm always tellin' ye? If ye don't stick a piece a wood straight into the vise, it won't come *out* straight, right?'

The boys rolled their eyes as if they'd heard this many times. Hoodlum idly cuffed Rowdy's arm and Rowdy gave him a Chinese burn.

'Lads, eh? Wotcha gunna do with 'em?' Buzzard sighed good naturedly.

~ * ~

The village clock showed five o'clock when Wicked left the market. With all the different feelings swirling inside him, he felt like one of those butter churns he'd seen near the bread stall.

He peered across the square into the fading light. It was too late now to find the library. *Prawns for brains!* – he'd dilly-dallied so long it would be dark soon. The stalls were being packed up for the night and people were calling goodbye. Out past the square, the bush was already inky.

Well, there were still a couple of days. He'd find the library tomorrow, when the light was good.

Now, instead, he'd wander down to the harbour and take a peep at Squid's Beach Bar. Who knew, he might not be back to these parts for a long time. And he had a powerful hunger to see how old Squid was shaping up to the landlubber world.

Doomsday, he could see, had had enough for the day. Sleepy, with a full stomach, he was wobbling on his perch. Wicked tucked him inside his shirt. It was a bit crowded in there, what with all the tasty packages and the little lamp in his pocket, but the bird didn't seem to notice. He didn't even open an eye.

By the time Wicked got down to the beach, the kerosene lamps were being lit on the tables and torches flamed along the shore. Red ribbons of light lay over the water and the beach looked dressed up for a fair. Wicked wandered down to the long wooden bar set among the tables. At one end was a row of shelves labeled with all kinds of goodies – Mango Marvel, Banana Beauty, Coconut and Honey, Blood Orange and Berry juices. Little dishes of whipped cream with a topping of nuts and chocolate dotted the bench top, with wafer biscuits that you could use to dip.

Folk stood for minutes at a time, deciding what to have.

And there, behind the bar, rushing back and forth between customers, was Squid. Thin as a whip, he crackled like a piece of lightning, mixing drinks, taking silver coins with a *Thank you!* and *Enjoy yourselves!* and sometimes, if his hand was free, a slap on the back.

Well now, Wicked thought, he'd seen everything! This place must be magic. Or that herb was more powerful than even Horrendo thought. The cramp in his belly came again and he had to sit down suddenly on one of the finely carved stools at the bar.

'What can I get ye?' asked Squid.

'Ah, er, nothing right now. Feeling a bit poorly.'

Squid nodded. 'I've got just the thing to settle yer stomach. It's on the house!' And he handed Wicked a creamy gold drink that looked as if it had been poured straight from heaven. He took a sip. It tasted like that, too.

Wicked sat and watched the lamps flickering on the tables and the folk deep in conversation until a customer sat down next to him.

'I'll have...let's see...a blood orange with a dash o' lime,' the man told Squid. 'Or, no, citrus fruit's bad for me stomick, Blusta said it'd give me grief. Oh, what about that sweet coconut milk, what do ye serve with that?'

'Honey,' said Squid, rolling his eyes. 'Why don't ye just 'ave what's on the menu, ye great looby?'

'Aye!' said the man. 'There's a good idea!'

'Dogfish Delight, coming up,' said Squid and vanished up the bar.

Under his hat, Wicked snuck a glance. His old mate. Well, not really, but maybe the closest thing he'd had to one. Dogfish was leaner and straighter somehow, sitting with his shoulders back, not bowed, and his head held high. Wicked would wager, if he had anyone to wager with, that Dogfish had lost his Disappointment.

'Bottoms up,' said Squid, returning with his drink. 'Now, if yer gunna be my assistant, then yer'll 'ave to work at least three nights a week. Can ye square that with yer missus?'

So, Dogfish was married now, was he? That was quick work!

Dogfish nodded. His eyes were closed as he savoured his drink. 'Bloomin' paradise,' he murmured. 'But mind you, when the baby comes I'll 'ave to take a few weeks off.'

'What? Yer only just startin' work and yer wanting time off? We'll have to see about that!'

'He's right, though, Mr Squid,' a voice said from the crowd waiting behind.

Wicked turned to see Blusta stride up, with Horrendo at her side. Quickly he inched his stool further down the bar, and pulled his hat down.

Dogfish shook hands with the pair. 'See?' he told Squid. 'You mightn't know everyfink about it, Squidman, seein' as *you* ain't in the family way yet.'

'Neither are you, ye great pudding, it's yer *wife* what is,' said Squid.

But Blusta butted in. 'Fathers are important in the family, too.'

'Aye,' said Dogfish. 'My Pandy's been readin' a library book all about it – first thing the little fella claps eyes on, he'll become attached. He'll follow it around everywhere and learn all his life's lessons, like how to quack and fly, an' dive for fish an' all.'

'That's ducks you're talking about, fathead,' said Squid.

'Oh, aye.' Dogfish finished his drink.

'But we're not so different,' Blusta said. 'My mamma says your whole life changes, Dogfish, and Pandemonium will be run off her feet…'

Wicked got up from his stool, and wandered down to the beach. He gazed out to the horizon, watching lights melt into the sea. Behind him the murmur of voices buzzed like bees around a hive. An accordion started up and the sound of clapping and happy cheers floated on the breeze.

Soon we'll sail to the Mainland and listen to the fiddles playing, his mother whispered in his ear. He was startled by the memory, so close and vivid. He almost looked around, as if she might be there. He hadn't thought of that in years.

He turned now to see the folk sitting at the tables, swaying with the music. One girl got up to dance, and then another. A woman was singing, but he couldn't catch the words. He wondered if he would always be watching life from the outside, straining to hear something just out of reach.

~ * ~

It was late when Wicked started back on his path to the cave. His feet felt heavy, taking him to a place he didn't want to go. Doomsday snored, tucked up under his ribs. He gave the little bundle a pat, and was comforted for a moment.

How lucky it was he'd found the lamp at market. He hadn't imagined he'd be returning so late. Still, he had to keep his eyes fixed on that small yellow glow at his feet.

He was dreading the climb back through the tunnel. Scaling down the wall of the cave was harder than climbing up. He was afraid he'd lose his footing. If he fell, no one would know he was there. He went down slowly, with care. 'But it's been this way since my mother left,' he told the sleeping Doomsday. 'Why am I worrying now?'

Doomsday said nothing. Wicked crawled on through the endless earth.

He didn't know what made him stop short just before he reached the last corner. The mouth of the cave, his 'parlour' as he called it, lay just around the bend. There was no new sound or smell, just a movement of air perhaps, something displaced. Keeping his back to the wall and sucking in his stomach, he peeped around.

Starlight streamed in, grainy with salt from the sea. In the shadows, nothing stirred. Maybe he'd imagined it. A presence. Tiptoeing in, he saw at the foot of the eastern wall a scatter of white powder. Directly above, stripes of exposed crystal the width of a knife blade shone smooth under his fingertips.

Someone had been here. Today, while he'd been out. He crept towards the entry, following more dusty patches of white. Whoever had come had entered from the rock pools and returned that way.

He'd been right to hang his hammock further back in the tunnel. No one would have seen it. Safe for now, he thought. Still, he'd sleep even further in tonight.

Later, as he lay in the dark, he took deep breaths as he did when he swam, and imagined himself in the sea off Turtle Island. A calm dropped over him. Sleep was near. But something was nagging, something about crystals and caves, a laboratory and a dog...

He sat up suddenly, and nearly fell out of the hammock. Rascal! What Horrendo said... Rascal could make things invisible. How was that possible – that puny weakling who'd worn mittens up in the rigging!

Wicked turned the conversation over in his mind. The Captain would be interested in a potion like that, without a doubt. Wicked imagined those shark eyes lighting up at the thought of how much gold he could get for it. Maybe he'd want it even more than the herb.

Wicked turned restlessly in the hammock. Then he sat bolt upright.

Why not hand over the *potion*, instead? Horrendo didn't seem to think it was important – not as important as the herb, anyway. And Rascal already had the formula; he could always make more. No one would mind if just a bit went missing, would they?

Wicked almost laughed out loud at his idea. It could work! The Captain hadn't known the plant was practically dead... Wicked could exaggerate a little, pretend he was unaware of the dried herb store in the library... and he'd have this magic potion to give the Captain instead. For sure it would fetch a pretty price. And he'd be free of the Captain!

Wicked climbed out of the hammock and paced the ground. Blimey, how was a fellow supposed to get any sleep? He gave up and went outside.

As he stood looking out at the silvery sea, a shiver of doubt ran through him. How in all the Cannonball Seas did he really know what the Captain would think or do? And what, really, would the villagers say? It would still be a theft – a lousy, wicked kind of thing to do.

But he couldn't stop hearing the music on the beach, remembering the laughing and limbo-dancing on the sand... He wanted more of that.

Oh, what was he going to do? Everything was muddled. He stood, frozen to the spot, as if he were stranded on a tightrope and had forgotten at which end lay the prize.

chapter 27

The science laboratory was a big bossy building that lined up at
the end of the school like an exclamation mark. Tall and made of
stone, it wasn't blessed with a friendly painting of coconut palms
and steel guitars and bowls of fruit like the other classrooms. It
housed fiery experiments and unpredictable explosions, and to
Wicked it looked sinister, and a little bit dangerous. Hovering
near, he thought he'd much rather visit the guitar room where
that lively music was coming from than open this dark door.

But someone was coming up the path. A boy carrying a
notebook was walking fast, followed by another puffing to keep
up with him – damn the wretch, Horrendo! The boy in front
must be Rascal, Wicked decided, even though he'd changed
so much Wicked wouldn't have recognised him. A head taller,
colour in his cheeks, confidence to his stride... Wicked hadn't
been away for so long – how could the lad look so different?

He slipped around the corner, and peeped his head out.
Rascal had stopped to scribble something while Horrendo
jabbered on about folk and whether they could change.

'You see, it's very hard to change completely,' Horrendo was explaining. 'Take Wicked for example—'

'Caterpillars do it all the time,' Rascal said. 'Grubs one day, butterflies the next. Did you see all those empty cocoons in the science lab? Amazing.'

'No, but I mean,' began Horrendo, 'it's very hard for *humans* to change. It takes a lot of work. Look how many classes in Anger Management and Household Budgeting we had to do with the pirates! Just imagine if Wicked had stayed instead of setting off alone to . . . well, to keep on being Wicked. I mean, if he was here with us now he could be going to Team Building classes, or working with the Librarian, or teaching the children to climb . . .'

Who was this librarian everyone was talking about every five minutes? An annoying bug that kept getting into your ears? An earwig!

'I thought I saw him yesterday,' Rascal said.

'No! Wicked? Where?'

'Over there' – and he pointed to the clock in the village square. 'He was wearing a hat. And he was thinner, scruffier than ever. But it was him all right. Something about the way he moved, sort of shifty, was familiar. But when I went over to see, there was nothing there. My mother said I must be having a flashback.'

'Well,' Horrendo said, 'I hope he *does* come back – if he's still alive that is. Such a bad diet he always had. He never ate anything good for him. He even refused my smoked salmon and potato cakes, remember?'

Rascal stared at Horrendo. 'You must be the only one in

the world who cares. Some people don't change. But chemical compounds now … when added together, *they* do. They make a reaction. You just have to find the right combination to make a change last.' He suddenly looked impatient to go.

But Horrendo clutched his arm, making him stop right there on the path. 'You know, I always see his leaving our island as my fault.'

Rascal looked longingly at the big doors of the laboratory. 'The trouble with you is you think everything is your fault. But we can't control anyone but ourselves. You should think about that, and lighten your load.'

Horrendo's eyebrows shot up. He nodded vigorously and let go of Rascal's arm. 'That's very interesting,' he said. 'I will.'

Rascal grinned. 'See you later then,' he waved, and hurried inside the lab, the heavy doors thudding behind him.

~ * ~

'Oh, it makes you want to puke,' Wicked whispered to Doomsday. He was going to have to stay very low. And that 'don't blame yourself' stuff – why, Horrendo had spewed a stream of hateful curses at him before he took off. And look at the way they talked about him now! He'd been fooling himself. How would he ever be welcomed here? All that cosy, do-gooder twaddle – it was exactly what he was rowing away from last time. Wicked shivered, and crept out from the shade into the sunshine. But a chill wind seemed to follow him wherever he went.

He waited until Horrendo stopped dithering on the steps and walked away. Then he tiptoed up to the window of the science lab.

With his nose pressed to the glass, he saw Rascal lighting a little burner on the bench. He was heating up a bowl of pale blue liquid. Next to his elbow was a tray with small containers filled with different mixtures. The boy added and stirred and wrote on his notepad, checking the time on the clock near the blackboard. Wicked stifled a sigh. His neck was hurting from straining up to see, and his fingers gripping the windowsill had gone numb. Oh, snails for brains, how long was the boy gunna be?

Wicked decided to wander down the path to get an earful of the music. In one of the classrooms a kettle drum had started up, accompanying the steel guitars, and he couldn't help tapping his foot. A lad was singing, a high voice that hadn't broken yet. He'd be, what, eight or nine years old? He sounded happy. Lucky mongrel won't have to go to sea like me, Wicked thought.

When he got back to the laboratory, Rascal had blown out the flame. He poured the liquid – now a bright purple – into a pocket-sized flask and placed it in a drawer under the bench. Whistling, he packed up all the little glass bottles and vials and headed for the door.

Wicked ducked down. He watched Rascal until he'd disappeared behind the doors to the pineapple-painted room, and then he went inside.

The thick stone walls of the laboratory kept the air cool, and goosebumps sprang up on Wicked's arms. He went straight to the drawer. A dizzying wave rose up in him, and just for a second he closed his eyes. Then, grabbing the silver flask, he tore out of there, his breath racing as if he'd run a mile without stopping.

~ * ~

But Wicked found it hard to leave the shady green clearing at the edge of the school. He dawdled under the spreading fig tree, sprawled on a bench. He counted the silver coins he'd brought from his treasure store and went into the village bakery to buy a cream bun. When he'd eaten it, he strolled back to the school to take one last peek.

At the classroom labelled ART, he could perch on the step to see in. A girl was standing with a bunch of flowers, and the children were seated at tables with scrolls of paper and charcoal, drawing her. There was a hush and the sunlight streamed in, buttering the wooden floor and the lemon mats, the children's faces and the glowing hibiscus the girl held.

'Change!' called the teacher, and the girl put down the flowers and resettled herself in a big armchair. The pupils took fresh sheets of paper and began drawing the new pose. They were silent, absorbed in their work as if under a spell. Wicked strained to see how they were getting on. One boy with spectacles was working intently. As he drew, Wicked watched the girl in the armchair appear. It was exactly like the model, only not. She seemed alive in the drawing as if she could get up and walk, but in among the flowers in her arms, he'd drawn mangrove roots and shells, birds, a lizard, crabs and turtles. It was as if she was holding his whole world in her hands.

'Mischief, how interesting!' said the teacher. 'I love that!' It was only when the boy looked up, his face shining, that Wicked recognised him. It was the spectacles – where had he got those?

Mischief pushed them back up his nose. 'Thanks, sir! It's these glasses the Librarian got for me. They're brilliant, like the world's suddenly jumped out at me. I never knew there were so many marvellous things to look at. Like, have ye ever truly looked at a mangrove root? It's grand, all curly and winding like a snake.'

The other children came over to look too. 'Teach me how to draw that lizard,' said one girl.

'It's easy,' said Mischief. 'Ye just gotta find one and study 'im. The more you look, the more you love the little fella. You gotta draw what you see and then when you get good, you can start makin' it up, as well.'

Wicked stood down from the step and rubbed his eyes. He tried looking at the fig tree nearby. Could he make out the details? The veins in the leaves, the yellowish tinge in the older ones? No, his vision was blurred. Maybe he needed glasses too...

'*The Librarian got them for me,*' he mimicked Mischief, scowling.

'When in doubt, get thee to a library,' said Doomsday, popping his head out for a moment.

'Oh go boil your beak,' growled Wicked. 'I don't want to hear any more about libraries!'

He kicked a stone on the path. He'd made his decision. He patted the flask in his pocket. And yet... even if he never clapped eyes on the precious herb, before he left these shores he had to see this earwig of a person with his own eyes.

~ * ~

A shipwrecked sailor lying under a palm tree was painted on the front door of the library. Wicked could hear children chattering inside. He knew it was risky to be standing there, but still he stood staring at the picture. He liked the way the sailor was lying on his stomach, reading a book.

Wicked was nearly knocked over when the door opened, and three girls came out. They were too busy talking about a prince who'd climbed up some lass's hair to a tower to notice Wicked. Maybe he hadn't heard right. That was just stupid, no one could climb up *hair*, could they? Not even on Devil Island.

He rounded the building, and at the back of the library found a large open window. He gazed inside the room and saw a rug the colour of a tomato, and books. Everywhere. The walls were covered with them and in the gaps were pictures of ships and stormy skies, maps and foreign ports. Lads and lasses sat cross-legged or sprawled on their stomachs like the sailor, reading. It was the most colourful room he'd ever seen ... except for one.

'Today I'm going to read from a book called *The Habits of Hermits*.' A woman's voice rang like a bell through the room. 'Can anyone tell me what it might be about?'

Hands shot up.

'Maria?'

'Hermit crabs, Miss. They eat worms and weed like Hermy in that box there.'

'Yes, splendid! Have you got to know Hermy yet? If you watch him for a while, you'll see him pop his head out for food. But he's curious, too. Likes to dig. You can talk to him, tell him anything and he won't blink an eye.'

'He can't blink, miss, 'cause he ain't got no eyelids.'

The Librarian laughed, moving into Wicked's sight, her back to him. 'How observant of you, Hoodlum! But if you look closely, you'll find he *does* have tiny little eyelashes. He's quite hairy, in fact, but the hair rubs off with all that digging he does.'

'Aye,' called out another boy. 'An' I like the way his eyes pop out of his head like he's always surprised.'

'Well, *isn't* the world a surprising place?' said the Librarian. 'One day I hope you'll be able to travel right round it and meet more fascinating creatures like Hermy.'

'How do you know when he's asleep then?' asked Maria.

'I seen him tuck his eyes down and go right back into his shell, with just his legs hangin' out,' said Hoodlum. 'I reckon that means he's asleep.'

'Yes,' said the Librarian. 'I suppose we do much the same when we're tired. But I'd rather eat watermelon than worms, wouldn't you?'

'In the bad old days Mamma used to grill worms and put 'em in me sandwiches,' a boy called out. 'But that was back in me old life. Now she puts curried egg in, an' I like 'em better.'

'I met a boy once who could make a hermit crab climb out of its shell at the first sound of his voice.' The Librarian went quiet for a moment, and the class did too, as if trying to picture it.

'How did he do that?' asked Hoodlum.

'He practised,' said the Librarian. 'Every morning he came to say hello to the crab, over and over again. He talked to it for ages each day. You can do that too, with our Hermy.'

'Where is he now?' asked Maria.

'I knew him when I was just a bit younger than you,' the Librarian said. 'He was so interested in the world – fascinated by every creature he saw. I wonder if he's still like that. He's the only person I ever met who asked as many questions as me.' She smiled.

'Is he still your friend?'

'He'll always be my friend, but I haven't seen him in a long, long time.' She sighed, and blinked. 'Now, has anyone brought a new shell for our Hermy? Not yet? Well, he's fast outgrowing this one...'

There was a low buzz in Wicked's head. An ache started at the pit of his stomach and spread up under his ribs. He remembered the time he'd collected worms and weed, caring for a creature just like that. And read lots of books. They'd filled him up, like the food filled that creature. His eyes prickled. He remembered the taste of something sweet ... guava jam. His saliva glands tingled. He needed to sit down. But he couldn't. What he needed more, right then, was to see the face of the dark-haired woman who sat with her back to him.

'Miss, there's a man at the window!' cried a sudden voice.

Wicked didn't wait to see if the Librarian turned around. His knees collapsed beneath him and he half-crawled, half-ran through the grass, his heart thudding inside him like a kettle drum.

At the edge of town, he didn't slow down. He crashed through the forest, blind to the branches whipping his face. He ran until the breath ran out of him, stumbling over a root, tumbling to earth with a thump.

Doomsday squawked with outrage. 'Madness and mayhem!'

Wicked lay panting on his back. 'Oh, put a lid on it,' he moaned.

Doomsday crawled out from under his shirt and sat on his chest. His feathers stood on end with offence. Cocking his head to the side, he studied Wicked. The squawking became a soft warbling, like purring, in his throat. His feathers subsided and he nibbled Wicked gently with his beak.

They lay like that until a twig snapped suddenly behind them. Wicked sat up with a start. He looked around. There was only a faint swish of leaves in the breeze. A dragonfly droned near his ear.

'We better keep going,' he said. 'Someone might be following us.'

He got to his feet, lifting Doomsday up to his shoulder. Now he had to find the path to the caves. He'd never been so deep inside this part of the forest. The air was throbbing with insects. He could hear the far-off boom of the ocean. He'd head that way.

They'd been walking for ten minutes when another sound broke the quiet. A cough, or maybe a clearing of the throat. A human noise. Wicked stood still, the hair on the back of his neck tingling. Doomsday scooted down to hide in his shirt. The cough came again, louder this time. It sounded … polite.

Wicked glanced up. Ahead was a cluster of coconut palms and beyond the trees he glimpsed the sandy path to the caves. Hovering among the bushes, half hidden by ferns, was an unmistakable, floppy-haired figure.

Wicked ducked behind a tree, his face burning.

'Hello there, Wicked. I wonder if I could have a word? Won't take long.'

'A picture can paint a thousand words,' Doomsday called back.

'Pardon? Is that you, Wicked?'

There was silence as Wicked tried to think what to do. 'Say *no* to the pesky varmint,' he whispered to Doomsday. 'Say no one's here!'

But Doomsday was silent.

'Horrendo here, Wicked. How are you? A thousand words indeed – that's so poetic of you. But you know, we can't all be artists. Clear communication and a bit of goodwill can solve just about anything, I reckon. So, have you made a tour of the island? I bet a lot of things have changed since you were last here. Is that stomach of yours still giving you grief?'

'The way to a man's heart is through his stomach,' Doomsday cried out.

'Well, yes, I couldn't agree more...at least,' Horrendo stuttered. He came out from the bushes. 'Is that really you, Wicked?' He took a few steps forward as Wicked inched out from behind the tree. 'My, you *have* lost weight, but look at all that muscle! And you have quite a beard. Why, you look...different.'

Doomsday poked his head out and hopped up to sit on Wicked's shoulder. Wicked couldn't help grinning at the look on Horrendo's face.

'Before you judge a man, walk a mile in his shoes,' Doomsday said haughtily.

Horrendo's mouth opened and closed, but nothing came out.

Wicked tipped his hat to him and made to pass.

'Wait, Wicked, please, I want to talk to you,' Horrendo gasped. 'And to you... er, Mr Bird. What a wise companion you've found there, Wicked. Not that you yourself aren't wise in your own way, I'm sure, but...'

'A man is known by the company he keeps,' Doomsday declared, preening his feathers.

'Indeed,' Horrendo agreed. 'And talking of friends, Wicked, have you seen how swimmingly *your* friends have got on? They're busy and cheerful and not one incident of sword fighting or ear-slicing since we set foot here four months ago.'

'They're no friends of mine,' growled Wicked.

'Well, life at sea was full of hardships, it's true. But if you were to come to the tavern tonight and eat with the men, exchange a story or two, you'd see how quickly they'd embrace you!'

Wicked snorted. 'I was just on my way home now.'

'Oh, yes, of course, you'll want to freshen up before dinner, what was I thinking?' Horrendo slapped his forehead. 'Where are you staying? The B&B is rather good, even if I do say so myself. My parents run it, and we have fresh sheets on the beds every day, hot baths...'

'Will you just leave off, damn it! I'm making camp in the forest and that's the way I like it.'

Horrendo's face fell. 'Oh, well, I see. Yes, perhaps it takes time to get used to the comforts of home when you've been sleeping rough.' His face cleared. 'Jolly good then, well, tonight I'll just tell everyone that you're here visiting, and then tomorrow...'

Wicked almost jumped in alarm. 'Just hold your tongue!' he yelled. 'Why don't you mind your own business, you irritating little horsefly?' The silver flask nestled in his jacket pocket, and the day after tomorrow the Captain would be waiting in the boat. He felt afraid and angry and strange from his visit to the library this afternoon and he wanted this pest of a boy to stop nattering and let him think. Why didn't somebody swat the lad?

Horrendo stepped back. But squaring his jaw, he said, 'I understand that this is difficult for you, Wicked, since you behaved so very...well, badly, before. I mean – you tried to steal treasure belonging to the lads not once, but *twice*. Oh, for a while there, every time I thought of you I'd get a terrible red rash on my neck, and once I came out in hives.' He shuddered, then pulled himself up straight. 'But everyone should be allowed a second chance, don't you agree?'

Wicked was already taking one, in his own way, if only the little nuisance would let him be. Horrendo had no idea of the bind Wicked was in. No idea at all.

He took a deep breath. 'Just give me a few more days. Please. I...er...wanna learn how to live here on the island with you all, I do. But I can't face folk, not yet. I'm...whadyercallit...shy. Have to prepare myself. Give me three days, and I'll be ready.' That should give him time to deliver the potion and be back, with a wash and a haircut and maybe, a fresh start...

Horrendo gazed at him. He scratched his neck then bit his nails. His face scrunched up with indecision. 'Can't I just tell...one person? I mean, it's a huge responsibility, keeping a secret like this. Who knows what you might do. Not that I don't trust you or anything. But just look at your past—'

'I'm asking you real polite: keep a lock on your tongue. This is part of my second chance, right? You said everyone deserves one.'

Horrendo held his gaze a fraction longer, and then gave a deep sigh. 'All right. If you give me your word, I'll give you mine. Three days.' He turned to go, then turned back again. 'Goodbye Wicked, goodbye Mr ... er, Bird.'

'Guts for garters,' said Doomsday.

Horrendo hesitated, frowning from Wicked to Doomsday and back again, then slowly walked away.

~ * ~

All the way back to the cave, Wicked's stomach churned and rumbled. 'Feel like puking,' he told Doomsday, who was pecking at something in his ear. Doomsday clucked sympathetically. Wicked wanted to break into a run. If he ran fast enough, he thought, he might leave behind this nagging ache in his belly.

But nothing did any good. Run, dawdle, count coconuts or coins, he couldn't stop the bad feeling. In the cave he lay down in the hammock and closed his eyes. Then he got up and found his bag of loot, spreading it out on the ground. He built a pile of gold coins, ran a finger over rubies, sapphires, slipped a diamond ring on his pinkie. But still he didn't feel any better.

He paced the floor of the cave, not daring to venture out now in case Horrendo had followed. But no, the boy had given his word.

It was he, Wicked, who couldn't be trusted.

He leant against the cave wall, a sudden cramp paralysing him. Closing his eyes he saw a room filled with paintings and books and a long table strewn with brightly coloured beads. Seated at the table was a girl with dark hair. She was buttering toast, spreading jam. She put a piece on his plate. But she had her back to him. No matter how much he tried to make her, she wouldn't turn around.

It couldn't be *her*, could it, that grown woman in the library with the voice like music? The voice that had sung him a lullaby, told him stories, showed him how fascinating the world could be. Don't say her name, or she might disappear…

He had to go back tomorrow. He had to make sure.

chapter 28

He was dreaming. As first light filtered into the cave, a cold voice jeered, 'Why would she want to know *you*? After all you've done; after all you are about to do?'

Wicked sprang up in the hammock, and tipped out. He landed hard on the stone. The flask bounced from his jacket and the stopper came loose, rolling away as the precious liquid spread over the ground into a greasy pool.

He stared at the growing stain. Trapped in sleep, his mind wouldn't move.

It all happened so quickly. Too quickly. He was still rubbing his eyes, trying to climb out of dreams, when Doomsday hopped over to taste the new drink.

'*No!*' yelled Wicked.

Doomsday jumped in fright. He slipped then tried to right himself, but only flipped onto his back, slap in the middle of the puddle.

From the shadows Wicked watched as the bird's feathers faded from purple, to light blue, to a cloudy grey. Even as

Wicked sprang to his knees, Doomsday gave a strangled scream, and disappeared.

~ * ~

Wicked waited in the cave until the sun outside was blazing. And then he waited some more. Still on his knees, he was afraid to move. He knelt there, hardly breathing, watching the spot where he'd last seen Doomsday.

If he moved, even just a step, he might tread on him. Where did folk go when they became invisible?

He couldn't stay still any longer. Gingerly, he touched the spot where Doomsday had lain. Nothing. The ground was dry now, empty. He stood up, feeling all around the walls, into cracks and crevices. His fingers traced the rough stone until they bled. He ran from one side of the cave to the other but no soft little body met his.

Doomsday wasn't just invisible; he had vanished.

Wicked's eyes stung from tears. He'd forgotten what it felt like – he mustn't have cried, he thought, since he was ten years old. But it didn't bring Doomsday back.

He tried to remember everything he'd heard about the potion. Horrendo had said its effects didn't last – why, that dog's dinner was still hot when he reappeared!

Wicked tried to cheer himself with the thought.

He waited another hour.

Oh, but why did that fool Rascal have to go and invent such a thing? Horrendo had called it an 'invisible' potion, but Doomsday was nowhere, melted away like a snowflake in sunlight. Wicked felt his eyes fill again. Of all the things the world didn't need, a *vanishing* potion! Drat it all, why go inventing new ways to make people disappear when, in his experience, they did it regularly of their own accord?

He checked the flask. It was still more than half full. He squeezed the stopper back on tightly and put it in his pocket. Something else was in there – the folded square of paper. He'd forgotten the Captain's note. He didn't want to think about that herb. Especially *now* ...

But the Captain didn't give anything to anyone without a reason.

On the paper was a black ink drawing of a leaf. Long and narrow, its veins looped together like running writing. The lines didn't flow out from the centre to the sides, they ran from one end of the leaf to the other like ... words! The blood pounded in his head. He turned the paper sideways, reading from left to right:

Heed well, Wicked, your Captain's advice,
For if you fail in your task to bring me the spice
The folk of Devil Island will be crushed by my hand
And what you most treasure will turn into sand.

Wicked folded the paper back up. Then he folded it again. He had to take extra care because his hands were shaking. He tried once more but the square wouldn't bend any further.

He needed the paper to be so small that the words didn't exist.

'*He will always be my friend* ...' She'd said that.

He slipped the ball of paper back into his pocket. Fear lit a burning trail from his gut to his heart. He couldn't think. All he knew was that this, now, changed everything.

The Captain was not only *his* burden anymore.

He remembered the lilt of her voice. That dark hair, shiny as polished wood.

And he understood, finally, what he had done. The weight of it dropped like a cannonball inside him, breaking his heart. He knew now what he had to do. No more doubt, no more chances. He had to get the Captain what he wanted.

But he'd have one glimpse of her. He had to see her face. He'd take that one last thing for himself, and see, just for a moment, what might have been.

~ * ~

It was midday by the time he stepped onto the path. He didn't notice the spicy whiff of nutmeg on the air or the sandpiper's call. He was lost in his regrets, and his feet trudged on as if walking through clay.

He arrived in the square at lunchtime. It was noisy with people selling and buying, eating fried calamari and pineapple slices from paper cones. They stood in groups, chatting, or sitting on benches, their faces lifted to the sunshine. He wove through the crowd, his hat lowered, and made his way to the library. Through the window he saw only a few lasses curled on the cushions reading, and a lad – Hoodlum – was whispering to Hermy.

Outside, Wicked kicked a stone. How long would he have to wait? If she didn't come soon he'd lose his nerve. He couldn't stand it any longer. He dragged his hat further down over his eyes and sidled back into town.

The smell of food made his mouth water. He'd eaten nothing since the afternoon before. With a pang he remembered Horrendo's careful preparations in the galley, his encouragement just yesterday for Wicked's return. Horrendo had trusted him. *The only one who cared.* In his mind he watched the worried way the lad had bitten his nails, the way he kept trying. Wicked felt worse. But he couldn't change things now.

At the tavern, he bought a tin of biscuits and wolfed down the fish pie. It would be a jolly place if you weren't about to lose everything. He liked the sparkly fish nets draped from the windows and the swordfish skeleton hanging from the ceiling. The pie was magnificent.

'Enjoy that, did ye sir?'

Wicked whipped around at that gravelly voice. The man wiping his hands on an apron was … the First Mate!

'Arrumph … er … aye,' stammered Wicked.

'That's the day's special, what you consumed just now. Had the devil's own job gettin' the pastry right though. Did you find it light yet satisfying, crisp not chewy?'

'Aye,' said Wicked again, getting up from his stool.

The First Mate nodded. 'I'm standin' in for Chef today. I'm his assistant, like. Been a challenge, an' no mistake.' He rubbed his hands together, beaming. 'But I'm not doin' too badly from all reports.'

'In a hurry,' mumbled Wicked, and fled out the door.

~ * ~

He sped down to the harbour, to clear his head. Pacing the sand, he tried to make a plan. But he'd never made one before – or at least, never one that worked. Life usually just washed over him, and he took what was left on the shore.

A sudden thought made him tremble. Would she look very different? Would he recognise her? Even in his mind he still couldn't say her name. She was grown up now, like him. Only she sounded *more* grown up. A warm feeling like melting toffee trickled through him. Hadn't it been like that from her very first hello?

He checked the angle of the sun. He'd go now. This time he'd take off his hat before he popped up his head. He'd make sure they were all busy before he inched his eyes above the windowsill. He'd take one look, then when no one was about, come back for the Captain's precious herbs. That was the plan.

He hurried up the sand, tingles of excitement bursting inside him. It was crazy; he could never even talk to her now. But he couldn't help the fluttery wings of his breath rushing him along.

Something sharp underfoot made him stop suddenly. He bent down to pick up a cone-shaped shell. He turned it over in his palm. The blue-green whorls rising to the point at the top were like the tidal marks on the shore. It would be just the right size for Hermy. He put it in his pocket and turned to walk back up to town.

~ * ~

The pumpkin vine under the library window made a good hiding place. He was just in time. From the deep green shade he heard the children's chatter as they trooped back into the room. A boy called out 'Story time!' and another child told him to 'Shoosh', and to 'Get off her cushion!'

A hush fell then, as sudden as a curtain dropping, and with a lurch of the heart, Wicked knew that *she* had walked into the room. It was so tempting to stand up and see. But he sat on his hands. Not yet.

'Now, whereabouts in the story were we?' the Librarian said. 'Does anyone remember?'

'The wife wanted the husband to get more of that sweet lettuce for her,' a girl called out. 'But it grew in the neighbour's garden. The husband loved his wife—'

'Aye,' called out a boy, 'but she was sad because she wanted to have a baby, an' couldn't. The husband wanted to make her happy, so he crept into the garden next door to steal the lettuce. Only when he was diggin' it up, the neighbour appeared. She was a beautiful witch, and she told 'im off for trying to steal her lettuce. The husband said he was real sorry, like, but his beloved wife was cravin' it. He said she was goin' mad for that lettuce …'

'I'm like that with buttered crabs,' another lad put in. 'No matter how much dinner I ate, if crabs are on the menu, I gotta have 'em!'

'Sssh, let's get on with the story,' a girl said. 'Who cares about you and your buttered crabs?'

'Well, the witch's heart softened when she heard the husband's story …'

Wicked almost leapt up and jumped right through the window at the sound of that voice. But he clenched his sweaty hands into fists under his legs. He wouldn't get up to see yet. Not yet.

'And the witch said he could have the delicious salad from her garden if he promised her one thing.'

'What, what?' the children cried.

'He must deliver to her his firstborn child. She said she would care for it like a mother, and tend to its every need. But he and his wife would never, ever, see it again.'

A quiet fell over the room then, and even Wicked under the pumpkin vine felt a terrible dread. *Don't promise, don't promise what you can't deliver*, he wanted to cry.

'The husband could only think about his wife waiting at home for her special treat and so the next night the husband tiptoed into the garden. He began pulling up the lettuce but it cried out as if it were in pain.'

The stillness in the room lengthened. What was happening in there? Why did the lettuce scream? Without warning his legs unfolded and he stood up. He peeped through the window.

The Librarian was sitting on a cushion with her legs tucked beneath her. Her long dark braid hung down her back. He could just see the tilt of her chin. She had her finger in the book, keeping her place. But she wasn't looking at the book. She was facing the door. Someone was coming through, and with an 'Excuse me,' she got up to meet him. As she turned, Wicked saw her face.

It was enough.

It was her.

Once, during a dark storm at sea, he'd stared at a candle for minutes on end. It had seemed like the only light the world had to offer. Afterwards, when he closed his eyes, everything behind his lids was lit up around it. He'd tried to hang on to the light but slowly it had disappeared.

He thought of that now and a tremendous happiness fanned up from his feet to his head. *She* lit up the world like that. He wanted to shout out loud, dance, and leap as high as a tree. The world tilted for a moment, dazzling him. There was her heart-shaped face, the little point of her chin, dark eyes shining. Her cheeks were thinner than he remembered, her body rounder. But it was her.

As soon as she gets rid of that person at the door, he told himself, I'll speak to her. As soon as the class has gone. His fingers raked through his beard. Maybe I should go and wash, he thought feverishly. I could get a trim at the barber. He looked at his nails, broken and black. He imagined picking up her hand, holding it in his.

His legs felt weak, as if they were filled with water. No, what was he *thinking*? It was impossible now. He was pinned against the wall by a memory. She was sitting on the couch, reading to him. 'I'll teach you,' she said. 'We'll be all right.' She had made him tea and they'd sat out on the porch outside, watching the hill roll away beneath them as the shadows gathered at their feet. And he'd never said thank you. He'd been nine years old, and she wasn't much older, and he'd left before he could tell her.

But now her voice was closer. She was right on the other side of the wall.

Bring me that herb, the Captain whispered to him.

She was talking with the person who had entered the room. 'Tell me, what is it, Horrendo?'

Oh, he should have known. Did that confounded wretch *always* have to be underfoot? Wicked wanted to stomp on him. But the boy's next words turned his anger into alarm.

'I hate to interrupt your lesson like this, Miss, but could you tell me something? If a person knew someone had come to the island who might do harm, and then the person doesn't tell anyone, is that like a *lie*? I mean, should a person tell the truth always? And what if he's given his word to the someone

[238]

not to tell? His promise would be broken. So either way he's doing the wrong thing, is that right? Oh, I just can't seem to get things straight in my head.'

There was a groan, and an answering murmur, like a hug. Wicked ground his teeth.

'I liked it better, almost, when I was cursed,' Horrendo went on. 'At least back then, even if I'd wanted to, I didn't have to make decisions. The curse made them for me. But now, well, what would *you* do, do you think?'

There was silence for a moment. 'I'd consult the person who put the curse on me. From what I hear, she is wise, even if her methods are ... hard to fathom.'

'You mean Gretel?' Horrendo wailed again. 'She's gone away – she has some business on the Mainland. Why she had to go now of all times, I don't know! Curse the catfish, she makes me so ...' and he kicked something that fell over.

'Perhaps you'd better tell me about it then.'

Wicked slid down the wall. He could hardly bear to listen. He closed his eyes, but he couldn't close his ears. And sure enough, Horrendo recited the long list of Wicked's sins; it was like being at sea and hearing the judgement read before he walked the plank. All his stealing and lying, his allegiance to the Captain, his unhelpful attitude. It was all there, flapping and gasping like a trail of stinking fish, all at the feet of *her*.

'Wicked said he wanted to come back and live peacefully, but ... should we believe him? I was prepared to, but then Rascal told me this morning that the invisibility potion was missing. I mean, who else on the island would take it? I can't help thinking it was Wicked. You know, I shouldn't have trusted him, I'm hopeless that way, always believing people to be their best selves, instead of seeing the truth. But I wanted him to have another chance. He was kidnapped earlier than the rest of us. And on top of that, did you know, Miss, he'd lost his mother? I mean, *our* mothers were waiting for us when we got back. But not Wicked's.'

'His mother? How?'

'One day she just vanished into thin air. I heard it from Gretel. It must have been terrible.'

'Do you know where he lived before he was taken?'

'No. Somewhere far from here. But Miss, what do you think we should do?'

Wicked's heart was thundering in the silence. From inside the room he could hear Maria's voice burbling along, reading the story to the class, and outside, in the bushes, the crickets were starting.

'We'll have to go and find him,' the Librarian said. 'Before it's too late – for him and for…'

But Wicked didn't hear her last words. A deafening *BOOM!* tore the air, blasting out every other sound.

Wicked fell back in shock. He gasped as his elbow caught a sharp stone, the roar still shuddering through his body.

What *was* that? He watched a plume of smoke rise over the rooftops. Like the silence after lightning, the air stood still until a thunder of shouts filled the sky. Children came running out of the classrooms, and people streamed onto the grass and into the square.

'There's been an explosion!' a villager cried. 'The laboratory has vanished! And so has Rascal!'

chapter 29

Behind the pumpkin vine, Wicked tried to steady his breathing. His mind raced with questions. He'd thought Rascal had everything under control ... but then, how could anyone be in control in a world where dreams always turn into disaster?

A pang shot through him. He saw Rascal shivering up the ratlines. Spluttering his lungs out ... Well, he couldn't think about that now, or anything else. This was his chance, and he had to be quick.

He waited until the last child had gone. Then he stole into the empty library. He crept like a cat over the cushions, listening for the whisper of returning feet. Even though he had to hurry, he couldn't resist pulling off his old boots to feel the soft red rug under his toes.

Oh, he almost wept for the pleasure of it! As soft and springy as fresh-cut grass. He remembered Treasure's lawn so neatly kept at the front, the verandah at the back where he'd slept. 'He'll catch the breeze out there,' Honey had said. 'The poor child's exhausted.' He could see that house

[241]

clear as day. He hadn't remembered it like that for years.

The shelves of the library were bright with books and he trailed a finger over the spines. Pulling out one, he opened it and put his nose right into the middle. He took a great sniff and another. The smell of stories. *She* had touched these books. Most likely she'd read every one. He shut the book and put it back where it belonged.

But the *Reference* section ... that's what he had to find now.

He didn't know the word. So many books, hundreds, just like Horrendo had said. How would he find the right one?

His eyes swept the room. On the low table near the Librarian's desk perched Hermy's little house. Wicked lifted up the glass lid. Taking the shell out of his pocket, he placed it carefully at the back of the box.

He stood for a moment looking at Hermy snuggled up to a rock. Most of him was tucked into his shell, but a single leg drooped out. He was asleep, as Hoodlum had described. What a grand surprise the little hermit would get when he saw his new home.

Wicked took the quilled pen from the desk and dipped it into the little jar of ink. Then he hesitated. It had been so long since he'd read or written. *For Hermy*, he wrote finally. *From* ... he hesitated again. A blot of black ink dropped on the paper ... *W*, he finished. He slipped the note under the shell and replaced the lid.

As he looked up, he saw, to his left, a yellow sign above the bookshelves.

Fiction. And to his right, *Non Fiction*.

Wicked scratched his head. One was the opposite of the

other, but how did that help if you didn't know what animal it was in the first place? He grunted in frustration. Far-off children were calling, and then came deeper, warning voices.

Little clay sculptures of people and dogs, model ships and books dotted the room. There were more signs he didn't understand. A faint perfume hung in the air ... roses? Was it *her* scent? A vase of red roses on her desk ... *Think!* His eyes darted like fish in a bowl until there, straight ahead at the other end of the room, hanging on a door, was the sign he was looking for.

Through the little window, he saw a smaller room with shelves stacked with books, each as thick as his wrist. *Reference* books.

He tried the handle. Locked. He tried again. It wouldn't budge. Weren't those voices getting closer? There was no time to do anything else. He clenched the muscles in his arms. He took a step back. Then he sprang at the door, his shoulder shoving into the lock with all the weight of his body behind it.

The door crashed open.

Inside, he stood for a moment, nursing his arm. The door was still on its hinges. But his stomach churned. This felt worse than anything he'd ever done. He might have fought and lied and stolen but ... *this*. He eyed the shiny lacquered table where the Librarian must work, and her jar of freshly sharpened pencils.

He bit down the bile rising in his throat and ran his hand over the books. *Assyria ... Battle Ships ... Spain ...* Somewhere inside these thousands of pages was a packet of dried herbs.

Blusta's password. What was it?

His mind went blank.

He wriggled his feet. The fresh-lawn feel of the carpet. It came back to him.

The Librarian's mother! At the Wise Woman's garden, he'd thought he would never guess her name.

A strange jolt of joy lit up inside him. This awful thing he was doing...it was for Honey, and her daughter. It was the only way to protect them from the Captain.

His fingers flew along the titles now until he came to *Habitats, Heiroglyphics, Houses*...He went back and started again. He pulled out books and flung them open. He riffled through pages... Was Blusta wrong? Was there some other trick?

He tried to think, staring at these big thick books. They must be concerned with big thick topics. Was the subject of *honey* enough to fill one of these?

Well, what made honey? *Battles, Bridges*...he needed *Bees*.

The door at the other end of the library creaked open.

'But Miss, I just wanted to borrow that dragonfly book,' a voice called. 'The one what told us they have three pairs of legs—'

'All insects have that many, Mischief.'

'Aye, but that book has big drawings you can copy. In real life a dragonfly won't stay still long enough for you to draw its—'

Insects! Insects deserved a big thick book – there must be millions of the pesky creatures. Frantically Wicked searched along the shelves.

'Mischief, you mightn't have noticed the explosion,' the voice sounded exasperated, 'but we're all in a hurry now looking for Rascal.'

'Yeah, I seen him running out of the lab just a minute before it exploded. He was going this brilliant shade of blue, fading into a sort of woolly grey...'

Insects of the World...yes! *Ants, Aphids...Bees...* An envelope fell out at page eighty-nine. Quickly Wicked grabbed it and tore it open. A marvellous scent rose up, spicy, delicious, mouth-watering.

'Have you told anyone this, Mischief? Good, he wasn't in the lab when it went up! Come on, there's a meeting in the town square...Yes, yes, we'll get the book later...'

The Librarian's voice trailed off as if she had stepped outside. Wicked quickly tucked the envelope into a pouch at his belt and put the book back on its shelf. Then he tiptoed from the little room, closing the door behind him.

Silently, he inched out into the library, past the bookshelves and the sculptures, towards the front door. He was nearly there when he heard footsteps on the stone path outside.

In a single leap he made it to the desk and dived beneath it. And he might have stayed hidden too if the vase of red roses hadn't wobbled with the impact then toppled over, crashing onto its side. A stream of water dripped onto the floor.

The footsteps came slowly towards him and stopped only inches away.

He heard a sharp intake of breath. 'Is...is someone there?'

Wicked closed his eyes. He'd lingered too long. What a fool he was! A *weak* fool.

'Come out and show yourself!' The voice had gathered strength, but quavered at the last word.

Wicked ached at the sound of it. He couldn't bear her fear, or the thought that he had caused it.

He crawled out from under the desk. But as he straightened he bumped against the corner, stumbling onto his knees, dropping something from his pocket.

The Librarian lunged at it.

The silver flask.

He let her take it. What did it matter now?

Slowly, he stood up, watching her glance from the flask to his face, to his scruffy beard and ragged jacket, his fraying trousers and bare, dirty feet. He didn't flinch or wriggle. He stood, drinking her in, this last taste of his Treasure.

'What are you doing in my library?' she demanded.

Those same dark eyes, black-lashed, scared, curious. Always curious. He could see it in her mouth – not set but slightly open, as if searching even now for the right question. A wave of longing rose up inside him.

They stood together in the small room, eye to eye.

It was too much.

'Treasure,' he whispered. He held out his hand.

She frowned at it. 'Did you steal this?' She held up the flask, waving it at him before placing it beside her on the desk. With her eyes, she dared him to snatch it back.

He nodded. But the tongue in his mouth was locked.

'But *why*?' Her voice broke. 'Why would you do such a thing?'

He studied the rim of grime around his toenails.

'Will?'

His head jerked up.

'Is it you?'

'I haven't heard that name in a long time.' Her voice shook his heart, making the blood charge through his body. He took a shuddering breath.

'But how could you have changed so much? You used to be so ... tender.' Her eyes glittered. 'You were my best friend.'

'And you, mine.'

In the silence they could hear a child wailing, a mother calling.

'Then you were gone.'

He straightened his shoulders. 'You helped me, an' I never had a chance to thank you back on Thunder Island. You and Honey saved me. And now you'll be wishing you hadn't.'

Treasure drew up her chin. 'You've seen some terrible things, I know. Done them, too. But you can change your life, Will. If you want to make amends, you can come back to live and work here like the others. It's a good life, Will. We could get to know each other again, and imagine,' her mouth suddenly twitched, 'you could even have a bath!'

He smiled. Then he looked down at his hands. 'I'm not like the other men. A bath won't get me clean. You don't know it all. I ... wouldn't fit in.'

'Why do you say that? It's a wicked crime to have stolen this potion – but if you say you're sorry, if you show how truly willing you are to do better, the village will forgive you. *I* will forgive you.'

He held her gaze until he couldn't bear it anymore.

What you treasure most will be turned to sand.

He set his jaw. 'You've got your potion, an' I've said my

thanks. What more do you want?' His voice was low and harsh. 'The Captain was right – you women, you're never satisfied. I've spent too long at sea to live a landlubber's life. My notion of treasure is different now.' And he turned on his heel, stopping only to pick up his boots as he strode out the door.

~ * ~

If he'd looked back, just a moment later, he'd have seen the hurt on her face. He'd have seen those stricken eyes, her mouth quivering in bewilderment before setting into a new bitter line. He'd have seen her fling the flask from the desk, then sink to the floor.

She stayed there, huddled, for a long time. When she was empty of tears, she sat up on her knees. Retrieving the flask, she shook it, relieved at the weight of liquid still inside. Then she spied something else on the carpet, just an inch away.

It was a tightly folded piece of paper. She opened it out. At first she thought the drawing was one of Mischief's sketches, with its remarkable detail. She wondered why he'd thrown away such a masterly drawing.

But then, smoothing down the creases, she saw that the remarkable detail wasn't an intricate pattern of veins in a leaf, but words.

And she began to read.

chapter 30

It wasn't until the caves were in sight that Wicked stopped running. He leant against a tree, his chest heaving. Against his face the late afternoon breeze blew cool and fragrant. Roses... where? Would he always, for every minute of his life, be imagining her?

There was no Doomsday to tell. No loony bird for comfort. He had an overpowering urge to shout her name. 'Damn and blast,' he cried instead.

There was nothing for it but to pick up his stride and walk on. But an old anger crept in. 'Bloomin' *everything!*' he muttered. 'Bloomin' village, bloomin' island, bloomin' potion, bloomin' Rascal!'

Aye, Rascal might have brains, and, he had to admit, plenty of pluck, but that bug-eyed boy was a damn fool. Look at all the trouble he'd caused, messing around with dangerous things! Didn't Horrendo tell the lad to stop? Why hadn't Rascal listened to the friend who'd sat up nights and knitted *mittens* for him?

As Wicked tore past, he'd seen the villagers hurrying into the square. People were calling out – 'No one else missing!' 'That smoke smells like boiled cabbage!' 'Didn't I always say that lab was trouble?' but still there was no sign of Rascal or what he'd been working on.

Wicked marched through the forest, snapping off branches, swiping at leaves. But then, struck by a thought, he stopped. If Rascal was no longer around – if he was gone for good – there'd be no hope for Doomsday, either.

With a stone in his stomach, Wicked descended into the cave. Slowly, he crawled through the dark tunnel. As he neared the last stretch, he went even slower. As long as he didn't arrive, as long as he didn't know the answer, he could still ponder the question. Would Doomsday be there, waiting for him?

~ * ~

He knew by the silence. Even before he shone the lamp around the walls, into every hollow and dip, he knew it. How empty the cave was without Doomsday. How empty everything felt. He wouldn't spend another night here; no, not another minute.

He tracked along the rocks, wading through pools, avoiding sharp shells and barnacles. All he wanted was to make the time pass until first light. He couldn't wait for this deal to be done, and yet he dreaded it like death.

Down at the shore he took out the envelope from his pouch and shook the dried herb into the empty biscuit tin he'd bought at the tavern. Then he tied it to his belt. He ran his finger over the edges. Airtight, it should hold against the sea. He gave the knot at his belt a final tug and felt his anger ebb away like the tide, leaving a nugget of satisfaction at a decision well made. It was a new feeling. A good feeling.

Soon the precious herb would be in the Captain's hands. And Treasure would be safe from harm.

~ * ~

Only a faint blush of rose lit the sea when the jolly-boat glided in. The air was grey with dawn, and the shadows in the rock pools were inky. Out past the furthest finger of land, the boat dropped anchor.

Wicked stood on the point and watched. With every second the sky grew lighter. Pink lifted into lemon into pearly blue. A dark figure stood up in the boat. Wicked narrowed his eyes to slits.

The figure giving the signal was heavy, not tall like the Captain. Unfamiliar. Seated behind him was the silhouette of another. Wicked strained his eyes. This wasn't the Captain, either.

Wicked swallowed. He'd reckoned on the Captain being there. The jolly-boat belonged to a bigger ship, most likely, manned by the rest of the Captain's new crew. The old devil hadn't even bothered to come himself, so sure was he of his willing slave.

Wicked looked back at the island. Such a morning, the air like crystal. Perhaps it would be his last.

He remembered racing down to the mangroves on mornings like this. The sky had streamed bright above the treetops. If he'd stretched high enough, he could have touched it. So many wonders he'd seen from those trees. Flowers and birds and the currents in the river. But back then, his mother had always been there to tell. He hadn't heard her voice in a long time.

He drew in a lungful of air. No use thinking about that now. Or *her*, or Horrendo or Rascal or Doomsday.

A shout came roiling out from across the water. The figure in the boat lifted his arm high, beckoning with an angry jerk of his fist.

It was time to go. It was like dying.

Oh, but just a moment more.

Remember the way the braid fell down her back? The light in her eyes?

No, it hurt too much.

Wicked took off, sprinting down to the sand.

He stripped off his jacket and shirt. His hands trembled. *Crushed,* he heard the Captain whisper. Wicked stood bare to the waist, swaying on the shore. He looked at the ragged bundle of belongings. Something was missing.

Idiot – he'd forgotten his loot! He gave a wild laugh. Not a gold coin to his name.

There was still time.

No. None of that mattered anymore. He'd lost the only treasure he'd ever wanted. He smiled grimly. A first-class pirate indeed. How the Captain would laugh.

He waded into the shallows. As the water rose up to his chest he dived under and began to swim. He remembered the first time he'd done this, and the joy. At least he'd had that. He ducked under the next wave, grateful for the cool slide of water on his skin, the breeze fresh on his face as he surfaced.

As he neared the jolly-boat, the seated man sprang up clumsily, and the boat rocked wildly.

'Sit down, you fathead!' the heavy man shouted at the other.

'You want to tip us over? The Captain *said* you were dumb. Thicker than a wooden plank. No wonder 'e named me First Mate and you Box-Brain.'

Treading water in the boat's shadow, Wicked caught Box-Brain's mortified smirk. He knew how the man felt. Not like a man anymore. That was what the Captain did to you.

Wicked's breath quickened. These men were dangerous. They had nothing left to lose. And that sort were the worst.

The First Mate put out his hand to haul Wicked up. The side was steep and Wicked clambered in, sprawling on his back. A boot clamped his chest. The man stared down at him, a mean smile on his lips, a callused thumb resting idly on the sword at his side.

'Have you got what the Captain ordered?' he growled.

'Let me up and I'll tell you,' he gasped.

'Don't do it,' said Box-Brain. 'He'll take a swing at you.'

'I'd listen to a jellyfish before I listened to you,' spat the First Mate, and took his foot off Wicked's chest.

Wicked considered giving the man a good kick to the belly to topple him. But a better idea was forming. *If you always do what you always did, you will always get what you always got.*

As he sat up, the First Mate grabbed his hands behind his back.

'Where's the goods then?' the man said.

'Told the Captain I'd hand it over myself.'

'Well, he ain't 'ere.'

'Where is he then?'

The First Mate waved at the horizon. 'Waitin' back at the ship with the rest of the crew. Think he'd bother to come himself?'

'So you're doin' his dirty work?'

The First Mate snorted. 'I'm carryin' out a very important job. Them plants is gunna make us rich. The Captain wouldn't want just anyone to help 'im. I'm his First Mate, see.'

Wicked grunted. 'An' I was his special look-out. I climbed those ratlines like magic. He valued me above other men, kept the best fish for my dinner, gave me the pick of the loot.'

'Oh aye, an' I'm yer fairy godmother.'

'It's the truth I'm telling you. An' now I'm just a slave doing his master's bidding. See how quick he changes favour?' Wicked twisted around to face the man. 'On Devil Island there's pirates doing an honest day's work and getting paid for it. There's delicious food and friends and music and women. It's a life for a man. Why would you choose to be the Captain's slave when you could be free?'

There was a small silence. Wicked felt the sweaty hold around his wrists loosen.

'Them pirates you're talkin' about,' the First Mate began. 'Were they once the Captain's men?'

'Aye,' said Wicked, straightening. 'An' they united against him.'

There was an awed hush.

'Wouldn't you rather be like them,' Wicked went on slyly, 'living the good life?'

'We could ask *you* the same question an' all,' Box-Brain suddenly piped up. 'Seems you were free as a bird back on that island. So what are ye doin' here then?'

Wicked's face darkened. 'I was stupid. Chose the wrong path and can't change it now. But you can. Think about it. You could be fillin' your bellies with fish pie, dancin' the hornpipe, sleepin' in a duck-feathered bed.'

'We been pirates all our lives,' mused the First Mate. 'We seen our fair share of devilish Captains, but I 'ave to say this one...'

'Is the worst,' said Box-Brain. 'I wish I hadn't signed up as his swab. But now, well, ye wouldn't wanna cross him.'

'Aye,' agreed the First Mate. 'There's somethin'...' He stopped, turning to Wicked with a frown. 'Why are ye tellin' us all this then?'

Wicked shrugged. 'Maybe I feel like givin' a bit of friendly advice. Or maybe I think we could overthrow the Captain. If we band together, we might have a chance. And the people of Devil Island would reward you.'

The First Mate guffawed. 'An' I believe in leprechauns!'

'I told you,' Wicked went on. 'It's happened before. Mutiny. Just think of those pirates back on Devil Island – all happy as larks.'

The First Mate gazed beyond the boat to the shore where a frill of waves sparkled in the morning light. His eyes had a faraway look as he imagined tucking into a dish of fish pie, a soft bed that didn't sag beneath him.

Wicked held his breath.

And then, the First Mate blinked. His eyes widened with surprise, just for a second, but Wicked followed the man's narrowed gaze. And what he saw turned his bowels to water.

There, past the rocky inlet and deep caves, standing straight-backed on the cliffs of Devil Island, was the distinct figure of the Captain.

chapter 31

Without another word, Wicked turned and dived overboard.

…what you treasure most…

He took stroke after stroke without a breath. He swam faster than he ever had in his life. He didn't wonder what the Captain was doing on the island or why the treacherous devil had changed their plan. He just knew he had to be stopped.

As Wicked ran dripping from the water, through broken barnacles and spiky rocks, his feet felt nothing. Only his heart pounded inside him, his thoughts thrumming to the beat, *no, no, no!*

He raced into his cave and entered the tunnel. Feeling his way in the dark, his breathing was loud in the close, damp silence. As the path rose and forked, he ran headfirst into a wall and stumbled to the ground, reeling, stars gathering behind his eyes. But he didn't stop.

He climbed up and out onto the headland. His left eye was filled with blood but even when he'd cleared it, he couldn't see the Captain. Desperately he traced the descent from the cliff, the sloping scrubland beneath it.

There. Striding through the bushes, the dark, mean figure.

Wicked hurtled down, falling, rolling. 'Captain!' he shouted. 'Wait!'

The Captain didn't stop. He was near enough to hear, Wicked was certain, but his step didn't falter as he took the turn to the right, the path that led to the village.

'Captain, I've got what you want! Why didn't you wait for me? Come back and we'll haul anchor!'

The Captain's pace slowed. He swung around to face Wicked. 'You giving me orders again, lad? That won't get you very far. Not with the ruler of the Cannonball Seas.'

'But I have the herb!'

'There are things more valuable.'

His tone had turned mild, almost conversational. 'The hearts and minds of men, Wicked. That's what I want. That's where the power comes from.' He opened his arms wide, taking in the island, the sea. 'A willing slave yields twice as much.'

'But we had a deal. I gave you my word and you...'

'Haven't you learnt anything, boy? Promises,' the Captain spat the word as if it were dirty. 'I told you not to believe in them.' He stared hard at Wicked across the distance. 'And I told you not to speak to anyone. Have you obeyed me?'

Wicked said nothing.

The Captain smiled. 'I thought so.' He turned back to face the path.

'Where are you going? What do you want?'

Over his shoulder the Captain called, 'I demand loyal

service for the long term, Wicked. I'm making sure you oblige. I've put a lot of effort into your education but I see your mind is weak and still unformed.' He stopped, and turned to face Wicked. 'Your … attachment to that girl needs to be severed.'

'No!'

'You'll thank me one day, lad. You don't know it yet but you'll be betrayed again. Your mother was only the first. You are just like I was but for me, all the way along, there was no one to turn to. For you it's different. You have your Captain to follow.' He pointed to the road ahead. 'And I will always be a step ahead of you.'

'That's right, sir,' Wicked said quickly. 'And I'm willing to set sail now like we said. Why bother with those stupid villagers? I don't care about them – or her, anymore. I learnt my lesson.'

'Ah, Wicked, your actions show otherwise. I demand complete commitment. How can I be sure of that, with a silly girl still around?'

'But no, I am, I will be! You'll see, let's go, I'm ready!'

The Captain gave a knowing smile, and shook his head. Then he started off again at a quick pace up the path.

As Wicked watched the distance growing between them, he understood no words would sway him. He clenched his fists, knowing they, too, would be useless. The Captain was like the stone wall he had just run into. And now he was making for Treasure.

He had to reach her first. Hide her. Warn her.

Ahead, the rope-bridge swung high above the river. The

hand ropes were frayed and dipped low, and a few of the slats were loose. He couldn't be sure of all the planks; only his feet and his weight would find out which parts were true.

He looked down at the grey-green water below and imagined the long drop through emptiness. The smack against the rocks would be killing.

As he stepped out onto the bridge, his stomach heaved. He tried to choke down his fear. Where was his centre? He couldn't feel it. Keep moving, that was it, wasn't it? But his legs were shaking – they used to be sure as tree trunks, there for him always like the earth, the rope, his mother. Look ahead...

He was almost halfway when the slat beneath his foot broke. As he slid through the bridge his fingers grabbed at the rope and he swung wildly in the air.

He flapped like a fish on a line. The rope burnt his palms. The faraway rocks spiking up through the water flooded him with panic; he could see his body falling through space, landing on stone, pierced through.

One hand began to slip.

'Don't look down!' A voice rang out from across the ravine.

Wicked twisted to see the path winding up into the forest. He glimpsed only bush and further back, boulders, framing the sandy track. Was it her, or just the voice in his head?

'If you can reach the next plank and haul yourself up, it'll take your weight.'

'Where are you, you wretched girl?' the Captain thundered. 'When I get my hands on you...'

'You'll never get me, I know every inch of this island. And that's a fact.'

He almost laughed. The girl with the notebook and a hundred things to say. The girl who'd found him when he was lost. Across all the years, all the loss and longing, the distance and the silence of the sea. She was here. Now. For him.

'See what that wench made you do? You're going to die in that river. And for what? Stupid boy!'

Hand over hand, he covered the distance to the next slat and swung himself up until he was lying on his stomach. But when he lifted his head and saw what was ahead, his courage leaked away. Fear snatched his breath, clamped his guts. It made him forget everything.

'Will, one foot in front of the other!'

Now her voice came from a different direction.

'Find your balance inside. Put your hand on your stomach, just like you taught me on Thunder Island.'

Treasure. He'd known her back when he'd known himself and suddenly, he knew what to do.

Will stood up. He took one careful step and held his breath. Good. He took another. And then, oh, he was walking! He didn't need the hand rope, he held his arms out straight, his centre a solid ball in his belly. Lifting his gaze to the end of the bridge, he focused on the prize.

Only fifteen, ten steps to go. Eyes steady on the base of the fig tree at the finish.

A figure appeared beside it, leaning casually against its knotty trunk. The Captain waited, with a coil of rope.

His step wavered.

The Captain tensed, watching.

Will pretended to waver again. Treasure had a chance if he kept hold of the Captain's attention. He hoped she was running now, back to the village.

He tried to slow his progress. Five, four more steps. There was no more calling out from Treasure. Even the breeze was still.

As he stepped onto the ground, the Captain's heavy rope caught him around his ribs. It tightened into a hold that made breathing hard. He didn't struggle. He stood inside it, quiet and still.

'Stubborn as a toad you are,' spat the Captain. 'But you're where you belong now.'

'Aye,' agreed Wicked. But his heart felt as if it had stopped beating.

'You see?' The Captain waited. 'Well, what have you got to say for yourself? What were you trying to do?'

Wicked's breath was loud in the quiet.

'You nearly killed yourself up there, and where did that leave you? Nowhere. Same place your mother left you.'

'Your mother didn't abandon you, Will. She was stolen, just like you.'

Treasure!

'Lying strumpet, I'll be coming back for you,' the Captain roared. He pulled at Will's ropes, dragging him back across the cliff.

'The man who came to chop wood. He was from the circus on the Mainland.' Treasure's voice followed them, but she was nowhere to be seen. 'Your mother tried to outrun him but he chased her downriver, all the way to the Cannonball Sea.

[261]

He caught her and took her away in his boat, and made her work for the Big Top. And you know who sent him to fetch her?'

'Bilge!' cried the Captain. 'You're a filthy baggage—'

'The Captain, Will. It was *he* who wanted her. He needed a star to draw the crowds and he fancied her, too. He was wild about her – met her back when your father did, but she didn't want him. So when your father died, he took her and made her work in his circus. Then he took the person most precious to her. But she escaped, Will, and sailed the seas to look for you. She even joined the pirates!'

'What? The Bonny Lasses?'

'Yes!'

'Codswallop, you foul-mouthed wench,' the Captain shouted. 'When I catch you, you'll wish you'd never been—'

'You might have found each other if the fires hadn't started. She was wounded, so badly…'

'Oh what balderdash! What does this wench want from you, a cut of your gold? You might want to believe her waffle, Wicked, but how can you trust her? I am the one who's saved your hide, time after time. The rest is just stories.'

A shudder ran through Will like lightning through a tree.

'Let the woman alone now,' he said quietly. 'I will be your slave.' His eyes were on fire. 'But know this, Captain. I will never be your *willing* slave. You are a monster. You suck the sweetness out of every good thing. You're like winter or disease or death, you wither… everything. Do what you like, you are dead to me.'

The Captain paled. His mouth opened, but no words came out.

'Will, catch!'

It must have been pure instinct, he thought later, but Will flung out his hand as Treasure threw an object from the thick of the bushes, his fingers closing over something square and silver. He flicked off the stopper, and hurled the flask at the Captain.

A gush of purple liquid shot out and drenched the Captain's face. His eyes widened in surprise then shut tight as the liquid streamed down his neck and torso, onto his legs, pooling into his boots.

Like a blob of paint splashed with water, the Captain's colours washed out. Fading towards the edges, he became an outline, a pencil drawing, until even that was rubbed out and the patch of sandy track where he once stood was rinsed clean. Only a silver belt buckle escaped, hovering bizarrely in the air. A heartbeat later, it fell *clunk* to the ground.

Will and Treasure stared at the empty space. The sky was silent. A curtain of air shifted, quaked, then twitched back into place with a final sigh.

Treasure put out her hand and Will took it in his and they stood like that, together, gazing in awe at the sunlit ocean where once there had been the shadow of the Captain.

chapter 32

As Will and Treasure made their way into the village, a crowd was gathering in the square. Villagers and pirates stood in huddles, shading their eyes, peering through the trees that fringed the market. Behind them, tourists looked on in interest. 'Is royalty visiting?' asked a man at the homewares stall.

'There she is!' shouted Horrendo, pointing. 'See, didn't I tell you we'd be all right? No need to worry. She's here, with ... oh!' He stopped suddenly.

Treasure kept hold of Will's hand, and as they stepped into the square, she held it up for all to see.

'We won,' she cried. 'The Captain's vanished,' and a cheer went up that deafened the gulls.

She pulled Will forward, but he hung back. His eyes were searching the crowd. When he saw Horrendo, hovering on one foot, he told Treasure, 'There's something I gotta do. Will you wait for me?'

Treasure grinned. 'What, another ten years? I'll be an old lady by then!'

Will hurried through the crowd. 'Horrendo! I have something for you.'

Horrendo lifted his head. 'Your name is Will, is that right?'

Will nodded.

'Pleased to ... er, meet you,' Horrendo said, and they both smiled.

'I took something that belongs to you.' Will put the biscuit tin of herbs into Horrendo's hands. 'I'm sorry for stealin' this, and for putting the island in such danger. All those things you said about me, back when we first arrived – well, they were all true. I've been a scoundrel and a blaggard. What can I do to put it right?'

'Such a good question! Sometimes asking the right question is more important than the answer.' Horrendo beamed broadly at him. 'The Wise Woman told us that when it was most important, you would act from love and kindness. She said you might have stolen the herb, but you wouldn't let the Captain have your heart. And that is what would save you – and us.'

'But how did she know?'

Horrendo sighed. 'I asked her once if she could see into the future, and she said, "Perhaps I see what folk are capable of, not just what they do."'

The two stood together, thinking.

'I wish I hadn't taken so long to understand things,' Will said slowly.

Horrendo nodded. 'Folk have to find their own way, in their own time. Sometimes there's nothing to be done until the person is ready. I thought I had to fix everything myself, and it was such a burden. Always worrying if every little thing wasn't perfect. But you made me see I can't change everyone – I'd have to use magic to do that and *ugh*, I've had enough of curses.'

'Speaking of magic…' Will sucked his cheek. 'Has Rascal come back, or … Doomsday?'

'Who?'

'The parrot. I…'

'Oh, yes, he's here. Or rather, he went with Rascal on an errand.'

Horrendo looked cagey, Will thought, which was an unusual expression for him.

'What kind of errand?'

'Oh you'll see soon enough.' Horrendo seemed to struggle with himself. 'It's not my place to meddle. Or push things along.' He bit his lip. 'Although of course we all need a little help sometimes, a bit of advice or reassurance. It's not wrong to ask for that, or to give it!'

At that moment, as if Treasure couldn't bear to have him out of her sight any longer, she came running towards Will. Her face was shining in the sunlight, her braid bouncing.

Will stretched out his arms and Treasure ran right into them.

~ * ~

At the tavern that night there was such a roar of voices that sometimes Will had to clap his hands over his ears. He wondered if he'd ever get used to it. The lonely quiet of the caves, Turtle Island, the crow's nest at sea – it still called to him. For a moment, sitting at the table with the sound washing over him, he wanted to obey its call. He could crawl back into the silence like diving under a wave, and make the world stop.

Then he looked at Treasure beside him. She was telling him

about a strange bitter fruit on the Mainland, and the face she made when she described the taste caused him to laugh out loud. *I never want you to stop telling me*, he thought. *I want to hear about every single place you've ever visited. And I want to go there with you.*

But Dogfish had risen to his feet. 'Good evenin', all. Ain't we celebratin' a great victory here tonight? Folk said the Captain was gone for good when he dropped off the edge of the world. But *I* always said the old devil would come back, I said—'

'Somebody shut him up!' shouted Squid.

Dogfish waved his hand. 'Ye all might jeer and jest, but didn't I always say...'

'*That man ain't human*,' voices chorused all around the tavern.

'An' we still don't know when he's gunna return from his ... er, retirement,' called out Goose.

'Aye,' everyone agreed, their faces turning to Gretel.

The Wise Woman stroked the cat on her lap. 'A spell of banishment will do wonders for the Captain's outlook. It's what he feared and loathed most. He hates to be invisible.' She sighed, and with a strange knowing look, she added, 'And he hates to lose. It quite crushes him.'

People were quiet as they waited for more.

'Be ready, for one day he will gather his strength and return.' Gretel looked down at her lap. 'But not in the form you know him. Remain united, and he won't be a threat to this island.'

'Well, that's all right then 'cause whatever faces us in the future,' Dogfish went on, 'we'll stand together an' defeat the evil blighter.'

'Let's give a cheer for Devil Island!' said Pandemonium. She led the whistles and shouts and when they subsided, she went on. 'This is the best place to raise nippers in all the Cannonball Seas. So ain't it time to think of another name for our home? Any ideas, put 'em in the Suggestion Box by the door.'

'Aye,' cried Squid from the end of the table. 'A snappy name could be good for business. What about "Magic Island" or "Delicious Delights"?'

'An' while we're celebratin',' Dogfish cut in, 'let's congratulate our chef, Horrendo, for the finest meal he's ever put before us.' He hauled Horrendo to his feet.

'Speech! Speech!' the crowd called.

Horrendo blushed. Biting his lip, he said, 'Well, actually, this time, I have to admit, I did do it all myself.'

'Steady on, *I* helped ye, remember?' the First Mate put in. 'I'm yer insistent!'

'Oh yes, indeed, you were a marvellous assistant,' Horrendo quickly agreed.

'I think what Horrendo is trying to say is that for the first time he cooked without using the magic ingredient.' Gretel smiled at him and her cat yawned, showing a long pink tongue. 'You know, Will did you a favour, Horrendo, by stealing that herb. You've proved your natural talent and reaped the rewards of your hard work.'

As folk went back to chatting over dessert, Will's eyes kept returning to Gretel. Finally she turned to him. 'Is there something you'd like to say to me?'

Will scowled. He tried to turn it into a smile, but his mouth kept turning down. 'I have to ask you something. How much heartache can you prevent? I mean, do you just let tragedy happen, and not lift a finger?'

Horrendo leant over and took Will's hand. 'Ssh, Will,' he whispered. 'That's a bit rude. She's a Wise Woman.'

'Aye, and doesn't a Wise Woman have the power to stop bad things happening?' said Will. 'Miss Gretel, what about Thunder Island? What about all those years at sea?'

Gretel's face stayed as cloudless as always. But her eyes shone brighter. 'Sadly, I don't possess the power that you imagine, Will. Those shoes I gave you were meant to keep you safe. But your love for your mother turned out to be greater than your fear, and you strayed into harm's way.' She looked away, through the windows, at the starlit sky. 'That was something I didn't know. Something new I learned, that I could never have foreseen.'

Will was quiet for a moment. He gazed into her eyes, and saw a deep sorrow. 'Thank you, then,' he said gently. He wanted to ask if he would ever see his mother, but something in her face stopped him, and the words died in his throat.

He looked around the room, at the living list of people he'd known ever since he'd been grown. There was Buzzard running his hand over the table, admiring its lacquered finish, and Squid and Goose arguing over the last piece of pie. Bombastic was having an arm wrestle with Rowdy, and Hoodlum had Hermy in the glass box on his lap. Even the two pirates from the jolly-boat were swilling Coconut Delight. As Will looked at the men he felt a wave of sympathy. In their bewildered faces, he saw himself just a short while ago. He knew their fear, their old angers and helplessness. Because now he knew himself.

Will nodded at them, and they raised their glasses to him. At the back of the room, perched on a stool, Mischief was drawing it all, a piece of charcoal in his hand and an absorbed expression on his face.

Will was glad they were all safe. But there was one boy missing. Where was Rascal?

An accordion started up, and Pandemonium took Dogfish's hand, whirling him into the centre of the room. Will looked to the small podium at the front where the music was playing. The accordion was so tall and wide, and the boy playing it so slight that Will had to stand up to see who it was. *Rip!* Those knuckles he used to crack when he was nervous flew over the keys, his foot tapping like a wild thing. Funny, the lad's hands didn't look nervous anymore, they looked as if they knew exactly what they were doing, just like Will's feet on the tightrope all those years ago.

Will grinned and started to sway to the music.

'Come on then,' said Treasure, leaping up. 'I love this tune!'

'Oh, I haven't danced for … I can't remember,' stammered Will. He stayed glued to the seat, reddening in the candlelight.

'You know, when I travelled to the Flamingo Islands, I saw a new dance,' said Treasure. She stood up. 'I've been waiting to try it. See, you go like this, it's very simple.' And she pulled him up.

But just as they were on their feet, the music stopped. Voices faded and an eerie hush crept over the room.

In the doorway, holding a flaming torch, stood Rascal. The cuffs of his pants were dripping, as if he'd just stepped off a boat and waded to shore. He grinned at the crowd and made a sweeping bow, then stood aside to let a woman with a parrot perched on her shoulder pass before him.

Whispers whirred through the air. 'Who is it? Who's that?'

The woman made her way through the room, looking neither left nor right. Although her pace was slowed by a limp, she glided through the crowd like a ship through the sea. Her chin was held high, the candlelight leaping in her eyes. Below the skirts of her velvet dress, her wooden leg tapped out a rhythm. *Tap* step *tap* step *tap*. She never turned to answer a query or a smile. Her eyes were fixed on one person, and she wouldn't stop until she'd reached him.

To Will, watching her progress across the room, she seemed like a dream. Her face had lit his lonely nights at sea, her words had whispered to him, her hand had held his. And he had lost her somehow. She'd stopped living inside him and a silence had closed over.

She came to a stop before him. He had been a boy when he'd seen her last. And now he was a man. He looked into her face. Older now, a little more lined, with grey streaks through her wild red hair, she was still his mother.

'All's well that ends well,' said Doomsday on her shoulder.

But Wanda Wetherto shook her head, and smiled at her son. 'This is just our beginning.'

epilogue

In the years that followed, Devil Island kept its name. Although there were many new suggestions, folk took a vote and decided they should not forget their history. As Doomsday reminded them, 'Those who cannot remember the past are condemned to repeat it.' And nobody wanted that.

Will set up a swimming school and spent his days down on the beach doing what he loved best. 'It'll be fun,' he told the children who were reluctant at first, 'and it may just save your life.' He was a good teacher and soon every child on the island could do the backstroke. His mother came to live nearby and when, much later, Will and Treasure had children, Wanda helped look after them.

She loved being a grandma and playing hide-and-seek with the youngsters (although she never stayed hidden for long), and when they grew older she taught them juggling and tightrope walking and magic tricks. When the other children saw how much fun they were having, they asked for lessons too. 'Well, I don't see why not,' said Mrs Wetherto, who liked to impart the skills she'd acquired in the world, even if she could no longer perform them herself. Will assisted on his mornings off, and with his share of the treasure he built a gymnasium with rope ladders to climb and trapezes to swing from.

The family went often to visit Honey on Thunder Island and the book in the library that was borrowed most, *Travels with Treasure*, was written right there on the verandah overlooking the hills, where all those years before Will had slung his hammock. Treasure continued to travel and write about her adventures all her life, and if her books needed maps or illustrations, Mischief was there to do a fine job.

The school expanded with a flood of new students from far away, and soon you could hear so many different languages in the square that you'd swear you were at the centre of the world. Rascal took to practically living at the new science laboratory (even though his mother worried about explosions) and invented a cure for warts. And with help from Blusta and her blossoming garden, Horrendo cooked up a recipe for pecan pie so sublime that a tyrant from the Mainland decided to stop making war and start a bakery instead.

As for the Captain, there was no news for a long time. Then a scrap of talk floated in with a French tourist... 'The strangest thing, *mon dieu*, a pirate ship looming up in the moonlight... no crew except one solitary figure. We froze in horror... but it glided past like a ghost, and vanished into the mist. Trick of the light, maybe, but it turned us all cold.'

When nothing more was heard – and as Dogfish remarked, 'No light trick never killed no one' – the islanders decided to ignore the idle fancies conjured by a moon on water.

And so it was generally agreed throughout the Cannonball Seas that the rules of funambulism could be applied to most things in daily life. If folk went about their business, checking their centre, keeping their balance and putting one foot in front of the other, they found that the joy of their journey, in most cases, became their prize.

Acknowledgements

Many thanks to Caribbean Kathy, who introduced me to hermit crabs, hummingbirds, and the gastronomic delights and nature of the islands.

Grateful thanks also to Kim Gamble for his valuable insights into what is needed to survive on a desert island, having once been stranded himself in just such a situation with only a fishing spear and a box of matches. (Kim was luckily rescued by a cruise ship and a friendly waitress, but that's another story.)

My gratitude, too, to Morris Gleitzman, who gave me excellent advice on structure, to Marie Claire for her reading and support, and to my mother Barbara, who was the first to read my manuscript, as always, and provide excellent feedback, creative suggestions and essential encouragement.

I am grateful, too, to Sue Flockhart for her challenging editorial analysis, and to Kate Whitfield for her unique understanding of magical concepts, her close attention to detail and structure, and her heartfelt enthusiasm just when I needed it.

About the author

Anna Fienberg is the author of many popular and award-winning books for children of all ages, including the Tashi series, *Figaro and Rumba, Louis Beside Himself, Number 8, The Witch in the Lake* and *Horrendo's Curse*, which was an Honour Book in the 2003 CBCA awards.

Anna began writing stories when she was only eight years old. She says: 'I've always had a passion for words. I used to collect them, like some people collect stamps. Certain words gave me a special, billionaire feeling, and when uttered, seemed to have a magical effect.' She also gets her ideas from her dreams, people she meets and snatches of overheard conversation.

Anna was once Editor of School magazine, where she read over a thousand books a year. She wrote plays and stories for the magazine, and then began writing her own stories. She has written picture books, short stories, junior novels, and fiction for young adults.

Horrendo's Curse

Anna Fienberg pictures by Kim Gamble

Horrendo's Curse

Honour Book, 2003 Children's Book
Council of Australia Awards